Dirty Business

Jack N. Lawson

Dirty Business

"Still want to eat?" asked Emily. Stephen answered by opening the door. The establishment was one of those wherein the owners wanted that old-fashioned, down-home look. Old signs and rusty farm implements decorated the walls. There were also plaques bearing well-used aphorisms. As their eyes were adjusting from the bright sunshine, they were accosted by an over-friendly greeter. "How y'all doin'? Hungry—I hope; 'cause we got some mighty fine specials today. My name's Charlene, and I'll be he'ping y'all today."

"That's great," mumbled Stephen as they were led to a table.

"Y'all take your time and I'll be back in a jiffy." And Charlene disappeared.

"That was oxymoronic," muttered Stephen. "How can we take our time if she'll return in a 'jiffy'?" Emily chuckled and Stephen joined in.

"Don'chu jest *lu-uv* being South'en?" teased Emily.

"Way-ull sorta," responded Stephen in kind, as he glanced over the menu. Then, looking all around him, he asked Emily, "Did you see a sign for the 'Twilight Zone' before we entered town? I mean, this has been a very *dis*-usual set of circumstances." Emily liked the way Stephen used neologisms or malapropisms to make a point.

Having not allowed her customers to 'take their time', Charlene was indeed back in a jiffy. "Y'all ready to order?"

"Not yet," replied Emily, "But could you just bring us some iced tea while we decide?"

"Sure enough, Hon," and 'poof'—Charlene was gone again.

"She should try out for the Olympics," said Stephen. No sooner had he spoken, and he and Emily had begun to laugh, than Charlene re-appeared with the tea.

"Y'all seem to be havin' a good time. That's what I like to see!" purred Charlene.

"We're on our second honeymoon," proffered Stephen, as he winked at Emily.

"Oh, that's so ro-MAN-tic," exclaimed Charlene. "How long'ave'y'all been married?"

At this point Emily took over. Her elbows on the table and her chin resting on her folded hands, she sighed, "Six—whole—months," as she gazed dreamily at her husband. Stephen reached over and took one of her hands and kissed it.

"*Six months* and y'all are going *ag'in*?!" exclaimed Charlene. And then, in a just-between-us-womenfolk tone, she leaned towards Emily and said, "Hon, you got more stamina than me!" and gave Emily a sisterly chuck on the shoulder. "Y'all are gonna need to eat!"

What They Are Saying About Dirty Business

Dirty Business by Jack N Lawson, is set in North Carolina in the 1980s. A young, newlywed couple face several challenges to their future together. These two main characters have very different education and focus: one is a scientist, one a man of God. Emily works at a local university while she completes her PhD. Stephen is a prison chaplain, recovering from a serious head wound, suffered during an incident at his prison. Both are committed not only to each other, but to their community.

There have been reports by local farmers of sick animals and reduced productivity. Some locals experience unexplained illness. As it becomes apparent that the land is being poisoned, the pollution coming from an unidentified source, the community faces continuing hardship. Can Emily and her students identify the perpetrators?

Stephen must decide his future career path, having made the decision to leave the prison service; will this influence his relationship with Emily? And who is Emily?

In this novella, many of the wide range of characters have interesting backstories. How will the protagonists pull together, and how will they find a way to serve their community and secure a safe future with each other?

While the novella is set in the late 20th century, its themes of justice and redemption are of relevance in every era. There is plenty of pacey dialogue: prison staff and inmates, police officers and local farmers come to life through banter and tense exchanges. As the plot unfolds, the reader is taken to a range of locales, from prison to mountain, 5-star hotel to university campus.

Where will Emily and Stephen settle, and how will their future be impacted by Emily's investigative work? Read *Dirty Business* to find out...

—Glenne Gibson
Kenilworth, England

Jack Lawson has faithfully re-created the story of arguably the nation's greatest environmental crime—the wilful spillage in the late 1970s of PCBs along hundreds of miles of rural highways in eastern North Carolina—all in order to avoid the financial cost of proper disposal and storage. I know, for I was reared there, and, as a young lawyer, I was involved in some of the litigation spawned by the spillage. That litigation has continued to the present day.

And that is not the only "dirty business" confronting the novel's heroes in this tale! Lawson spins a tale bringing to life the people and cultural experience of that time and place, told with sensitivity and insight informed by keen observation worthy of Mark Twain.

—Steve Coggins
Wilmington, North Carolina

Dirty Business

Jack N. Lawson

Crime Novel

RESOURCE *Publications* · Eugene, Oregon

Resource Publications
A division of Wipf and Stock Publishers
199 W 8th Ave, Suite 3
Eugene, OR 97401

Dirty Business
By Lawson, Jack N.
Copyright © 2022 by Lawson, Jack N. All rights reserved.
Softcover ISBN-13: 979-8-3852-6904-4
Hardcover ISBN-13: 979-8-3852-6905-1
eBook ISBN-13: 979-8-3852-6906-8
Publication date 10/31/2025
Previously published by Wings ePress, Inc., 2022

This edition is a scanned facsimile of the original edition published in 2022.

Dedication

This book is lovingly dedicated to two people of great
encouragement: Jeanne R. Smith
and Richard C. Prust.

One

"Do you think they'll all die?" Clarence wiped the sweat from his brow with the back of his hand. The sweat was as much from fear as from the incipient spring heat in eastern North Carolina. "I mean, I know you're not a veterinarian, but have you got some idea?"

Emily cast her eyes over the Holsteins, each wearing its distinct pattern of black and white patches. As she squinted in the bright spring sunshine, the cattle appeared to Emily as a negative photo. She walked patiently from cow to cow, looking at their eyes, checking their tongues and occasionally testing their temperatures; then turned to look at Clarence, "No. I don't have any ideas at present. But you said they were all healthy until when?"

"About three weeks ago. Then they started acting funny—kinda like they were drunk. And then several of their calves died—more than usual. Then some of them began coughing—just like that." He pointed to a nearby cow. "And a number of them have some sort of mucus running out of their noses." Clarence folded his arms across his chest, almost as though he were trying to protect himself from the bad news that was evolving before his eyes. It was every dairy farmer's worst nightmare—some unknown disease which could take out his entire herd...and his family's income.

"And you haven't changed anything with regard to their feed?"

"Nope. Not a thing." He waved his hand toward the pastures. "They have plenty of grass and I buy the same grain I've done for years to supplement the hay."

"May I take some samples of it?"

"Sure. Take as much as you want."

"And water? I see the wind pump over by the barn, but surely that's not enough for whole herd?"

"Not by a long shot. No, there's a branch over beyond that stand of pines. It runs down to the Tar River, about a half-mile from here. That's where they tend to drink."

Emily stood with her hands on her hips for a brief moment before breaking her silence. "I'd like to drive down there. I have collection bottles in my truck—for the water—and bags for the feed samples—oh, and poop samples, if you don't mind helping."

"Not at all," replied Clarence. "But that brings us to another thing. Come have a look at this." He gestured toward a fresh cow pat. "Some of them have been passing blood."

Emily knelt, studying the bloody manure. Looking up, she said, "Find some old cow pats from a few weeks back and then some fresh ones, so I can compare them. I'll also want to take some blood and milk samples. Everything's in my truck." They turned to walk back to where the truck was parked outside the farmhouse. As they approached, Stephen Travis sat up, having been napping on the pickup's bench seat.

"You didn't tell me you had a helper with you. He coulda come with us or waited in the house."

2

"Well, my *helper* is actually my husband, the Reverend Stephen Travis. He's been working part-time since...well, since having an injury a few months ago. The drive down from Raleigh left him feeling tired, didn't it, babe?" Emily casually kissed her husband.

Stephen stepped down from the truck and shook Clarence Moore's hand while they exchanged greetings.

"Feel like helping?" asked Emily.

"Absolutely!"

Emily walked to the pickup's cargo area and unlocked a box containing various supplies. She produced a handful of plastic zip bags and handed them to Clarence. "Use about three for the feed and the rest for the manure, if you're okay with that."

Clarence made a face and shook his head. "Honey, I'm a *dairy farmer*. I spend half my life in cow manure."

"Sorry, it's a habit from working with students. But still, you might want this." She handed Clarence a trowel and smiled warmly at him.

"Mighty thoughtful of you, young lady."

Stephen and I will drive down to the branch and collect some water. We'll also pick up some manure samples down there. Back in a jiffy." Clarence headed to the barn while Emily and Stephen drove across the pasture toward the creek.

"Got any idea what's wrong with his herd?" asked Stephen.

"As I told Clarence, I have no idea at all. But his animals are becoming very sick. I'm going to need all of my student lab assistants on this case if we're going to save the herd." Emily bit her lower lip in silence. Although they could still be classed as newlyweds—they had been married four months—Stephen knew her well enough by then to know she was as concerned for the Moore family as for her primary concern: what was ailing the cattle. Emily stopped the truck before the ground became too marshy. "Now you see why I brought extra pairs of rubber boots." She winked at Stephen. "Ready to play in the mud?"

"As ready as you are, my lovely mad scientist." The two donned their boots, picked up the sample bottles and waded into the stream.

'Tell you what," offered Emily, "collect some water along the edge where the cattle have made puddles with their hooves. It will more than likely contain some of their urine. Two birds with one bottle, so to speak."

The cattle had trodden the banks into a marshy quagmire resembling a muddy moonscape. Both Stephen and Emily had to keep freeing their boots from the muck. It produced a comical *schlupping* sound, which made them both laugh. Emily flung one bottle of water at her husband.

"Hey! Be careful I don't fling some of this brown slush at you!" But Emily knew he wouldn't and Stephen reflected on how much he adored her playfulness. "Let it not be said that you don't know how to mix work and pleasure."

Ten minutes later and their job was done. They took careful giant steps out of the slush, kicking the mud off their boots as they made their way to the pickup. Emily took all of the samples and carefully dated them before placing them in another locker. She closed and fastened the lid and said, "C'mon, Rev, let's go see what Clarence has for us."

As Emily eased the truck over the bumpy pasture, she turned to Stephen. "How's your head?"

"I've only banged it hard once against the rear window. I have to admit that didn't feel very nice, but I know you're doing your best. Couldn't the university have provided you with a pickup with better shocks?"

"I'm just lucky to have this." Emily squeezed Stephen's left knee as a gesture of love and concern. "Sometimes lately I can barely tell you've got that steel plate in your head. Your hair's nearly grown back. But I'd love you even if the plate looked like a trap door."

4

Stephen chuckled at his wife's sense of humor. "I have just enough vanity to admit I'm glad it doesn't *look* like a trap door; but I'm just happy you love me." He laid his hand on hers. "I'm just glad to be alive. Sometimes it almost overwhelms me how close that bullet came to ending everything—not just for me, but for both of us...you know?"

"Yeah, I do know. If you hadn't rammed the shooter's car off the road that precise moment—" Emily shivered involuntarily. She squeezed Stephen's knee tighter. "I never want to lose you."

Stephen nodded and said, "About that...I've been thinking...as it was prison that nearly got me killed...what if I didn't go back?"

"To full-time chaplaincy?"

"To chaplaincy full stop."

"Wow..." Emily rolled the truck to a gentle stop outside the Moores' farmhouse. As she pulled up the handbrake she turned to Stephen and said, "Looks like we have a lot to talk about on the way home, eh? But I'm with you—regardless. Let's get those blood samples." Emily again fished in the truck's locker for syringes and vials into which the samples would be saved. Stephen held the equipment in a steel tray while Emily took blood from four cows and two calves. "That should do it. Let's store these in the truck and get back to Clarence—I know he's anxious."

Moore was sitting out of the sun on his front porch. As Emily and Stephen mounted the stairs, he pointed to the swing and said, "Thought I'd save the best seat for you two. Marcie's bringing out some tea in a minute. I hope you're not in a rush?"

Stephen turned to Emily with a cheeky grin. "She's in charge. I'm just along for the ride."

"Nice to hear a man talking sense," Marcie jibed as she pushed open the screen door with her hip and began handing out glasses of tea. She thrust her hand to both Emily and Stephen. "I'm Marcie." Pointing over her shoulder with her thumb, she added, "Clarence minds the cattle and I mind Clarence."

5

"And all is right with the world and universe," chimed in Clarence. Then he added, *sotto voce*, "Except that it ain't right now." He was silent for few seconds, then said, "But that's why Dr. Travis is here, right?"

"That's right, and you can call me Emily—please. I won't officially become 'doctor' until May, when my thesis is presented."

"Oh, Clarence, let the young lady drink her tea!" interjected Marcie. Looking at Stephen she said, "Clarence tells me you're a minister and that you two are married."

Stephen nodded. "Clarence is right. Emily and I were married on New Year's Day—just four months ago."

Marcie clapped her hands together. "Newlyweds! Ain't nothing like it!" Then, addressing Stephen again, she asked, "Where's your church?"

"Well, I don't actually have a church per se, I'm a prison chaplain—at least right now." Stephen's right hand unconsciously went to the plate on the rear of his head and patted it gently.

"Say your name is Stephen Travis?" Clarence asked.

"Yes sir, it is."

"If you don't mind me asking, aren't you the fellow who was in the news a few months back—uncovered some kind of money-making scam the prison staff were running on the inmates? I believe I read where you were shot—is that right?"

"Oh, Clarence," chided Marcie, "Don't give our guest the third degree."

"Well, you saw it in the *News and Observer* just like I did," retorted Clarence. "The reverend doesn't have to answer if he doesn't want to."

Stephen began to laugh. "Don't y'all fall out over this. I'm guilty as charged. In short, I blew the cover on a terrible scheme to extort money from inmates' families. And yep, I got shot in the back of the head for my troubles. I have a shiny new plate back here as a souvenir." He knocked gently on the plate and turned his head toward the Moores.

"Land's sakes!" Marcie placed her hand over her heart. "Does it hurt?"

"Only if I bump it! It did hurt at first, but it's got better over time. Oh—and I have to stay away from big magnets!"

Continuing in her motherly concern, Marcie asked, "Well, are you taking time off from prison work now?"

"Now who's giving the man the third degree?" Clarence chortled.

Marcie waved her husband off with a motion of her hand. "I'm just concerned is all."

"The short answer is that I'm working part-time at present—and keeping my lovely bride company and trying to be of help when she lets me." He winked at Emily. "Funnily enough, I was just saying to Emily that my prison chaplaincy days might be nearing an end. But we'll see...Em and I have a lot to talk about. However, right now I sense she needs to talk with you two about your cattle."

Emily took a long sip of iced tea before she began. "Well, as I told you earlier, I have no solid idea of what is affecting your cattle. But I can assure you of this: in my lab back at the university, I have access to state-of-the-art equipment—unavailable to most vets—which will be able to identify what is in their bloodstream and digestive systems. Once I have that information, I will pass it straightaway to your vet, and to you, of course."

"How long do you think that might be?" asked Clarence.

Thinking out loud, Emily said, "Today's Tuesday. We won't get back to the lab before four. I'll need to assign some students assistants to the case. I think we'll have preliminary results in forty-eight hours. In any case, I'll call you on Friday to give you an update. How is that?"

"Fair enough." Clarence said. Watching the toe of his shoe trace a pattern on the porch floor—and not looking up—he cleared his throat. "We...um...haven't discussed money. How much is this going to cost us?" He shot a worried look at Marcie.

"I'm so sorry," blurted Emily, "I should have told you earlier that this won't cost you a penny. I have a research grant from a company in the Research Triangle which is covering my work. I think you have enough to worry about without having to pay for this diagnosis."

Clarence breathed an audible sigh of relief, and both he and Marcie were visibly reassured.

"Well, don't let us keep you. I can't pretend I don't want you to get the samples back to your lab as soon as possible." Stephen and Emily stood and shook Clarence's hand, but Marcie declared that she was a hugger and embraced the younger couple. "You two take care of each other—especially after what you've already been through."

Two

"So you're planning a prison break?" Emily glanced at Stephen as the truck rolled along the two-lane blacktop county road which was punctuated with 'Reagan for President' signs. "What's prompted your decision?"

Stephen's right arm was riding the wind currents from the truck's open window. "Dreams, I suppose—or rather, nightmares. You're probably aware of the number I've had over the last four months. Add to that my being in the place where it all happened, regularly seeing some of the victims, expecting to see Vance Strader sitting at the desk, worrying when I see car lights closing in on me at night. I believe I just need a clean break from it all."

Emily turned her eyes toward Stephen for a moment and then back at the road ahead. "I guess I've kinda been expecting this— for all the reasons you've mentioned." She paused for a short while, collecting her thoughts. "I suppose both of us needed to hear you voice these things. Have you said anything to your therapist?"

"Anthony? No, not yet. We've concentrated on my dreams a lot—particularly the repetitive nightmares. But also the pleasant dreams. Being a good Jungian, he wants me to engage in the analysis of them—the patterns, the emotions, the fearful and hopeful things. All that has helped, to some degree, but I'm coming to the conclusion that without a change of scenery, the nightmares and the feeling of powerlessness they produce won't stop anytime soon. The only way I'll know for sure is to make the break. I think that's what the dreams are pushing me to do. What does my scientist wife think of that?"

"Hmmm," mused Emily. "Well, I'd say you have defined the problem, collected the evidence and analyzed it...and it seems you've reached a preliminary conclusion."

"Preliminary?"

"Yes. Until you make the break—i.e. act on the evidence—you won't know for sure, will you? But look, my sweetheart, getting shot in the head—and surviving it—is no small thing! Some people might think you'd have been justified in leaving the prison system as soon as you were out of the hospital."

"Are you one of those people?"

"If I had been, don't you think you'd have known it by now? You've had a lot to process; and no one else could do it for you. I've simply accompanied you on the journey—much like you're with me right now." Emily reached over and gave Stephen's ribs a tickle. She had a sense of when levity was needed.

"Hey!" Stephen jumped reflexively. "And you know I can't retaliate because you're driving!"

"Funny thing about that, eh? But look, if you do decide to leave prison chaplaincy, have you thought about what you might do next?"

"A little bit—but not in detail. I really can't see myself in a typical parish. That's the easiest thing for the district superintendent to do—as I'm white, assign me to a middle-class church. That's never been my aspiration. The few Black United

10

Methodist ministers we have in the district are rightfully assigned to predominantly black churches. But after all of these years working in prison, I can't see working in any monochrome environment. There are a number of outreach and mission projects between Raleigh and Durham, so I might start investigating any openings. How much does it pay to be your lab assistant?"

"You should know—I let you sleep with me. Just be glad I don't pay all of my assistants the same way." They both had a chuckle. "In any case, let's just be happy that I have a year of post-doc work lined up. We can survive for a while on my income if need be. I just want you to feel fulfilled in whatever you choose to do...and if it happens to be a less dangerous environment, that would be a bonus." She extended her hand and stroked his wavy brown hair.

"Melvin Strader, that great extortionist of inmates, could have taken both of us out that night. If his bullet had killed me, you know he would have come for you—" Emily's hand moved from Stephen's hair to seal his lips.

"Sorry, babe, but enough. You managed to run Strader off the road, he's dead, but *we are alive*. You know your therapist tells you not to keep replaying the event. It doesn't do you any good—quite the opposite. And believe me, I know how tempting it is to relive it because *I was there too*. I just didn't get injured like you did. We have today, and we can plan for tomorrow. *Right*?"

Stephen had to fight the urge to say he couldn't help reliving the event, to say *it felt like it helped*, even if it didn't. His mind flipped through the images of the dozens of Vietnam vets he had worked with behind bars and the countless times he had listened to their stories of watching friends die or of killing women and children in fits of rage.

"Stephen? You still here?"

"Yeah—sorry. And you're right...and my therapist is right. It's just hard sometimes."

"When you fell away from the wheel that night, Stephen, I really thought I was a goner. I mean, speeding along in a driverless car and knowing a maniac was trying to kill us. I didn't know Strader's car had plunged into the lake. But if my time in prison taught me anything, it was this: the story works out the same every time you go back over it. My friends and I did something stupid when we tried to buy dope in Mexico; we got busted and I had to serve time for it. My brain would have cooked itself if I had spent those sixteen months replaying it all. And, *of course* I did dwell on it for a while. But not knowing exactly how long I was going to spend behind bars taught me to focus on other things. What is that quote of Kierkegaard's that you like?"

"'We remember life backwards, but we must live it forwards.'"

"*Pre*-cisely! God willing, we have a lot of years ahead of us. I'm looking forward to all of the adventures we're going to have...it certainly hasn't been boring so far."

"No shit!" came Stephen's terse reply—but he was laughing.

Three

Stephen liked watching his wife do her work. He liked the way Emily thought out loud—both to herself and for the benefit of the undergraduate lab assistants. He enjoyed watching her methodical brain sort through a problem. Stephen had helped her carry in the various samples gathered at the Moores' farm. Each of the students working with Emily was assigned a particular machine in which to test the samples. They worked in pairs. "This is a gas chromatograph," Emily indicated to Stephen. "In short, the liquid samples will be heated, vaporized and then transported by a carrier gas. Then they are ionized in a flame in the detector. If the cattle on Clarence's farm have ingested some sort of toxin, it can be identified by the peaks along the base timeline of the chromatogram printout. The concentration or amount of the toxin is shown by the width of the peak at the baseline." Emily pointed to a printout on the adjoining desk as an example. "We will know the peaks of the carrier gas, so they can easily be ruled out, leaving

13

my fine helpers here with comparing the peaks with those of hundreds of other known substances and toxins until an identification can be made. Make sense?"

Stephen raised his eyebrows. "Yeah...well sorta. Are you gonna test me on this when we get home?" The lab assistants laughed.

"You'd better believe it." She directed Stephen to another machine. "And this over here is an infrared spectrophotometer. Our samples are passed through an infrared light. Each substance has different levels of infrared absorption, reflection or emission. This machine also produces a printout of peaks, but along the infrared spectrum, which must then be compared with other known substances."

"Sounds like it could be time consuming...and perhaps even a bit tedious?" He turned his eyes toward the assistants, a couple of whom grunted.

"And that, dear husband of mine, is why God made undergraduates—just like the four specimens you see before you here." Emily gestured toward each student and introduced them by name to Stephen. "They love working with me." She then made a grim face. "*Isn't that so?*" They all responded in the affirmative, giggling and jabbing each other.

"They have too many names," said Stephen. "How about we just call them the Gang of Four?"

"Call us what you like as long as working here helps pay for tuition!" chirped one of them.

"I know how that feels," replied Stephen. "I worked student jobs every semester. But it beats debt."

"Amen to that," added another. "And I like the 'Gang of Four'—it makes us sound like badasses, whereas 'lab assistants' sounds a bit namby-pamby."

"See how easy that was, Em?" said Stephen, who smiled broadly. He took Emily's water bottle and splashed the four students. "There, as an ordained minister, I christen you all the Gang of Four." Emily shook her head at Stephen's antics, while the Gang laughed. Then, changing tack, Stephen asked, "So how long might all the testing take?"

"Longer than our farmer friends might like, if we don't leave these guys—sorry—the Gang of Four to get on with it." She jokingly pushed Stephen toward the door. Before she followed, Emily turned. "How long can you each give to this project? This dairy herd looks in bad shape; the animals' lives and the livelihood of the farmers depends on our work. Oh, and I'm willing to pay for the extra hours."

One of the newly-christened Gang of Four, Alison, who was a pre-veterinary student, spoke first. "I'll give it whatever it takes—forget the extra money." She looked at her colleagues. One by one they each gave their vocal assent.

"Great!" beamed Emily. "I'll drive Stephen home and come straight back. Shall I order us some pizzas for supper? At least let me pay for that." There was no argument from the assistants.

As the couple walked to their car, Stephen had to stop and search for it. His previous car had been totaled in the crash following the attack five months previously. As Stephen had not been allowed to drive for some time after being released from the trauma unit, he had to remind himself they now had a different car. His entire family had joined together to buy Emily and Stephen a fairly recent Volvo, joking that if they had to suffer future attacks on the road and roll the car, he should have one with a good safety record. It was also the case that Stephen's brother-in-law—and attorney—Dave Andrews, was suing the state for damages on Stephen's behalf. Stephen had tried to report the extortion racket that was being run by prison staff on the inmates at a pre-release facility and their families. The families had been pressured into buying worn-out, used cars from one of the prison guards and his brother, or face seeing their loved ones go back to close custody and serve out their sentences. Stephen's chain of command in the correctional system covered up his findings, leaving him vulnerable to threats, and finally the attack that nearly took his—and Emily's—life.

Emily said nothing—partly because she did not want to pre-empt Stephen's exercising his memory 'muscles', but also because she was concerned to note Stephen's progression following his brain trauma.

At that moment, shaking his head, Stephen turned to look at Emily. He mocked himself by rolling his eyes and pretending to slap himself on the forehead. "Duh! The new car. I'll remember one day."

"Stephen, you're doing fine. Besides, how long did you drive the old Pontiac?"

"Gosh," Stephen seemed to search the sky. "Maybe five years?"

"And we've had this car about six weeks. You'll get there." Getting 'there' was that unspecified place in the future that any person who has suffered a traumatic injury sets before him or herself. That state of being that will become as close to what normal was before the injury—and often a completely new normal. Emily unlocked the car and they got in. As Stephen buckled his seatbelt, he asked, "Are you more concerned now than you were back on the farm? Your words to your young minions didn't bode well."

"I've been uneasy since we saw the cattle. Some—and I stress *some*—of their symptoms remind me of what I've read and heard about a 'prion disease' like scrapie.

"Um...want to explain?"

"In short, prions are abnormal forms of a protein that is found in the brain. This malformation can cause fatal neurodegenerative diseases in animals."

16

"I like the 'short'," quipped Stephen. "Will the lab tests confirm if they have it?"

"Maybe...I don't know. I think the only way of knowing for sure is to examine the brain tissue of a dead cow. There's a problem, however: scrapie is usually found in sheep and goats—not cattle."

"Is it contagious?"

"Unfortunately, yes. And it would probably mean the end of Clarence's herd. In any case, I've got a lot of homework to do. Sorry, babe, but it's going to be a long night. Oh, are you going to the prison tomorrow?"

"Yeah, I think so, but I won't get up too early, if that's what you're concerned about."

"No, it's not that...but I have to admit I'm still nervous about your being in the car alone...driving."

"Um, I haven't had any blackouts, seizures or 'anything nefarious' as the neurologist put it. I think I'm 'out of the woods'. I'll be all right—but thanks for the concern."

"And your planned resignation?"

"I'll run it past James and Lincoln once I'm at the unit tomorrow." James Fowler and Lincoln Parker were not only Stephen's colleagues, the three had become close friends, and had particularly bonded in their struggle against corruption at the Fairborn Advancement Center for Men. Fowler was a prison officer with ten years' experience. He had been promoted after the previous warden and two correctional officers had been fired, due to acts of omission or commission in the extortion scandal. In fact, three officers would have been fired except that Melvin Strader, who had been the linchpin for the scheme, had gone missing and was later found dead from presumed suicide. James now had seniority over the rest of the correctional staff—a good thing for staff and inmates alike. Lincoln Parker was the unit's social worker, specializing in helping the men find both jobs and places to live, which were the necessary final steps before their release. James and Lincoln had served as joint best men at Stephen's wedding.

Emily pulled the car into the drive that led to their one-bedroom cottage set among oak trees. "Guess I'll head straight back. You okay with that? I'll stop by that pizza joint on Hillsborough Street and grab supper for the team." Emily leaned over and gave Stephen a hug and kiss. "Keep the bed warm for me."

"You can count on it," replied Stephen as he got out of the car. Emily reversed up the drive to the road, gave the horn a toot and was gone.

Stephen walked up the steps to the front door and stood on the little porch for a few moments. The spring sun was behind the grand oaks that gave this old, established neighborhood its character. The fresh new leaves were translucent, and in the soft breeze created a natural kaleidoscope that Stephen found mesmerizing. He could feel when the leaves parted enough for the sunshine to caress his face. He mused about how it was only a year before that he and Emily had met while riding their bikes around town—each de-stressing from work. Until that time, he had lived alone in the tiny cottage, renting from the family that lived next door. The woods around and behind the property belied the fact that it was situated in the busy state capital. Stephen pulled open the screen door and unlocked the main door, leaving it open so the sounds and smells of spring might enter the house. He found himself looking at Emily's things and thinking: *One year together and now I can't imagine being without her.* His mind quickly jumped to the night of the gun attack, in which he and Emily were nearly killed. But just as quickly, he heard Emily and Anthony Morley, his therapist, chiding him for doing so.

"Refocus!" he said aloud. "It's dinner time." Stephen found that speaking aloud to himself helped deal with the trauma barely five months past. Hearing his voice actually helped him to turn his awareness to outside himself. Stephen also took seriously his therapist's recommendation to adopt an 'attitude of gratitude'— thankfulness for his survival, his medical care, his marriage to Emily, the many people who supported him. Stephen realized the list could go on and on, and that, of course, was the point. The brush with death was just that—a brush; death had bypassed him, but life was full-on and abundant, always right here and right now. Before getting started in the kitchen, Stephen put a record on the turntable: *The Allman Brothers live at the Fillmore*, one of his favorite albums. He played 'air guitar' between cracking eggs for an omelet, and washing bean sprouts and asparagus to accompany it.

The telephone rang. It was on the wall just outside the kitchen, but with an ample cord. Stephen held the receiver between his ear and shoulder. "Hello? Linc? Hey buddy, what's up?"

Lincoln's tones were plaintive. "Can you sing lullabies? I can't get this baby to sleep."

"'This baby'? Man, it must be bad to call Clarissa—my goddaughter—'this baby'. I could croak a few songs over the telephone line, but that might just make her cry more. Where's Marcella?"

"Oh, she's at a church meeting, or so she says. But I think's it's just an excuse for a bunch of the sisters who recently had babies to have an evening off. She'll be back about ten."

"Are you looking for an invitation? If so, the door's unlocked. Have you eaten?"

"No, man, I haven't eaten, but you don't have to do—" Stephen cut him off.

"It's no problem, if you don't mind an omelet. I'm just preparing one now. Oh, and one more thing: don't forget to bring a bottle for Clarissa...maybe two."

"Thanks, man. See you in fifteen."

"You got it. Drive carefully."

~ * ~

Three hours later, when Emily came home, she found Stephen asleep in his rocking chair with a baby in his lap and two empty bottles on the floor. Lincoln was flopped across the sofa, equally dead to the world. It was almost a shame to have to wake them.

Four

The alarm clock rang at seven-thirty. Two sleepy people made waking-up noises and turned to look at one another's somnolent eyes. "You didn't tell me you were going to have a pajama party when I dropped you off." Emily kissed the tip of Stephen's nose.

"It kinda surprised me too," croaked Stephen. "Poor Lincoln couldn't get Clarissa to sleep, so he brought her to Uncle Stephen's. I guess it worked." Stephen smacked his dry lips and reached for a glass of water.

"I wish I had a camera when I came in last night. Seeing you three racked out like that—and little Clarissa asleep on your lap. You looked a natural."

"Gosh. Do I hear a hint of broody?"

"Why not? We're not getting any younger—and both of us turning thirty this year. We've certainly done a lot of practicing."

"Speaking of which..." Stephen kissed Emily, then lifted up the covers and began kissing her belly.

"Hey! What's going on? I can't linger this morning—much as I'd like to."

"I'm just checking out your baby basket, wondering how you'd look with a bump."

"Pregnant, I guess. But we'll have to discuss this at another time."

"You brought it up," chided Stephen as he nipped Emily's hip.

"Ouch!" She whacked him with a pillow. "Let's get up and fix breakfast. I have worried dairy farmers counting on me."

"And I have a limitless supply of inmates awaiting me. Are you showering first?"

"Yes," replied a still dozy Emily. "I need the water to wake me up."

"Scrambled or fried?" Stephen asked as he slipped on shorts and a T-shirt.

"Any way you like. Thanks—I'll make it up to you." She kissed his neck and grabbed his bottom.

"Promises, promises!"

~ * ~

Driving to the university, Emily was feeling both energized and reflective. She mused that she usually felt one or the other, but not both at the same time. She was having mixed feelings over having brought up the idea of children. The topic was something she and Stephen had flitted over several times, and both were open to the idea, but neither had made an opening gambit. *Wow. This is real adult stuff. Here I am with a husband and a job—no more of the student lifestyle.* Emily laughed out loud. *Come back to earth head and feet; we have sick cattle to diagnose.* She was soon at NC State and drove down to the animal science labs. When she opened the door to her lab, she found two assistants already there. "When did you two get here?"

"What day is it?" groaned Alison.

"Thursday," replied Emily.

"Then Mark and I got here Wednesday, just after lunch." She looked at her watch, "So it must be half-past yesterday. Terry and Stewart should be in soon. They left about eleven last night."

Alison yawned and ran her hand through her hair. "Oh—and they borrowed a centrifuge in Professor Anson's lab to run some tests on the blood. They said you had okayed it." She winked at her supervisor. "Hope that's all right with you?" She smiled wearily and Emily noted that Alison's eyes looked like brake lights against her pale skin.

"Well, that was a good bit of thinking—and I would have approved. So maybe it's simply a case of it being easier to ask for forgiveness than to request permission," said Emily as she returned the wink to Alison. "Any initial results?"

"We can definitely rule out some things," Mark spoke up from his desk, his eyes rimmed red like Alison's. "You had mentioned the nasal congestion or mucus in the cattle? Well, it's not malignant catarrhal fever, so that's good. And it's not bovine rhinotracheitis—nasty stuff!" he gave a shudder. "From the symptoms, those seemed to be the most likely—but nope." Mark tapped a pencil on his note pad.

"Their feed has been showing no signs of contamination," added Alison, "so that's good too." She yawned

"Look, you two. Go back to"—Emily realized she didn't know whether her young assistants lived in dorms or in off-campus accommodation—"...to wherever it is you sleep and, well, get some. Meanwhile I'll look over your lab reports until Terry and Stewart arrive." Neither lab assistant objected. "Oh—and I don't want to know if you've skipped any classes, okay?"

"We won't hold you accountable," mumbled Mark as he walked toward the door, giving a little wave over his shoulder. Alison laid out her lab books neatly for Emily.

"Where would I be without you guys?" she mused aloud.

"Left with a lot more work. That's for sure," said Alison.

Emily began looking over the lab notebooks left by her younger colleagues. "Do you know what I like about science?"

Alison shook her blond curly locks in the negative.

"I love the fact that *negative* results are still *positive*. They still give us information. They tell us not to follow this trail, but find another. Happily, we know the cows are not infected with two distinctly *ungood* diseases." Alison chuckled at her supervisor's neologism. "Now we have to identify *what is* ailing those cows. Go get some rest." No further encouragement was needed.

~ * ~

Stephen noticed a distinctly heavy feeling as he turned down the road leading to the Fairborn Advancement Center for Men. It wasn't exactly dread—but perhaps a first cousin? *Why aren't I feeling joy or relief? All the people who had made incarceration even more hellish for these long-timers awaiting their release were either dead, gone or themselves in prison.* What Stephen felt was more like an intense pressure—the inexorable pressure of *time.* As he often thought in images, the image which appeared in his mind was that of the massive hands on the clock tower at the Palace of Westminster, pushing him forward. As a student in London, he had often stopped to listen to 'Big Ben' and the other bells peel the hour. That was it. He felt the time to move on had come, that those intense years of prison chaplaincy had served their purpose—his purpose. Stephen was so deeply in thought he nearly passed the turn into the parking lot. He slowed and steered the car into a space, but before he got out of the car, his mind was made up. He practically ran up the steps into the administration building.

Although the previous warden and several of the custodial staff were gone—thanks to the sleuthing done by Stephen, James Fowler and Lincoln Parker—good old Maxine Willerby, the main secretary, was still there. And her nasally Southern twang was just as present. "Well, hey there, Chapl'in Travis! Yer lookin' mighty fine today." She unconsciously primped her cotton-candy hair. She was white enough to be the paper cone on which the sugar was spun.

"Thanks, Maxine, and I'm feeling it. Is James in?"

"He sure ee-iz (ah, the diphthongs of Southern American English, wherein single syllables are elongated into two!) and I'm sure he'll be glad to see you lookin' so well."

Stephen smiled and, as he entered the corridor, almost tiptoed to James' office where he found the door half-open. Knocking vigorously and standing out of sight, he put on his best redneck voice. "Officer Fowler, you seen a 'spicious lookin' white boy 'round here, 'bout six foot tall and sportin' a steel plate in his head?"

Taking the bait, Fowler replied, "It all depends on who's asking. Why don't you come on in?"

Stephen pushed open the door. "Aw man, Stephen! You know I've had it up to here," he brushed the top of his head, "with SBI and others sniffing around here. Don't mess with me like that!" He was laughing as he pointed at a chair. "You coming in to actually work today or just to pull stunts like that?" The two friends shook hands.

"Both I guess. But first, have you got a few minutes?"

"Please don't let it be anything serious. Things are just settling down here. But, yeah, for you I can make more than a few minutes. Whatcha got?"

"Let me close the door," Stephen spoke softly as he got up and went to the door.

"I don't know if I like the sound of that," groaned James, but Stephen waved his hand as though dispelling whatever thoughts Fowler might have.

"It's nothing to do with our former colleagues here at the center—it's about me."

"Shoot," spouted James before he could consider his choice of words. "Damn, brother, I'm sorry."

"It's okay. It only hurts when there's a real bullet being shot at me. But it is fun going through metal detectors at the other units. The guards who know me don't worry about it, but one or two zealous new guards frisk me up and down. I've invited them to knock on the plate in my head, but they freak out!"

"I'll just bet they do. Anyway, what it is with your fine self, brother man?"

"To cut to the chase, I'm thinking about resigning from prison chaplaincy. Just wanted to run it past you and Linc to see what you think." Stephen sat back in his chair and waited for James' response—which wasn't long in coming.

"Hallelujah!"

"You that glad to be rid of me?" Stephen feigned hurt feelings.

"Diane and I were talking about you the other night. She asked if a wound like yours would have been a ticket home from 'Nam. And I told her, 'Damn right it would!' So she asked if I thought it was doing you any good to be around this place, and I told her, 'Probably not'." He stopped and looked at Stephen for emphasis. Stephen simply nodded. James interpreted the gesture correctly to mean, 'I'm listening. Carry on.'

"Look, man, in Vietnam the decision would have been taken away from you, lying there in a coma with a swollen brain. You'da been evac'ed stateside as soon as they thought you could travel. So if you have *any* concerns about leaving prison work as a sign of weakness or that you're scared—if you're thinking *any shit like that*—forget it! You've served your time and paid a price for it! So git, while the gitting's good!" Fowler intoned in a countryfied manner.

Stephen laughed quietly. "You haven't been speaking to Emily, have you?"

"No, but I would put money on it that she feels the same as Diane and I—and Lincoln! He's in today, so ask him!"

"I'm planning on it, James. And you're right about Em. Yesterday she told me it had to be my decision to leave prison work. And she was right. It's just to say that I'm not feeling like a coward per se, but that I really and truly believe God called me to

26

prison chaplaincy. I'm more concerned about letting the Almighty down than some pissant cracker shooting at me."

"Did God ever tell you *how long* you were supposed to work in prison?" asked James pointedly.

"Actually, no."

"Well, there's your 'get out of jail free' card! Take it, brother, and use it. And sorry for preaching to the chaplain, but don't you think God speaks to your heart—and to the hearts of those who love and care about you?"

Stephen simply nodded again, slowly and thoughtfully.

"Listen, man, soon as my pension is topped up, you better believe I'm out of here! It's good, honest—*usually*—and important work, but you and I both know that the prison system is a...a...what?"

"A parallel universe?"

"Exactly! And it does things to your head! Am I right?"

"Completely." Stephen felt tears welling up in his eyes. Was it from sadness or relief at making this momentous decision—or a combination of things?

James saw Stephen biting his lip and holding back the tears. He got up from his chair and came around the desk. "Unh-unh—no tears bro, not today! If you let it go, you'll get me going, and then what're we gonna look like to the rest of the folks here? So get out of my office and go to yours and start typing that letter!" But before Stephen could leave, James' six-foot-three frame enfolded him in a quick bear hug. "Love you man! *Now git!*"

Stephen greeted a few of the 'residents'—as they were called in this pre-release unit—in the dayroom, who were watching television or reading. As every man in the unit had to have a job in order to pay for his room and board as a way of adjusting to 'life outside,' these men were those who worked night shifts. Their final hurdle to clear before their release was to have a 'home plan'. Lincoln Parker, the social worker and Stephen's office partner, helped the men with both job and home plans. Stephen knocked at the door of their shared office before entering, knowing Lincoln could be carrying on a confidential conversation with a resident. "Enter," came Lincoln's voice from within.

Attempting to sound like a 'brother', Stephen said, "Mistuh Parker, I gots to get me a home plan."

Without looking up, Lincoln said, "Stick with the voices you know, Rev."

"And I thought that wasn't too far off."

Lincoln looked and smiled broadly. "Well, it was close. Shouldn't you be at home, nursing your head in the arms of that beautiful lady of yours?"

"Well, I would, except she's at work and I have to show up for work occasionally so the state keeps paying me."

"Damn, bro, they oughta be paying you big time after the shit they've put you through. Any news on the case?"

"Not yet, but my brother-in-law-cum-lawyer thinks the state wants this finished soon—and out of court—so hopefully there will be news before long." Stephen sat in his chair and swiveled a bit from side to side. "And speaking of news..." Lincoln looked up from his work, "I plan to resign from prison chaplaincy."

"Break—out—the—champagne!" declaimed Lincoln. "Man, I've been wondering when you were going to get over that head-wound of yours enough to come to your senses! That is great news! Where are you going? I mean, have you found another job?"

"In the order of your questions: no idea and no." Stephen shrugged. "But James told me you'd be in agreement with him that it's about time I moved on."

"Yes indeed! What does Emily say?"

"She's of the same opinion as you and James. She said I just needed to come to that decision myself."

"Smart woman! Have you sent your letter yet?"

"Nope. I'm about to write it now. Do you need the typewriter?"

"If I did, I'd stand aside for you, bro. Hey, I know how to begin your letter."

"How's that?"

"You remember that crazy redneck saying you told me about that you heard from the mouth of that guard up at the women's prison—the guy who got fired?" Travis laughed at the memory.

"You mean: 'Yew kin kiss mah ice and go to hell and I'm just the man to do it'?" They both laughed.

"Yeah, man, that's the one! There's your letter in one sentence!"

"It's tempting, but I think it will have to be a bit more diplomatic." And with that, Stephen pulled out some correctional system stationery.

Five

"You mean to say there are other herds suffering from the same symptoms?" Emily switched the receiver to her left hand so she could write. "Slow down, please, Clarence. I need to get their names and locations. Yep, go ahead."

The Gang of Four froze at their stations and listened attentively to Emily's end of the conversation. "Yeah, got that. Hog farms, too?" Emily ran her hand through her hair nervously. "Jeez," she mumbled under her breath. "All with the same symptoms? ...When is your local farm bureau meeting again? I'd like to be there, but I also want to bring some colleagues from the university as well as from the Environmental Protection Agency...Well, I was going to call you today, as a matter of fact, and the news is disturbing...No, I don't think it's anything you've done, unless you have access to PCBs...No, P-C-Bs, polychlorinated biphenyls...I know you're not a chemist. They're particularly toxic chemicals that are used in electronic equipment, insulators and such, because they are highly heat resistant. We found them in the water samples from the stream that runs across your property. PCBs are bad news for all animal life—including humans—which begs the question: do you have well water?"

Now all the student assistants were gathered around Emily, their faces tired and yet full of tension. The next thing she said surprised them: "Shit!" She made an embarrassed face at her younger colleagues and apologized to Clarence. "I know, I know—and me a preacher's wife. At least I know he'll pray for me." She winked at the students. "Listen, Clarence, we can be with you by ten a.m. tomorrow. Is that okay? There might be a bunch of us, as we need to start tracking the source of the PCB contamination...Okay, try not to worry too much, but to be on the safe side, go buy some bottled water until we can test yours. See you tomorrow. Bye." Emily put the phone down and rubbed her ear as she looked from face to face.

Alison was the first to speak. "I can be free tomorrow—all day." The three young men each agreed to be part of the team. Emily's face beamed with gratitude as she nodded in thanks.

"I'll buy food and drinks for tomorrow, but let me know if there's anything you don't like. Oh, and bring plenty of extra water. You know just what we're dealing with. For anyone who can stick around for a while, here are some other farmers and livestock owners we need to contact." Emily scribbled out each name and telephone number on a separate piece of paper. "Let's get to it!"

~ * ~

Stephen had never seen Emily so tired. He thought her head might drop onto her dinner plate. "Em? How'd it go today?"

Emily smiled weakly at her husband. "I'm sorry, babe. I don't mean to be so quiet...I'm just—"

"Exhausted?" Stephen finished her sentence. Emily nodded. "What about the mystery illness? Make any headway?" With that question, Stephen thought she might actually start to cry. He held his hand up. "I retract the question. Just get some dinner in you, and a bit more wine." Stephen refilled Emily's glass. "After this, why don't you hit the hay? We can talk in the morning—I'm all yours tomorrow...and pretty soon, all of the time."

Emily's eyes lit up. "Does that mean what I think it means?"

"Yes. I've sent in my letter of resignation, effective in eight weeks. I'm busting outta prison!" Upon hearing this, Emily did start crying.

"I'm sorry, Stephen—I really am happy." She pointed at her exhausted face and said, "See? These are happy tears."

"And if you turned your head upside down, you'd be smiling too!" Stephen kissed his hand, leaned over the table, touched Emily's lips and face and then wiped her tears away. "We can talk tomorrow. You finish eating and get ready for bed. I'll come tuck you in and maybe even read you a story."

"I love you," said Emily.

"Yes, but will you say that in the morning?" Stephen chuckled as she threw her napkin at him. "Eat. Drink. Bed. Got that?"

"Yes, Reverend...but..."

"But what?"

"But I have to drive down to Bryce County in the morning to see the Moores about their cattle, as well as some other farmers about their livestock." She smiled unconvincingly and gave a Gallic shrug.

"Okay. First, you're not driving—I am. Second, I'll help you organize whatever it is you'll need down there."

"Happily, the second part is done—the pickup's in the driveway. It's why I was late for supper. But we'll need to stop and buy sandwiches for the Gang of Four—they're all coming down, but in Stewart's and Alison's cars—that will help us cover more territory." As she finished the last bites of supper, she added, "Oh, please get the cooler out of the cellar. We'll buy ice on the way."

Stephen put his index finger over his lip. "Enough, my beautiful, caring, tired scientist! We'll sort these things in the morning." He walked around the table and helped pull back Emily's chair. "The bedroom's that way." Stephen gently turned

Emily's torso and pointed. "It's about eighteen feet from here—can you make it?"

"Just about. It's a good thing we live in such a small cottage."

"Indeed. Shout if you need me."

~ * ~

The muffled alarm took several moments to wake Stephen. He had put it under his pillow so as not to wake Emily. His hand groped under the pillow until it found the travel alarm clock. He switched it off and turned to see if Emily was waking. She wasn't. Stephen slipped gently out of bed, put on some shorts and slippers, carried out some ablutions and then went to the kitchen to prepare breakfast. He lifted the waffle iron out of the cupboard—it had been a wedding present, and this was its first outing. Stephen mixed the batter while the iron was heating and then broke some eggs for scrambling. He hoped the scent of breakfast cooking might have a rousing effect. As he went to the boiling kettle to pour water on the tea, the various aromas had done their job. Emily's croaky morning voice made its way to the kitchen, "Zat brea'fast I smell?" Followed by, "Wha'timezit?"

So as not to let anything burn, Stephen made a mad dash to the bedroom door. "Scrambled eggs, waffles and tea in five minutes. It's eight o'clock. We need to leave in thirty minutes." As Stephen returned to the kitchen, he heard the rustling of a waking Emily, followed by the sound of running water and the flushing of the toilet. Emily's long brown hair was still mussed from a night's sleep as she came and flopped onto one of the ladderback dining chairs. Stephen pulled the plates from the oven, each with a stack of waffles. He added the eggs and brought the plates to the table. Emily's eyes widened as she saw the source of the aromas. Her bleary eyes fixed on Stephen as she said, "This is why I married you."

"Well, it sure wasn't for my money," he replied as he kissed her somnolent eyes. "You can nap some more on the way to the Moores' farm, if you like."

"We'll fee," she said, talking with her mouth full. "I 'ave a wot to tell 'ou."

Between bites, Stephen asked, "How did you sleep?"

"Wif my eyes closed." Stephen gave her a gentle kick under the table. "No, I swept wike an'zausted doc'oral can'inate."

"You can wait until you've swallowed to tell me," teased Stephen.

"What fun woul' 'at be?"

"Your sense of humor is certainly refreshed—so that's a good sign." Looking at his watch, he said, "I'll put the rest of the tea in a thermos; we can take it with us. We'd better roll if you want to be there by ten o'clock."

~ * ~

As they drove eastward from Raleigh, Stephen caught Emily up on his chats with James and Lincoln, and their delight that he was getting out of prison work. Emily returned the favor, giving Stephen the bad news about the PCB contamination, and the need for her team and others to find the source—and soon. They drove along for several miles, both thinking about the gravity of both situations. It was Emily who spoke first.

"Is it scary?"

"Driving you to the Moores' farm or leaving prison chaplaincy?"

Emily reached over and tweaked his nose. "Wise ass!" But as usual, she was smiling. "I mean is it scary to leave your job before you find another?"

"A little bit, I suppose, but overall, it just feels right, or what we used to call in theology classes a '*kairos* moment'."

"Now you've lost me the I way lost you with the PCB explanation."

"Well, the Greeks had two basic words for time: *kronos* and *kairos*. *Kronos* refers to measured time: hours, minutes, days, weeks and months—that sort of thing. *Kairos* refers to...well, the *right time* for doing something. Rosa Parks refusing to give up her seat on the bus; Martin Luther King's "I have a dream" speech. *Kairos* is more like God's time wherein good things are meant to happen."

"Like when we met on that bike ride last year?"

"Exactly! I nearly didn't take my bike out that day...but because I *did*, well..." He flashed his wedding ring at Emily, who leaned over and kissed it.

"But back to the job business...well...I'd be happy to spend a few months being your flunky—driving you around or even being your house-husband. Happily, I'm not worried about it."

Emily shook her hair in the spring breeze flooding through the open window, cocked her head and smiled at Stephen. Then she laughed out loud.

"What?" queried Stephen.

"Oh, I'm just picturing you in a skimpy butler's uniform, attending to my beck and call. I could get used to that." She snuggled close and kissed him on the neck, as her hand started exploring his anatomy.

"Hey, I thought you were going to catch some z's while I drove! And be careful what you touch if you want me to stay on the road."

"Well, we could pull over, if that would help," Emily playfully twisted Stephen's longish hair.

"And your promise to be with Clarence Moore at ten? Not to mention meeting your Gang of Four? What's made you so horny?"

"Maybe overwork and stress..." Then, feigning disappointment and pouting, Emily grumbled, "Oh, I guess you're right. Cows' udders are certainly more interesting than mine." She lifted her T-shirt. Stephen nearly ran the truck off the road. But then he checked the mirrors, hit the brakes and pulled the pickup onto the shoulder of the road.

"Let's just hope no one stops to 'help' us," he said. They rolled up their shirts with the side windows for a modicum of privacy.

35

Six

"Just glad I don't wear make-up," muttered Emily, brushing her hair in the rearview mirror as they pulled into the drive leading up to the Moores' farmhouse.

"I think I've just about dried out," replied Stephen. "But at least we have a warm day and no air-conditioning to blame for our appearance." He winked at Emily and they both broke out laughing. They could see the student assistants sitting on the porch talking with the Moores. Stephen switched off the engine and got out first.

"I could barely wake Emily this morning." He shrugged helplessly. "Sorry if we're a bit late."

Alison chirped up, "Hey, it's fine. The Moores have been filling us in about their situation and the other farms in the area.

After Emily and Stephen greeted everyone, Emily took charge. "Okay, we've got a lot of ground to cover. Stewart and Terry, why don't you go to the Longacres' farm and the Pattersons', okay? Mark and Alison, you're getting three farms as they are all close together. Stephen and I are going to follow the creek upstream. Clarence is coming with us in case the landowners worry about what we're doing. But before we leave, take a look at the map—y'all notice anything about the locations of all these farms?"

"Well, yeah," proffered Stewart, tracing his finger along the map, "they're all along State Road 58. But they must be along a thirty mile stretch of road..." His voice trailed away as the gravity of the situation began to sink in. "Someone's dumped the stuff along the roadside!"

"It's beginning to look like that. The problem is that PCBs have no discernable odor, but they can leave a waxy residue—depending upon the type. So, all of you are going to need to stop every mile or so and look for anything suspicious. In any case, you're going to need to bag soil every three stops or so. Be sure to mark where each sample was taken. Oh—I bought some Instamatic cameras last night. Take pictures if you need to identify a site. Okay?" The team members nodded. "Great, let's get over to the truck and I'll give you your equipment." Emily methodically handed out the tools and containers for taking samples, while Stephen handed out the prepared lunch bags.

"Thanks, Dad!" quipped Mark. Stephen pretended to throw a punch at him.

"Oh, and one more thing. Don't take any chances whatsoever with any samples you collect—soil or water. Wear these protective gloves. You've all done enough research in the last forty-eight hours to know what PCBs can do to your health. And some of you might even want to have children one day—so no shortcuts! Got that?"

"Mom and Dad really care about us, don't they?" Mark again.

"Do you really want to stay after school, Mark?" Emily tried to give him her fierce look, but after hers and Stephen's roadside pause not even an hour ago, she just grinned widely. "And finally, Mrs. Moore has kindly agreed to take any messages, if need be, when you stop at the other farms. Shall we try to meet back here say..." she looked at her watch, "about half-past two? If you find you need more time, just ring Mrs. Moore."

"Please, just call me Marcie. We're not very formal around here."

"Well thanks for being 'mission control' for this operation of ours, Marcie; it's a real help."

"Heavens, young'un, it's y'all who are helping us—and many other farmers around here. It's the least I can do. Nothing worse than standing on the sidelines unable to do anything."

Emily looked at her team. "We'd better get moving. Clarence—Stephen and I are with you."

"We can take my truck, if you want. Locals are likely to recognize it. Want me to help put anything you need in the back?" The spring sunshine was starting to assert its power as they moved the required equipment into Clarence's pickup. The metal was hot to touch. Marcie walked over and handed Clarence a bagged lunch.

"His brain will be wanting food before his stomach," offered Marcie. "He's been fretting about this contamination business for days now, and it's shown in his appetite. Oops! I nearly forgot..." Marcie darted back to the house. She soon re-appeared with two bottles of water. 'We've been following your advice," she added.

With that, Emily pulled out a sample bottle and asked Marcie to fill it from the kitchen tap. "Just make sure to give it to me before we leave for Raleigh, okay?"

"Don't you worry," smiled Marcie as she patted Emily on the arm. "Y'all get going now."

~ * ~

None of the group made it back to the Moores' place before three. Terry and Stewart were the first to arrive, followed by Alison and Mark. It was nearly three-thirty when Clarence's truck pulled up the drive. Stewart and Terry, who had been pacing the porch, stopped in their tracks when they saw their team leader approaching, glasses of Marcie's omnipresent iced tea in hand.

The mid-afternoon heat was releasing the fragrance of the wisteria which grew along the porch rail. Chairs awaited Clarence, Emily and Stephen, but before the latter two could be seated, Stewart and Terry approached them, barely containing their anxious excitement. "We found this shit everywhere!" blurted Terry as he held forth a plastic bag with waxy-looking soil. Immediately he turned and apologized to the Moores.

"It's okay, son," replied Clarence. "As I've told the pastor and Dr. Emily here, when you live on a dairy farm you get used to a lot of shit! Of course, we aren't used to *this kind* of shit," he added.

Emily gently took hold of Terry's arm. "Is it okay if Stephen and I sit down and catch our breath? We've all been more than a little busy."

"Oh...uh, yeah...sorry. Guess I got a little carried away."

"I think the reverend and Emily could use some of this," Marcie said as she supplied them with two brim-full glasses of tea.

"Please, y'all can all call me Stephen. As a fellow Southerner, I know it's custom to call a minister reverend or pastor, but I prefer just plain old Stephen—*except for you two*," he pointed at Stewart and Terry, who looked nonplussed—until Stephen laughed. Stephen took a long draught on his tea and then rubbed the glass across his forehead. His eye lit on Clarence, who was doing the exact same thing. Clarence looked up at Stephen and beamed, as he nudged Marcie and said, "See the rev—um, Stephen understands farmhouse air-conditioning. And you tell me not to do it in front of guests." He lifted his glass in a toast to his fellow brow-wiper.

Stephen returned the toast and said, "If it helps."

Emily saw that Stewart and Terry were about to burst, so she invited them first to sit and then deliver their findings slowly and without expletives.

"Okay," began Terry, trying his best to remain calm, "before Stewart and I even got to the two farms you assigned us, we began finding evidence of this...this...um..."

"Shit?" offered Clarence.

Terry laughed and said, "It was all along the roadside."

Stewart nodded in agreement and added, "It was on both sides of the road for miles. It must've been a tanker full."

Clarence rubbed his face with both hands and muttered something under his breath. Marcie reached out and took his hand, squeezing it. He looked up at his wife with a face etched with despair. "Somebody's poisoned our land and water..."

Marcie looked at Emily and her team. "Why would anyone do something like this—kill our animals and endanger our lives? Why?"

"I can give you an answer in one word," responded Emily. Every face turned toward her. "Money."

"Money?!" spat Clarence as he stood upright and stamped his way across the porch and down the steps to the front lawn. He lifted his arms helplessly as he looked around his farm.

"Please tell me how somebody makes money on doing something like this?" He waited in silence.

Emily cleared her throat. "PCBs are long-lasting and expensive to get rid of. It's not so much *making* money as trying to *save* it—by not paying to have it properly and safely removed. That's what I got from my friend, Craig, over at the EPA in the Research Triangle." Seeing the puzzlement on Marcie's face, Emily explained. "That's the Environmental Protection Agency. Craig told me there have been other cases like this around the country. Sometimes the company that makes or uses the PCBs dumps them; other times they pay someone else to do it."

"This place has been in my family for three generations," declaimed Clarence. "It would have been four generations if we hadn't lost our only son, Alan, in Vietnam. Marcie and I...well, we put what was left of our love and energy into our dairy herd these last eleven years. And now this."

Emily bit her lower lip and looked at Stephen, unsure of what to say or do next. At that moment, Marcie slowly got up and

40

walked across the porch and down to her husband. As she put her arm around his waist, his arm made its way around her shoulders, pulling her close. If they spoke to one another, no one on the porch could hear it.

Stephen called gently to the distraught couple, "Marcie and Clarence, would y'all prefer that we gave you some time alone? We could clear off for a while and compare notes—or even head back to Raleigh."

"You'll do nothing of the sort!" came Marcie's reply. She wiped her eyes before she turned around. "Matter of fact, I've got supper cooking for all of you. I meant to tell you earlier, but things kinda got busy fast. So y'all do what you've got to do and I'll arm twist Clarence into helping me prepare dinner. It'll be early so y'all can get back to Raleigh before evening." She gave her husband a friendly nudge and pulled him by the arm. "C'mon Farmer Brown, this herd of young'uns needs feeding. We can see to the milking while they're eating." Clarence silently nodded and followed his wife.

Mark looked each team member in the eye and then said, "It's easy to think we're 'just doing science'," he made quotation marks with his fingers. He then turned to Emily, "But now I see why you have been so...well...*driven* in this case; and why you've pushed us. In the end, this is all about the lives of *real people*. I mean...it's not that the cattle don't matter, but they're part of a bigger picture. I guess I've missed that by simply carrying out tests in the lab—it's all so clinical and removed from life." Mark sat back in his chair, deep inside his personal reflections and revelations.

Alison added her thoughts into the mix. "If I realize my dream of becoming a veterinarian, I don't think I'll be able to walk onto a farm and just consider what's wrong with an animal. I mean, how do you deal with the fact that the Moores have lost their only son and heir, and that they see him in all of this?" She lifted her hands wide, indicating the entire farm complex.

"I don't mean this to be funny," interjected Stephen, "but just like doctors have to work on their 'bedside manner,' it seems you'll need to do the same with *barnside* manner. Everything we do in life is invested with *us*; it's all part of our individual stories. And those stories need to be treated with respect. It's no different than my work in prisons. It's all too easy to look at men and women behind bars simply as 'inmates,' and to assume that's all they are. But they were children once. They had families and friends. And yes, at some point they took a wrong direction—but they are more than inmates. They are full, three-dimensional human beings, just like you and me."

They all sat in quiet reflection for a few moments and then Stewart piped up. "Emily, does your husband preach like that?"

Smiling at Stephen and looking him over quizzically, she replied, "I suppose he does—not that I've heard him that often, because he's usually behind bars when he preaches." This brought a chuckle from the undergraduates, but Stewart persisted. "I probably would've kept going to church if our preacher had made that kind of sense...like you just did," he looked at Stephen, "but I'll pass on hearing you in prison!"

"I don't blame you, but I'll accept your compliment with thanks." Then turning to Emily, Stephen added, "Methinks my scientist wife needs to discuss your findings with you, right?" Emily nodded her assent and they launched into reports from the five other farms, as well as the roadside 'gunk' samples collected by Stewart and Terry. The water from the creek, along with all the other samples would have to wait until they were back at the lab. The most disturbing news of all was the fact that each farm reported news from other farms whose animals were displaying similar symptoms as those of the Moores' cattle. "Did you get their locations?" asked a hopeful Emily.

All four assistants gave a resounding, "Yes!"

"We don't work for just anybody, *Dr. Travis*," came Terry's mock ingratiating response.

"Let's just be clear that I can't help you with your grades, Terry. But if you ever need a reference for being a lab assistant, you've got it!" offered Emily. She looked from one undergraduate to another. "That goes for all of you. But right now, let's get to mapping those other farms." Emily unfolded the North Carolina map and laid it on the table.

"I'm afraid we're going to need county maps, 'cause some of these farms are on tiny state roads," Mark said.

"Right. Well, let's do the best we can then," stated Emily. It didn't take them long to determine that whoever had dumped the toxic waste had, according to the locations of the farms, made a loop onto Route 43.

"Damn," Mark muttered under his breath, "that's four counties—that we know of—and more than sixty miles of road. And these are from the farms which have reported their problems. There must be others, I'll bet."

Emily tapped one spot on the map: the Tar River Reservoir. "Nearly every creek in the southern part of our study area flows into the Tar River. And the reservoir is right between two good-sized cities: Rocky Mount and Wilson. And Greenville is also on the Tar River. I've got to get onto Craig at the EPA. There are more than livestock at risk." Standing up, Emily peeked through the screen door into the house. "I'll just go see if I can use the Moores' phone to call Craig. This can't wait until tomorrow." She knocked and then entered, following the sound of voices to the kitchen at the rear of the house.

In the meantime, Alison asked Stephen, "How did it go with you, Emily and Mr. Moore?"

"We followed the creek, taking samples, until it joined the Tar River, then we drove back northward until we couldn't get to the creek anymore. As Mark said, we're going to need detailed county maps to be sure which creek is which. It got a little confusing crisscrossing farms and back roads. What about you four? Were you dealing with creeks, ponds or wells?"

Stewart answered first. "All three in our case. One was a wind pump. If that's clean, at least we'll know the PCBs haven't entered the aquifer." All agreed that would be a hoped-for outcome.

Somewhat timidly, Stewart put a question to Stephen. "You've worked in criminal justice for quite some time and...I mean...I know you're not a cop or anything, but do you have any idea if whoever dumped the PCBs can ever be found? Emily has told us a little bit about the case you blew open in the prison system."

"Oh yeah, that's me, a real Sherlock Holmes." They all laughed. "I wish I could tell you, but your guess is as good as mine. I know one thing I'd bet on—those dumpings must have taken place at night. The communities around here are too small for some stranger in a tanker truck—or whatever—to go cruising along while pouring or spraying this stuff along the roadside. Let's just hope that as news gets out, someone will have noticed something." As Stephen finished speaking, Marcie appeared at the screen door. "Y'all come on in and wash your hands before dinner. There's a bathroom along this hallway on the right and another one at the top of the stairs. Emily's already at the table." When everyone had gathered at the table, Marcie turned to Stephen. "We can't have a preacher at the table and not ask him to ask the blessing. Emily here tells me you can do it in Hebrew—just be sure to translate it for the rest of us. Marcie and Clarence reached out to take the hands of those sitting next to them. Mark and Terry showed some embarrassment, dropping their faces, but followed the household tradition. Stephen intoned the traditional Jewish blessing for meals, *haMotsi*, much to the amazement of the four undergraduates. He then translated: "Blessed art Thou O Lord our God, King of the universe, who brings forth bread from the earth. Amen."

"Hey," remarked Terry, "'amen' is the same in Hebrew—I heard it!"

"Funny thing about that," jibed Stephen.

"How did you come to learn Hebrew?" asked Clarence. "You rattled that off just like it was in English."

"I suppose I learned it the same way you learned the dairy trade. You had an abiding interest in it."

"Now this is a good topic," interjected Marcie, "because I've already told Clarence and your lovely wife that we are *not* talking about PBCs or whatever they are at dinner. Please continue, Stephen."

Seven

Emily and Stephen clinked their beer bottles in a toast as they watched the WRAL Late News on television. For once, there was a story that bumped the Iran-hostage affair—which had dominated most of 1980 so far—out of its place as top story. As the TV reporter interviewed Emily, Stephen could be seen in the background talking with a newspaper reporter from the *News and Observer* outside the animal science building at the university.

"Do you have any proof that someone deliberately dumped the PCBs into the water supplies for farms in four counties?" asked the WRAL reporter, wearing more makeup than Jackie Collins.

"It's four counties *that we know of*, four counties *so far*," responded Emily with clear determination in her voice. Then she looked directly at the camera. "Polychlorinated biphenyls, or PCBs," she stated with emphasis, "are not naturally occurring substances. And they are deadly to humans and animals—make no mistake. Do we have proof of *who* did it? Not yet."

"Great response," blurted Stephen as he gave Emily a hug. She was leaning into his shoulder as they sat on the sofa.

"But again," continued Emily, "and I want your listeners to be clear about this: PCBs don't just suddenly appear along *more than sixty miles of highway* without human agency. And any animals drinking from contaminated water sources will, more than likely, need to be slaughtered." At that moment in the news footage, the reporter from the *News and Observer* could be seen almost dragging Stephen into the frame. She could be heard almost shouting, "Do you know who this is?" indicating Stephen. But the pushy TV reporter was not about to share the air with a newspaper reporter. The *News and Observer* would have to run its story in the morning.

"Aren't you being a bit alarmist?" asked the WRAL reporter, playing the people's advocate. "These animals are people's livelihoods." The camera caught Emily taking a slow, deep breath and biting her lower lip to stop herself from saying whatever was on the tip of her tongue.

"What were you about to say?" queried Stephen.

"Oh, probably something like, 'You ignorant bitch.'" She looked at Stephen and they both laughed. On the television Emily was explaining that PCBs are cumulative for animals and for the humans who eat the animal products—milk, eggs, meat and the like. "This goes for fish, too. The streams we tested flow into the Tar River."

The sassy reporter couldn't stop her cynical line of questioning. "So, if humans consume contaminated cows' milk or pork from contaminated pigs, what happens to them? Surely *they* can't be slaughtered?" Again, looking directly at the camera, and by extension, thousands of viewers, Emily made a 'what the F?' face as she pointed at the reporter and simply said, "Look lady, I'm an animal scientist, not a physician. Just give it time. There will be plenty of doctors to interview." As that news segment ended, Stephen and Emily howled at the aplomb with which she had handled the reporter.

~ * ~

The telephone rang before the alarm clock. "What timezit?" mumbled Emily. Stephen rubbed his sleep-fused eyes and picked up the bedside clock.

"Six-thirty...shit! Who's calling us at this hour?"

"Dunno," muttered Emily as she used both hands and feet to push her husband from the bed. "You go."

Stephen moved wearily toward the living/dining room to the side table where the telephone kept bleating at him. He swilled saliva around his tongue and grumbled, "Hello?"

"You lookin' to get another bullet in your head?"

"Who is this?" demanded Stephen.

"Or what about that pretty wife of yours? How'd she look with a hole in her head? Y'all just keep doing what you've been doing and see what happens."

"You pissant little coward! If you want me, come and face me instead of hiding behind an anonymous call, you pathetic prick!" The line went dead.

Emily was calling out to Stephen from the bedroom. "What on earth is going on? Who were you shouting at?!"

"Oh, just some asshole who offered to put another bullet in my head. You know, everyday stuff." He let go a streak of expletives that ministers—in common lay opinion—are not supposed to know, much less use.

"What?" exclaimed Emily who was already out of bed and tying her dressing gown at the waist.

"It was an anonymous caller who threatened me—and you—if we don't stop doing what we're doing." Before they could continue, the telephone rang again. Both stopped and stared at it.

"Let me answer," insisted Emily. Stephen deferred to her with a wave of the hand. She lifted the received like it was broken glass. "Hello?"

48

Emily's face changed from alarm to a half-smile. "No, we haven't seen the morning paper." She mouthed, "It's Mother" to Stephen and ran her hand through her tousled hair. "No, you didn't; we were already awake." She raised her eyes heavenward "Why? It says *what*? Yes, I did chat to reporters from several newspapers last night. One practically wouldn't let Stephen go until I spoke with her—yes, the *News and Observer* and its affiliates." Emily's mouth opened wide and she placed her hand over it in astonishment. "You're kidding! Really? Well, what a hoot! Stephen will get a kick out of it. Thanks, Mom. We love you too. Bye."

Emily set the receiver on its cradle and walked over to Stephen, put her arms around his waist and kissed him fully on the lips. "I don't think she was your anonymous caller." Stephen chuckled despite himself. "Nah, your mom would have the guts to face me." He squeezed Emily tightly and put his face in her hair. "It really lit my fuse when that asshole threatened you. If he'd been in front of me, I would've torn his head off his shoulders."

"My hero," teased Emily, "the Killer Chaplain."

"Hey, I'm serious!" he pulled back from their embrace and looked Emily in the eyes.

"I know you are—and I'm touched...but also worried. It feels like *déjà vu*." She placed both hands on his face. "*You don't need this.*"

"Well, neither do you. But it's happening." Stephen looked at the clock on the wall. "It's quarter to seven...what do you say to a morning bike ride? We can get some fresh air and I can burn off the adrenalin rush I got from the friendly caller. What do you say?"

Emily thought it over for a brief moment. "You're on—but only thirty minutes. You know what's in store for me at the lab."

"Done! I'll wear my watch. I'll even come help you in the lab, if you like." The couple hastily donned their bike gear, but before they could get their bikes off the back porch, the telephone rang again. Stephen rolled his eyes. "My turn?"

"Let's both answer it," suggested Emily. They walked back inside. Stephen lifted the receiver and they both put their ears to the phone. Emily silently counted by showing one-two-three fingers. "Hello?" they both intoned.

"Hey—um, Stephen—Emily? Have I got you both on the line?" It was James at the Advancement Center. Emily nodded to Stephen to take over. "Yeah, we both answered the phone...Yeah, you're right, we only have one phone," spoke Stephen, "Look man, I'll explain it to you tomorrow when I come in for the worship service." Stephen motioned for Emily to place her ear at the receiver again. "Yeah, she's right here with me. No, I haven't seen the newspaper yet—funnily enough, you're second person to call and ask us that this morning."

James' energetic voice spoke with enthusiasm. "Brother man, you must only be happy when you're busting crime—am I right? And now you got Emily involved with you. Listen to this, listen..." Stephen could hear the newspaper crinkling in the background. "This is in the editorial section: 'The name of the Rev. Stephen Travis should be familiar to regular readers of this paper, as he recently helped break up a criminal ring involving state correctional staff. Now Raleigh's own 'Sherlock Travis' has teamed up with his very own 'Dr. Watson,' otherwise known as his scientist wife, Dr. Emily Webster, to break open a case of toxic waste dumping in eastern North Carolina.'" Stephen and Emily looked at each other in amusement. "Listen to this," continued James, "'Where the NC Highway Patrol, county sheriffs and police fail, this intrepid duo step into the breach.' No wonder you're resigning from prison chaplaincy, my man, you're too busy out fighting crime." Fowler finally took a breath—perhaps just so he could laugh.

Emily used the break to speak to James. "Well, you've saved me from having to tell Stephen the same thing all over again. My mom called us a short while ago after having read the same article in her newspaper this morning. You called us just after I had put the phone down." Then, looking at Stephen, she asked, "James, will you be at the unit tomorrow?"

"Sure thing—in the afternoon. Why?"

"I just think Stephen will want to talk to you about this 'crime busting' activity of ours, that's all." Stephen nodded toward the door and their bikes. Emily acknowledged the message with a return nod. "Well look, James, we have to dash. Thanks for calling. Stephen will see you tomorrow. Bye." Putting the receiver down, Emily blurted out, "Run! Before the phone rings again!"

As they pedaled away from the cottage, Emily asked, "Are you aware you hold your breath when you're dealing with negative things? Even driving?"

"Vaguely aware, I guess. Why?"

"It's just something I've noticed in our life together. Not many romances have a car chase and gunplay as a lead up to marriage vows." Stephen let out a guffaw despite himself. "As your wife, and a scientist, I just wanted to make sure you knew that breathing was important."

"I'll try to bear that in mind."

"Try not to think about it too hard—it's much better when you breathe automatically."

Stephen made a mock rude gesture at Emily, upon which she feigned shock, pulled her bike close in to Stephen's and smacked his bottom. Stephen dropped a gear and pedaled hard, leaving Emily to catch up.

"Your ass is mine, Reverend Travis!" she growled as she bore down in hot pursuit.

Eight

Stephen arrived at the center an hour before the Sunday morning worship was to start. He wanted time to sort through his mail and prepare his thoughts for the service—both for the spiritual content as well as what he planned to say afterward. The service was always at ten-thirty so the men could have a little slower start to the day, attend the service and have lunch before afternoon visits with their families.

Officer Martin, a newbie, was on the main desk when Stephen arrived. When Stephen greeted him, Martin smiled in such a way as to indicate he was concealing something. The dayroom, across from Stephen's office, was totally deserted—unusual for a Sunday morning. A few of the men were in the kitchen preparing Sunday's lunch—which smelled particularly appetizing. When Stephen arrived at his office door, he was greeted by a poster containing a silhouette of Sherlock Holmes, with deerstalker and pipe, and '221B Baker Street.' Underneath was a new name plate: 'S. Travis, Det.' The 'Travis' was lightly marked through with a felt-tip pen, with 'Holmes' written above. As Stephen stood and shook his head in amusement, the empty dayroom started filling with men. There followed spontaneous applause and laughter. Before Stephen could react, he was enclosed by two score men who were pumping his hand, slapping his back, hugging him. One of the crowd pointed out the name plate: "Look, Rev, you only got to change your last name!" Each man wanted Stephen to hear how they had learned about the part he had played in Emily's discovery of the toxic waste dumping—be it television news, newspaper or radio. Three of the men were from counties affected by the PCB pollution and expressed concern for their rural relatives.

All of a sudden, Stephen felt a kinship with the men he had never felt. Somehow, the former, clearly delineated line between incarcerated and free vanished, like the morning dew on these increasingly warmer spring days. In spite of the joyful chaos surrounding him, mentally he was trying to work out why he was feeling this way...*now*. Certainly, he had felt a pastoral love and care for his 'flock' when he had taken their revelations seriously—regarding the scheme run by the now-deceased Officer Melvin Strader.

Stephen never made it into his office. Rather, the surrounding group of men moved him into the dayroom where he sat, chatting, joking and laughing with the men. Before he knew it, the clock on the wall was reading ten twenty-five. Stephen glanced at his watch to make sure that was the correct time. This did not go unnoticed by the residents, who began jibing him. "Got somewhere to go, Rev?" "S'matter? You gettin' tired of our company?"

Stephen protested as nicely as he could that he had a service to lead in just a few minutes. "Oh," said Marvin Jacobs, one of the men who had come to Stephen with evidence regarding the used car scam. "You think we wanna listen to *you* preach again?" He let Stephen sweat it out for a brief moment and then laughed out loud. He turned to his fellow long-timers and said, "We really had the rev going there for a minute!" He then waved his hand at Stephen. "Naw, man, you ain't gotta do nuthin' this morning. We got it covered. You just relax and listen." Stephen was in a mild state of shock, not knowing what to say or how to respond. Marvin continued, "A little jailbird told us you're a short-timer." Instinctively, Stephen looked around. "Ain't no good lookin' at the fellas," continued Marvin. "*You know* there ain't no secrets in prison." He let loose his distinctive laugh, a string of heh-hehs like the staccato of a machine gun. "It's like this, Rev. Couple of us gonna be outta here soon—including me. So we wanted to do this for you, while we're all still together. Delbert here is gonna read the Gospel and Tyrone Mason is preachin'. So you just kick back and relax. Got that?"

"Hey, you're in charge." Stephen put up his hands in surrender. At that same moment he caught a glimpse of James Fowler and Lincoln Parker in the corridor. One of whom, Stephen was sure, had let the residents know about his resignation. As Delbert Moore got up to read, James and Lincoln grabbed chairs from the dining hall and sat behind the men. Delbert was one of only two short-timers in this unit intended for men who had spent long years in prison to re-adjust before release back into the free world. He had been set up for a marijuana bust by a crooked sheriff in eastern North Carolina, where Delbert was a town councilor. The town governing body had been looking into the sheriff's wheelings and dealings, when he got wind of it and framed Delbert for drug trafficking. Because Delbert was a first offender, who was white, and with a hitherto untarnished record, the judge showed 'leniency,' giving Delbert eighteen months in an open prison. He used his time working toward a master's degree in Elizabethan English via an extension program at UNC. Delbert read from John's Gospel, chapter 15:12-13. "This is my commandment, that you love one another as I have loved you. Greater love has no man than this, that a man lay down his life for his friends." Biting his lip, Delbert pointed at Travis. "You are that man." Stephen felt the air being punched out of his lungs and tears well up in his eyes, so taken aback was he by those words.

54

Hands slapped his back and shoulders and Stephen grasped as many of them as he could.

As two-thirds of the men were African-American, the hymns they sang were usually with a gospel flavor—something Stephen enjoyed. Marvin put on a cassette of Mahalia Jackson singing, "Move on up a Little Bit Higher," and asked everyone who knew it to join in. The song relates the hope of meeting in heaven all those who have gone before us in faith—from biblical times to our own families and friends. Travis knew full well that some of these men had lost many of their nearest and dearest while serving decades behind bars. It was their song and their story of hope. As the song ended, Tyrone Mason—a multi-muscled specimen of a man—stood to bring the Word to the gathered throng.

"Y'all know me," he began, slowly letting his gaze engage each man in the dayroom. "Some of you might even be wonderin' why I'm standin' here. Not just because I ain't a preacher, but because of the kind of man I am. And that's fine. You'd be right to think that way. I rode the fence so long between doing what's right and doing what's wrong in this place—and you all know what I'm talking about—that my butt crack is deeper than the Grand Canyon!"

The congregation erupted with laughter and applause, and shouts of "Tell it!"

"Yeah, I got caught by them Strader brothers in their crappy-ass car scheme. And I didn't want to see no more time behind them prison walls—not after gettin' so close to release." He held up his thumb and forefinger a hair's breadth apart to emphasize his point. He nodded and looked around the room again. "So I played their game...enough to keep my butt here...but I also tried to help our brother, the chaplain," Tyrone opened his outstretched right palm toward Stephen, "to be aware of the...the..." Tyrone waved his hand around as though trying to capture the right word.

"All the shit that was going down?" called out one of his fellow residents.

Tyrone smiled and pointed to the man who had spoken. "Yeah, you named it! The shit that caught a lot of us just like quicksand."

Another round of "Yeah!" "Tell it!" and "Amen!" followed.

But then the smile left Tyrone's face and his head dropped as he stood in silence for a few moments. In *mea culpa* fashion, his right fist began to beat his firm pectoral muscles. Still looking at the floor, Tyrone recommenced, "Most of y'all know I'm workin' out whenever I'm not out workin'." He let out a snort of laughter. "I like to think I'm tough...maybe even hard." He shook his head, "Hell, I'm not hard, I'm not strong. Now Walter Jackson—he died trying to call the Strader brothers on what they was doing to him, to me and a lot of y'all. Jesus says "Greater love has no man than to lay down his life for his friends. Jackson had the courage to do that." Tyrone's audience made noises of approbation as they nodded thoughtfully. "And *me*, what did I do? When it was clear Chaplain Travis was figuring things out here, I did what Strader tole me to do and stuck a bullet under his windshield wiper." Tyrone's head rose up as he looked straight at Stephen. "I-I tole myself I was protecting you, by...by sending you a warning to back off. I knew why Jackson got hi'self shot when he tried to run that night. I didn't want to see the same thing happen to you..." Tyrone's head dropped again, "But I sure as hell didn't want it to happen to *me*...I wanted my freedom more than anything...more than doing the right thing. Jackson done more time than most of us here. He was on the way *out*! But he done the right thing and *died* for it. His was the 'greater love.' And that brings me to our chaplain here." Tyrone shook his head and smiled at an inward thought. "Jackson gets killed, I tried to warn Rev off with the bullet—and, oh yeah, I punctured your car tires as well—" At this comment the men started shaking their heads and shouting out rude comments at Tyrone—mainly in jest. Tyrone waved his hands at himself and said, "Yeah, I got it comin'. Y'all bring it on!"

56

"Kinda figured it was you," called out Stephen, with a smile.

"And then, and then, what happens?" asked a fully animated Tyrone. "Chaplain Travis and the two brothers in the back," he pointed toward James and Lincoln, "throw us a Christmas party as—I might add—a way to speak to all of the families who'd had the Straders lean on 'em to buy a used car. And on the way home our man, Sherlock Travis, gets a bullet in his head, that come pretty close to killing him. That bullet could just as well have been for me—or you, Marvin—or many others here today." The men became more audible with their acknowledgments of the truth Tyrone was telling. "You see, 'greater love has no man.' Travis has a steel plate in his head because of what was happening *to us*! He coulda backed off-but he didn't! That's the greater love."

The men surrounding Stephen began clapping and pushing him forward. As he got to his feet, he gave up the battle to hold back his tears. Tyrone put one of his stout arms around Travis's shoulders. For his part, Stephen was fishing out his handkerchief to wipe his streaming eyes.

Tyrone raised his hand for silence. "And that's not all. Who speaks in my defense when the state investigators come 'round to find out who all was involved in the Straders' dirty business?" He looked at Stephen. "My man here." Now Tyrone's eyes were reddening and he gave them a swipe with the back of his hand. Pointing at Stephen, his voice broke. "Didn't hafta say anything— for or against me. Coulda let justice takes its course. Had every reason to let my ass get sent back behind them walls for another four years." Now Tyrone was biting his lower lip. "Greater love." He used his index finger for emphasis. "That's what that is, greater love. I thank God for you, my man." Tyrone hugged Stephen and then asked for the closing hymn. All the men hastily pulled out sheets of folded paper from their pockets.

Delbert stood up and said, "This is a variation on a well-known hymn." He gave the men a count and in unison they sang:

"What a friend we have in Travis

All our sins and grief to bear.
What a privilege to share them,
With the rev with shaggy hair.
Killers, thieves, it does not matter;
What we've done, he doesn't care,
We can share whatever we like,
With the rev with shaggy hair!"

Everyone cheered and clapped following the 'hymn.' Delbert shouted above the din, "Sorry, Rev, but that's all the lyrics I could write with such short notice. It will have to do!"

Stephen's tears had been quickly replaced by joyful laughter. "That was just fine, Delbert! I only wish that Emily could have heard it!"

"Oh, I think she heard it just fine," yelled Lincoln from behind the main group of men. He motioned for Emily to come from around the corner where she had been secreted by Lincoln and James. She was dabbing her eyes with a tissue and smiling at the same time. The residents parted like the Red Sea and pulled her forward to be with Stephen. The couple were both overcome by their mutual surprise, emotion and joy. But, in fact, Stephen was flabbergasted.

"Who pulled all of this together? The only three people I told about my resignation are here in this room. I just wrote my letter of resignation three days ago." Stephen shook his head in disbelief.

"Look at that," said Lincoln, "the man can't keep himself from investigating things!" Lincoln walked over to Travis, laid his hands on Stephen's shoulders, and said, "Stop—asking—questions! Just for a little while, okay?" Extending his right arm and indicating everyone around Stephen and Emily, Lincoln added, "This is simply one of life's mysteries."

Still astonished by all that was happening, Stephen looked at Emily and asked, "Wh-when did you find out about all of this?"

"Just after you left this morning. An...um...*anonymous* caller said I wouldn't want to miss the surprise they had in store for you today—so here I am. Oh, and as Lincoln said, stop asking questions!"

From the kitchen a voice hollered, "Lunch will be ready in ten minutes!" With that, the gathered throng began migrating toward the tables, which were set with tablecloths—a rarity in correctional facilities, except for perhaps Christmas, and even then, it depended upon what level of security the unit was. Just when Stephen thought the surprises were over, in walked Ben Katz, the staff psychologist from the women's prison adjacent to the Fairborn Advancement Center. He was hand-in-hand with Kate McIntyre, his psychologist colleague and steady date. Their blossoming relationship was a spark of joy and hope in the drab, grey environment of prison life and work. Ben had served as one of Stephen's three best men, along with James and Lincoln.

"*Nu?*" said Ben, as he approached Stephen with outstretched hand. "It's good you keep doing things like getting married and resigning from prison chaplaincy. It gives Kate and me an excuse to go out together. What's next, a *bris?*"

Stephen laughed as he shook Ben's hand. "No thanks. I'm covered in that department." Stephen kissed Kate's cheek as they greeted each other.

"Watch it, Travis! That's my future wife you're kissing," snapped Ben in jest.

Stephen's eyes widened with delight. "*Mazel tov!* Just for that, I'll kiss her again!"

"I think Ben and I must have drunk something at your wedding," beamed Kate, "Or maybe we've spent too much time with you and Emily. Who knows? But in any case, Ben and I have been delighted to discover we have more in common than clinical psychology and prison."

"That's just her polite way of saying she's hot for me," blurted Ben.

59

Kate opened her mouth wide in feigned shock and gave Ben a soft smack. "You naughty man!"

"You know you love it," retorted the irrepressible Ben. And then, to Emily and Stephen, "Dirty talking—Kate can't get enough of it."

"Time out!" called James as he placed both of his large hands on Stephen's shoulders and turned him toward his place at a table. "Everybody find a seat so our chaplain can say grace." Conversations came to a halt as the men, joined by Kate and Emily, gathered at the tables.

Stephen cleared his throat and began. "For food that came not from our planting, our tending or gathering, but which sustains us in this gift which is life, may God our Creator make us truly grateful..." Stephen paused, for he had intended to end his prayer at that point, "and, Lord, thank you for your gifts of forgiveness, love and renewal, which you freely offer all of us here, making it possible for us all to have new beginnings...particularly these men who have spent too much of their lives away from those they love and who love them. Bless them and keep them. Amen."

Amens resounded around the dining hall. The staff cook, as well as his resident helpers, had outdone themselves with roast chicken and gravy, baked potatoes, green beans and corn bread—a veritable Southern feast.

During the meal, several of the men came over to congratulate Emily on her work exposing the dumping of PCBs in several of North Carolina's most rural, and poorest, counties. All but a few of the men at the center had come from rural areas—it stood to reason. It wasn't so much the nature of the crimes that put them behind bars for so long, as the crime of being poor, or worse, poor and black. The counties where the PCBs were dumped had a few sizeable black-owned farms, but for the most part the biggest financial losers were white. Yet when it came to the endangerment of human health, all suffered equally. Toxic waste does not discriminate.

~ * ~

Following the meal, Kate and Ben stuck around to chat with Stephen and Emily. "I don't know how much I've told you about my family," began Ben. "Half of my family thought I'd gone beyond the pale when I moved to North Carolina...and now, I'm marrying a shicksa. Guess I'll find out what it's like to be the living dead."

"Is it really that bad?" asked Stephen.

Ben looked at Stephen with mock sympathy. "*Nu*? The *only* son with three—count 'em—*three* sisters? You work it out." Then he turned to Kate, who wore a half-smile, while her eyes expressed pain for Ben. "This woman can't make a brisket, has never eaten gefilte fish or lox and bagels and probably hasn't a clue what latkes is. But I love her gentile ass!" At this Kate rolled her eyes.

"He is endearing, isn't he?" joked Stephen. "But what can you do? We find love where we find it. Emily and I are happy for you."

"Are you so happy you'd be willing to help conduct the wedding?—along with a rabbi, providing I can find one, of course. But, if I can't, well...at least you're circumcised—that's a start. And you can read Hebrew." He turned to Emily and asked, "How do you think he'd look in a yarmulke?"

"I'm prejudiced, Ben. I think he'd look good in anything—or nothing." She winked at Ben, who bellowed with laughter.

"No nudist weddings—I draw the line there. A Jewish-Christian marriage is enough to deal with. With the help of *haShem baruk-hu*, I might be able to get my younger sister Esther, and her husband, to attend...and perhaps some cousins. We shall see."

"Do you really think you'll have trouble getting a rabbi to officiate?" asked Stephen.

"I'll let you know. Truth to tell, I've been splitting my Shabbats between the Conservative and Reform synagogues. I'm pretty sure the Reform rabbi will consider it. Once I've spoken to him, I'll let you know. *Vey ist mir*! A Christian wife, a Reform rabbi and a—what are you anyway," teased Ben.

"Methodist, the last time I checked," grinned Stephen.

"Sounds like the beginning of a joke: A Christian woman, a rabbi and a Methodist minister go into a bar..."

"Better work on the punchline," jibed Stephen. "Especially if you're going to use it at the wedding feast."

Nine

"So, our phone line has a trace on it?" asked Stephen between bites over supper.

"Yeath," replied Emily, having just shoved a last forkful of spaghetti into her mouth. She slurped at the sauce which was about to slide off her lower lip. "Wif all 'at was goin' on, we 'idn't 'ave time to 'iscuss it."

"Ah, my beautiful, bright—but messy—eater." Stephen leaned across the table with his napkin and wiped Emily's lips. "You are so...so..."

"So'isticated?" interjected Emily.

"Yes, that's exactly the word I was looking for. "You know, an older ministerial colleague of mine once told me that, in his pre-marital counselling, he always tells young couples to think of the one annoying habit their partner has and then multiply it by, say, fifty years. He then tells them to consider whether they could live with that habit for that long. If the answer is 'no,' then bail out now."

"Did you use his formula with me?" enquired Emily.

"I sure did."

"And?"

"I cheated."

"You cheated? How?"

"I multiplied by forty-nine years!" Stephen gave a cheeky grin. Emily threw her napkin at him, grabbed the beer she was drinking, took a large gulp and began gargling with it. When Stephen nearly choked with laughter, so did Emily—with the effect that beer splattered everything on the table, as well as Stephen.

"You are a crazy woman!"

"Well, you married me!" retorted Emily.

~ * ~

As they lay in bed a little while later, they sniggered at the fact that recently they had made love anywhere except their bed. "At least we haven't fallen into a routine so early in our marriage," offered Stephen. He propped his head on his hand as he gazed upon his wife and lover. His hand traced its way along the contours of her face. Then a thought sprang into his mind. "Say, weren't you telling me about our phone calls being traced, before we...ah...were so sensuously interrupted?"

Emily took his finger in her hand and kissed it. "Yes. I called the phone company yesterday and told them about the threatening call we had, so they're monitoring calls for the next two weeks or so. The guy I spoke with also said we should let the police know, so I did that as well. I told them to read the article in the *News and Observer* if they wanted more background. It seems that's all we can do for now. After all that you—well *we*—have been through in recent months, there's no point in waiting for something to happen."

"No, you're right about that. Thanks for being on the ball, Em," mumbled Stephen, who was falling into slumber.

Emily patted his chest, before laying her head over his heart. "We are in this together." She listened as the rhythm of Stephen's breathing and heartbeat slowed down, but just as she was drifting into the blissful oblivion of sleep, Stephen's whole body jerked and he called out her name. Realizing he was dreaming, she gave him a firm, but gentle shake.

With dazed eyes, he looked at Emily who was now propped on her elbows over him. "Oh, God, not again?" he groaned.

"Yep," replied Emily. "Same nightmare?"

"Variation on a theme," he replied. "Except you were being shot instead of me."

"When do you see your counsellor next?"

"Tuesday."

"That's good. Be sure to tell him about that call...and the nightmares, okay?"

"Be sure of it," Stephen replied. "Em?"

"Yes?"

"Glad you were at the center today..."

"Me too. Now take some slow, deep breaths, my love." Emily lightly stroked Stephen's brow. "Think about our lovely honeymoon in Asheville...sitting by that big roaring fireplace...the mountaintops covered in snow...our walks...making love in the that big four-poster bed..." Stephen twitched a bit and then slipped into a peaceful somnolence. He was soon joined by Emily.

Ten

"Okay, team, fill me in. What did I miss yesterday?"

"A day of work when you should be off on Sunday anyway," teased Stewart. He looked at his colleagues who gave him the nod to continue. "Now that we have tested all of our samples, it's become clear that the PCB spillage was done all along the roads we traveled. It continued over the bridges, which is how it got into the streams."

"Bastards!" grimaced Emily.

"Fucking bastards, in our opinion," added Alison. They all laughed with dark humor. "Mark and I drove back out to Bryce County yesterday morning and took samples to see how far from the road the PCBs were sprayed in order to estimate how many gallons were dumped. The average distance from the tarmac to the end of the spread was six feet." She looked at Emily and she signaled for her to continue. "We found the penetration was deeper immediately by the tarmac than further out, so even if we reduced the figure to something more conservative, we're looking at maybe thirty thousand gallons per mile." Emily's mouth fell open and she searched for a chair.

"But of course, we didn't stop but every few miles," added Mark, fearful his supervisor might faint. "Still...it is *a lot*." The four undergraduates looked at each other nervously.

Sensing there was more to be said, Emily demanded, "Okay, out with it. What other happy news is there?"

"There were some messages on the office answerphone," mumbled Terry. "I...I played them when I got in...um, do you want to hear them or shall I read my notes?"

Emily' face looked drawn as she asked Terry to read his notes.

"Well, the first one was from the Longacres...their son and daughter-in-law have been trying to get pregnant over the last few months, but no luck...and...em, they live in a trailer down near one of the springs. Oh, and neither the son nor his wife have been feeling very well of late. They want to know if the PCBs could be responsible."

Emily ran her hand over her brow several times and then over her chestnut hair. "Continue."

Stewart was clearly nervous, as his voice trembled when he read the next one. "Uh...this next one is kinda nasty and is aimed at you. I'd rather not read it, if you don't mind?"

"That's okay, Terry. What's the upshot?'

"Well, it was a man and he called you all sorts of bad names and made threats against you. I—uh—have saved the recording in case you want to call the police. I also called campus security, just to be safe. One of the officers should be here any minute now."

Emily made a fist with her right hand and softly pounded her thigh. She looked at each team member slowly, and then pronounced with deliberation, "Y'all know that this puts you at risk, don't you? I wouldn't blame you if you wanted to pull out. It's my name that's been associated with this mess, but if we—or I— am getting threats here...well, who knows? Anyway, you don't have to make a decision now; just think about it."

"Hell," blurted Mark. "I've never done anything this important—not important enough to get threats—" At that moment there was a knock at the open lab door. Two officers stood in the doorway. One was a campus policeman, the other from the city. Emily invited them in and introduced herself.

"Hope you don't mind, but I invited a colleague from the Raleigh police. He tells me you've already been in touch about a threatening call at your home, right?"

"Yes, that's right. I'm glad you're here together. It will save having to go through it all a second time." Although Emily smiled, the tension in her face betrayed her worry.

After taking all of the team members' names, addresses and listening to the recording, the campus policeman asked if he could take the tape and make a copy for himself and for the Raleigh department.

The Raleigh cop gave each team member his card. "If y'all have any more threats or see anything suspicious around your homes—anything—y'all let me know. All right?"

Terry found himself reading the card out loud. "Sergeant Eric Longacre..." He looked up at the policeman. "That's the name of one of the farmers we visited."

"My uncle and his family. So I got a personal—as well as professional—interest in this." He looked at Emily. "There are a lot more of us behind you than you might realize. It might not seem that way when...well...when you get a message like that jerk left you. We'll put a trace on this phone as well—as long as it's all right with y'all?"

"She's the boss," said Alison. "It's her decision," indicating Emily.

"Ma'am?"

Somewhat absent-mindedly, Emily responded, "Oh—sorry—I was lost in thought for a moment. Yes, please put a trace on this line." Then she took the policeman's arm. "You might or might not be aware of this—but my husband, Stephen, was shot and wounded several months ago. None of this is helping him...well, *heal*. If you know what I mean."

"I received two Purple Hearts in Vietnam, ma'am, so yes, I do know exactly what you mean. Don't worry—we'll look out for both of you."

"Thank you, I appreciate it. May I ask you one thing?"

"Yes, ma'am."

"What is the likelihood that you can find whoever is making these calls?"

"To be honest, I hear the voice of a desperate man on that tape. He's done something that's illegal and endangers human life...and, well...now he knows someone's on to him. My guess is he's simply trying to scare you—to bluff you into stopping your work. In my experience, his desperation will cause him to slip up. Whether he's the guy who actually dumped the...what is it again?"

"PCBs."

"Yeah, thanks. So whether he dumped them or created the mess and paid someone else to dump it, he's now got you, me—and the Raleigh police force—the county sheriffs, the EPA and others on his trail. Let's hope he keeps calling you. It will make my job easier. Oh—and his accent, it was local. I grew up here in Wake County. But he'll screw up; they almost always do. Try not to let it get to you, okay?"

"I'll try, thanks again."

~ * ~

Stephen stopped to look at the Sherlock Holmes poster on his office door. Some wit had inked in an arrow pointing toward the deerstalker hat and written: Bullet proof. The door was partially open, so he knew Lincoln Parker was in their shared office.

"Hey, Linc. How's it going?"

"Just fine," replied Lincoln. "How's our resident Sherlock Travis? Although, this time around, I wonder whether you might be Dr. Watson to Emily's Sherlock. Gotta think about that."

"You do that." Stephen looked at the mail on his desk. A manila envelope marked inter-office for the prison system lay on top. He opened that first.

"Is that what I think it is," queried Lincoln, drumming a pencil between his thumb and forefinger. "Who is the new Director of Chaplaincy Services since Ralph Martin's unceremonious departure?"

"A chaplain named Richard Blaylock. He's worked at Polk Youth Center, Central Prison and more recently at Western Youth Institution."

"You know him?"

"Yeah, a bit. Seems okay. At least they picked someone who's worked behind bars for fourteen or fifteen years—unlike Martin. He just drew his salary, smoked like a chimney and tried not to rock the boat." Stephen shook his head in disgust.

"Well, he fucked up big time when he ignored the information you gave him on the scam that was going down here. He's lucky he didn't get jail time. So what has Blaylock got to say? Is he letting you go?"

"As though he could keep me here," chortled Travis. "He's said all the stuff he has to say: thanks for the service, dedication, wishes me good health after my injury sustained in the line of duty, etc."

"So the countdown has really begun..." Lincoln leaned back in his chair and cocked his head as he seemed to study Stephen. After a moment he said, "I'm going to miss working with your honky ass."

"Thanks, Linc...I'm strangely moved by your words. But in all honesty, I'll miss working alongside you and James. You've both been great colleagues and friends. And you know where I live—in case you need a babysitter."

Lincoln's eyes rolled upward as he seemed to be trying to recall something. Then he began to laugh.

"Okay, Linc, what is it?"

"Oh, I was just picturing our leaving Clarissa with you and Emily, and what your white neighbors would think if they saw you two out with a black baby! That would get their tongues wagging!" he laughed again at the mental image. In a nasally send-up of a white person, Lincoln said, "The poor pastor! It's clear she's been messing around on him."

Travis laughed along with Lincoln, but added, "Be careful my friend, because this street goes both ways."

"Wait a minute!" blurted Lincoln as he sat upright, "Are you and Emily expecting?"

"Not that I know of," responded Stephen. "But who knows? Watch this space. But enough chatter for now. I've got to go through all of my mail and then get up the hill to the women's prison to let them know what's happening."

"Ben Katz is going to miss you."

"The reverse is true for me," replied Stephen. "He's also my best source for jokes."

"No man, I mean *really*. Moving his Jewish ass from the Big Apple down to North Carolina, and *prison work*, whoa!" Lincoln lifted his hands for emphasis. "From what I've seen, you're one of the few Southerners he really has warmed to. You mean a lot to him, is what I'm saying."

"Ben is a great friend. Happily, Emily and I aren't leaving Raleigh—at least not anytime soon. She's got a grant to sustain us through her post-doc year of research. We hope to see all of you in more relaxed circumstances from now on. Oh—did you hear the news yesterday? Ben and Kate McIntyre are planning to get married."

"Really? That's great! They'll be good for each other. Um...he's not going to want three best men like you did, is he?"

"I have no idea," but he has asked me to help conduct the wedding, so I'm out."

"Will you be the rabbi or a minister?" joked Lincoln.

"You laugh—but I might have to do both if Ben can't find a rabbi to help with a mixed marriage."

"Mixed marriage." Lincoln chuckled again to himself. "Time was, that meant a black and white couple...is that a problem for him?"

"Ben's family in New York are a mix of Orthodox and Conservative Jews...so sadly for him, it is a problem. Some will treat him as though he were dead."

"Jeez," Lincoln whistled through his teeth. "So not a million miles from ol' Jim Crow."

"Except they don't lynch people for that. They just treat him like a dead man."

"Ain't it great being human?" Lincoln shook his head

~ * ~

"We'll be sorry to see you go," said Karen Watkins, the relatively new warden of the women's prison. Stephen mused over the fact that in the space of six years, he had worked under five different wardens—such was the political nature of those appointments. "But I guess after what you've been through," Watkins unconsciously pointed toward her head, "a change must be in order." The warden stood and proffered Stephen her hand.

"Oh, I'll be around until the end of June," responded Stephen as he took the outstretched hand. "I'll make some rounds today and let folk know."

But before he could leave, Karen asked him to take a seat. She came around her desk and closed the office door before taking a seat in the chair opposite the chaplain.

"You know, Stephen, I have to admit that at first, I wasn't sure about a male chaplain in a women's prison. And I'm embarrassed to say that I did more than a little asking around about you." She paused to let her words sink in, and her eyes darted nervously. "After the business with Chaplain Goodman a few years back—well! I mean, a chaplain running a prostitution ring with female inmates?"

Stephen nodded. "I think I can understand your concern. The buck stops with you. In any case, I'm not offended." Stephen waited to see if she had more to say. She seemed to be searching for words.

"The thing I've learned about you is...well, it's simply that you might be the first man for many—if not most—of these women who didn't want to take advantage of them." The faces of many women passed through the chaplain's mind as he listened to the warden. "Perhaps you know what I mean?"

"Yes, believe me, I do know what you mean. The stories I've heard from these women—the abuse they have suffered..." Stephen shook his head. "Some of the accounts I wish I could forget, but I don't suppose I ever will." He paused for a moment and wondered whether he should say what was on his mind. But in the same instant, he felt the liberation of having tendered his resignation. "Ms. Watkins, I don't know you that well, but I want to say this: a lot of these women don't deserve to be here. It's their menfolk who ought to be serving time. Oh, I know some *are* doing time, but many aren't. And even the women who killed their husbands or boyfriends—when you read the police and court records, and what they'd suffered—they didn't deserve to be convicted of murder. At worst it was justifiable homicide, manslaughter. But after the men who used and abused them, then came the arresting male police or deputies, followed by male prosecutors, male judges and bailiffs. In so many ways, the so-called justice system has failed them at every turn. And finally, I have learned that for so many of these women, this prison in the safest environment in which they've ever lived. I hope that doesn't escape you in your time here."

Karen sat with Stephen's remarks for a few moments before responding. "When I asked around about you, someone did tell me that if I wanted to know what was on your mind, you'd tell me—straight up. Thanks for your honesty. In some ways, I'm sorry you and I won't have the chance to work together longer. Do you know what you plan to do after chaplaincy...*Sherlock*?" She laughed despite her best efforts to control it. "I'm sorry, but yeah,

I read the papers. You have to read them when you're a political appointee. That's how you find out if you've been fired."

"I don't plan to be a private detective...not if I can help it. Things kinda fell into my lap down at the Advancement Center—and I guess you could say the same about my wife's work. When the truth hits you in the face, and people's lives are in danger, it's time to act, the consequences be damned."

"Now I really am sorry you're leaving. But I wish you Godspeed in whatever it is you choose to do." She stood and once more extended her hand.

~ * ~

As Stephen entered the building where Ben and Kate had their offices, he was amused to see a paper-chain of hearts connecting their doors. Ben's door was open so Stephen peeped in. "Heard any good ones lately?"

Without looking up from his desk, Ben responded, "What is natural childbirth for a Jewish American princess?"

"Beats me."

"No make-up or jewelry. Pull up a chair."

"Shall I make us a cup of tea first?"

"Always a good idea," Ben looked up and smiled.

Travis rummaged through Ben's extensive tea collection. "What'll it be? Mint?"

"That'll do."

As Stephen put the water on to boil, he pointed toward the door. "Looks like Cupid—or someone—has been busy."

"Yeah, that's the work of one of Kate's support groups. Sentimental, eh?"

"That's you all over: Benjamin, the sentimental New York Jew. They'll write stories about you one day." Stephen brought the mugs of tea over to Ben's desk.

"L'khai'im," Ben raised his cup to Stephen. "Well, at least a bunch of convicts are excited about my impending marriage to

74

Kate. And get this—they want us to have our wedding in the prison chapel."

"That's funny," responded Stephen. "But, at the same time, it's also somehow appropriate—as long as you don't mind it being a Christian chapel."

"*Nu*," said Ben, "...some of my best friends are Christians."

"What does Kate think about it?"

"I think she's...um...warming to the idea. I mean, why not? A New York Jew marrying an Episcopalian Southern Belle—and we met behind bars. It's beginning to have its appeal. The inmates are more interested than my own family...hmm, maybe that's something I share with many inmates—an indifferent or hostile family?"

"And the reform rabbi—is he willing to officiate?"

"I'll catch him after shul on Shabbat. But don't worry, I'll keep you posted."

Eleven

"The date for my execution has been set," Emily said in a matter-of-fact tone, as they sat at the dinner table.

Stephen set down his fork. "Your *what*?"

Emily laughed. "Just wanted to make sure I have your attention. You seem a little preoccupied this evening. My dissertation defense—it's two weeks from tomorrow."

"Well, hopefully it won't be as dire as an execution. Are you feeling ready?"

"Oh, as ready as I'll ever be. I seem to have a reasonable panel. Want to come?"

"Oh, really? I didn't know guests were allowed."

"I had asked for you and my mother to be allowed in. I've been told it's fine as long as you don't hold up signs to coach me on answers to their questions."

"Very funny." Stephen scooped up a pea from his plate and flicked it at Emily.

"Watch out, Rev, unless you want to start a food fight."

"I seem to remember the last one ended well." Stephen offered up a sly smile.

76

"No time for that tonight—I've got to go back to the lab for an hour or so. Want to cycle over with me?" Emily placed her face in Stephen's line of sight, raising her eyebrows in querulous fashion. "Maybe you can even talk to me along the way?"

"Sorry, love. I've just been replaying some of my conversation with Anthony in therapy today. But, yeah, let's talk as we ride. I can use the exercise as well."

~ * ~

The humid air enveloped them like an invisible cloud. Stephen's face was dripping perspiration within five minutes of starting out. "Good ol' muggy Raleigh," he puffed. "They ought to rename it 'Sauna City'."

"You're not just going to talk about the weather, are you? But at the same time, I really don't want to pry...it's just that we have a *shared* trauma. Sometimes I think I ought to go with you to the therapy—it's just that I felt you were in greater need—I was there, but *you* got shot."

"I know, Em. And maybe you should come along. I'll bring it up with him, if you like."

"I think I'd like that. At least I won't have to repeat everything about the event."

"In any case, I'm not hiding anything," said Stephen. "It's just that Anthony has made it clear just how important my new ministry position will be—in the sense that...well, it needs to be a place where my healing can continue."

"And?"

Stephen drew a deep breath. "And, he doesn't feel that most churches would be a place of great understanding. He's seen too many Vietnam vets who couldn't find the sort of *understanding* they needed in the average church. Instead, they are given the old 'just pray about it and everything will be fine.' And then, if the vets still display...well, symptoms of what is now being called 'post-traumatic stress disorder,' then people give up on them. It's kinda like saying, 'Well, if God won't fix you then there's nothing we can

77

do for you either.' Hell, Em, I've seen enough Viet Nam vets in prison to know that sometimes all you can do is *accompany* them on their journey of healing."

"I guess we're different in that not many wives or girlfriends got shot at along with their men in Vietnam. Maybe my preoccupation with seeing you get well from your head wound, along with finishing my PhD dissertation, has helped me not to dwell about what we went through...but there are times that it comes back to haunt me as well." Emily paused to catch her breath as they were cycling at a brisk pace. "So what about your future ministry?"

"Well, obviously, Anthony's not a career guidance counsellor—but he knows enough about people who have suffered traumas to know we don't need to be in positions where we have to hide our feelings, weaknesses—in other words, most parish jobs in America."

"But you have said yourself that you wouldn't want to be in an all-white middle-class parish, so what's the issue?"

"The issue, lovely animal scientist wife, is that my training has largely qualified me for jobs I don't want...and, frankly, I have never had any interest in doing. Let's slow down—I want to be able to talk, breathe and pedal!" Stephen took in long, deep breaths before restarting. "I studied theology because I wanted to know more about what makes us truly human...and, as I believe in a Creator God, Great Spirit, Unifying Principle—call it what you will—I wanted to read my faith tradition's sacred texts in detail. With me so far?"

"Yep."

"And so I learned Greek and Hebrew in order to understand the scriptures more fully. So to make this long story a bit shorter, I fell in love with the prophetic texts and the message of Mr. Jesus—largely because they point us toward our societies' weaknesses: the disenfranchised, the poor, the voiceless, the strung-out, the imprisoned—people who actually need our help. You know most of this about me. And so, it hits me that most churches are not interested in preaching good news to the poor, much less doing anything about it, and they certainly don't want the captives released—or anywhere near their pews. Almost every month for the last five or six years, I've preached in churches so they can hear from a real-live prison chaplain and see where their mission money is going. And frankly, they're happy I'm doing what I've been doing all these years so they don't have to 'visit the imprisoned' as Jesus enjoined his followers to do. And now...well...I'm a genuine shot-in-the-head news-making nearly ex-chaplain who is wrestling with the big question: *now what?*" At that point they wheeled up to the bike rack outside Emily's lab.

"Well, *now* we lock up our bikes and go to my lab, where we can either continue this discussion or you can help me a bit, if you want a break. Your choice." As they climbed the stairs to Emily's lab, she laid her hand on Stephen's shoulder and stopped him. "There's one thing you haven't put into the equation as to 'what now?' for you. Aren't you forgetting something?"

Stephen returned Emily's gaze with a puzzled look.

"Your brother-in-law, our lawyer, Dave Andrews is beavering away on a damages suit on your behalf, against the state of North Carolina. And, as the state is not contesting the suit, it has become a matter of negotiating how much they are going to pay you for your exposing the wrongdoing of various state employees and getting shot in the head in the process—sound familiar?"

"Well, yeah...it's just that I haven't wanted to count on any money coming from the lawsuit—just in case it doesn't amount to anything."

"Stephen, my sometimes-cynical love, what has Dave told you several times about the case?"

Stephen felt and looked sheepish, "Um, why don't you tell me?"

"'Substantial damages' is what he has told you and me. Heavens, every major newspaper in the state picked up the story of the scam being run by prison guards, as well as the hush-up from the warden and your chaplaincy supervisor. The state is over a barrel—all the more so since you, my unusual man, fell into the five percent of headshot victims who survive—and in your case, without permanent damage. If they try to stiff you, you can tell your story to every paper in the land, if you want to. I'm sure *60 Minutes* would be interested—seriously. Let's just say that if I were a gold-digger, I'd marry you. In any case, I married you before there was a lawsuit. For richer or poorer, remember?"

"I do remember. But frankly, I'm just glad you married me at all."

"Great, so now let's clear one thing up right now," Emily held Stephen by both upper arms, her hazel eyes fixating on his chestnut-colored eyes. "You take as much time as you need, both to heal and to find a ministry to which you can give yourself wholeheartedly, okay? I can pay the bills for the foreseeable future. Got that? Now kiss me, you fool!" Emily's hands sprang from Stephen's biceps to the back of his neck, as she pressed her lips firmly against his.

After holding the kiss for several moments, Stephen drew back and said, "Yes, ma'am, Dr. Emily. Whatever you say."

"And now—to work—so we can get home at a reasonable hour." Emily's lab assistants had left results from their work on her desk. Before she could start reading them, her eyes were drawn to the flashing light on the answerphone. Emily took a deep breath. The first message was from Bert Longacre, one of the farmers her team had visited the previous week. It was a message thanking Terry for looking into his son's 'problem'—but without stating what it was. The second message was short and bitter. "You fucking bitch!" spat out from the recording. "I warned you!" And then the phone was slammed down. The message had been left shortly after Emily had left for home. She and Stephen stood looking at one another in silence, which was soon broken by Stephen.

"I think the Raleigh policeman was right. I think this guy's desperate—and scared."

"What makes you so sure?"

"Because he's only called here when you're unlikely to be in. I don't think he has the courage to talk with you. But this time, your phone line is being monitored. Time to ring Sergeant Longacre."

Looking overburdened all of a sudden, Emily said, "Would you be a love and call him? I'd like to dig into these reports." She indicated the files on her desk.

Stephen kissed her on the forehead and bowed. "Your servant, ma'am." Emily smiled and handed Stephen the officer's card.

Stewart's report was sitting on top. He had scribbled 'Read me first!' on the file folder. The contents provided an explanation for the voice message left by Bert Longacre. In a hastily scribbled note, Stewart had written, "As my dear, departed English grandmother used to say: 'In for a penny, in for a pound.' I hope you don't mind, but I did the Longacres' son, Eric, a favor. As you might recall, he and his wife have been having trouble getting pregnant and they hadn't been feeling well—so I drove down there and took some blood from both of them. Eric also gave me a sperm sample. When I checked his blood and sperm in the lab, the results were worrying. He's definitely showing reduced sperm count, as well as traces of PCB contamination in his blood—same for his wife. I've told him to see his doctor as soon as possible. Look, I know we're supposed to concern ourselves with farm animals, but—hey—Bert's son is an animal and lives on a farm, and well, we have the equipment to provide some answers. (At this point, he had drawn a smiley face.) Hope you're okay with what I've done. See you tomorrow."

Emily smiled to herself and silently congratulated Stewart on his initiative, reflecting that she would have done the same thing. The only cost was the team member's time—a real boon to Eric and his wife, who now had serious problems to deal with and didn't need the expense of going to a private lab. She then read through Stewart's lab report and the same for those of the other three assistants. Stephen had finished his call to the Raleigh police department, but waited for Emily to come up for air. When she finally lifted her eyes from the paperwork, Stephen was watching her with a mixture of adoration and amusement. Emily suddenly remembered asking Stephen to call the police.

"Oh! Sorry, I guess I forgot."

"Good," Stephen replied, "It means you're not letting the threats get to you. In short, Sergeant Longacre wasn't there, but he will receive a message to meet you here tomorrow morning at nine sharp. I gave them the time of the call, so hopefully they'll find the number...but unless the caller is a total idiot, he's probably used a pay phone. Time will tell."

Emily then related to Stephen what Stewart had done on behalf of the Longacre family.

"You know, you've really got a great bunch of young'uns working with you."

"Don't I know it. We wouldn't be anywhere near this far in the case had I been working alone."

Stephen's brow was furrowed and his mind seemed to be churning something. "What is it?" asked Emily.

"Well, I was wondering...just *how toxic* are PCBs for human beings? You've mentioned that cattle and other animals can die from ingesting too much of these toxins—so what about humans? Could we soon be looking at a murder case?"

Emily seemed mildly startled. "Talk about not seeing the forest for the trees...I've been so involved in the research aspect of this case I hadn't thought about other outcomes."

"Well, happily, that's not your job. It's the police that can prefer charges, but it might be worth filling in Sergeant Longacre about the possible lethal effects of PCBs on the rural communities. I have a gut feeling this whole PCB business is about to become a lot bigger.

Twelve

The meeting began at ten o'clock. In the three weeks that had transpired since her first visit to the Moores' farm, Emily's team had grown from her and Stephen, to include the Gang of Four, two colleagues from the Environmental Protection Agency, a member of the North Carolina Department of Agriculture, an officer from the State Bureau of Investigation, Sgt. Longacre from the Raleigh police and a deputy sheriff from both Bryce and Warren counties. Because Emily's lab had become the epicenter of the PCB dumping investigation, her department had given her a classroom for the use of the expanded team. Having both the legal and research investigative personnel in one room saved time and shortened the communication loop. Naturally, the university liked the positive publicity brought by one of their own, so lunch was provided as a small acknowledgment.

Emily welcomed everyone and began. "You have in front of you the highlights of our research work so far, so rather than repeat it, let's cut to the chase and see what each of us has discovered in relation to this investigation." She turned to a large map of eastern North Carolina on the wall. "The color key is simple. Yellow highlighting marks the roads on which my team has found evidence of PCBs. Orange highlighting is for the farms and properties we have visited and tested to date. Blue is, appropriately, water sources that have been contaminated." She gave everyone a moment to take in the scope of the toxic waste problem. "The news from my end is bad. Less than two weeks ago, we had identified PCB dumping along sixty miles of highway. That number now stands at something just over two hundred miles...and we're still testing." There was an audible groan. "And those two hundred or so miles are in eleven different counties." The two deputies both shook their heads in dismay and mumbled to one another.

Noting their consternation, Emily said, "Yep, guys, you're going to need help from the sheriff's departments of neighboring counties. This thing...this *problem* is huge. It can't be understated because we haven't yet determined the extent of it. As many of you already know," she nodded to Sgt. Longacre, "people's lives have been adversely affected—and seriously so. There have been no reported deaths that we know of, but PCBs can take months to do their damage. I don't need to tell the law enforcement officers here that we are looking at a major crime. Lives—human and animal— are being ruined, and livelihoods destroyed. This is going to take a major toll on the economy of eastern North Carolina. I'll leave it to our colleagues at the EPA to determine an estimated cost of cleaning up the spillage—but I'm sure it will have a lot of zeros." The two employees of the EPA nodded sullenly. "May I ask our two deputy sheriffs to report on their findings?" Emily stepped aside to let the men use the map board.

Deputy Linville from Bryce County took the lead, although it was clear he was not comfortable addressing such a group. Each county's sheriff's department had initiated calls to homes along the roads affected, as well as door-to-door questions about slow-moving tankers at night. So far, the only confirmed sighting was, ironically, by one of Bryce County's deputies. He had seen an out-of-state tanker, which he thought had broken down, on Highway 58, but the driver had reported that all was well and that he had just taken a nap break. Linville scratched his head and rubbed his jaw nervously as he tried to cover a grin. "Um, the deputy in question is undergoing...uh...hypnosis to see whether he can recall any details about the tanker truck." Linville paused, his eyes darting about, expecting sniggers or laughter, but none came.

Sgt. Longacre called out, "Good idea."

Encouraged, Linville continued, "The deputy thought the background color on the plate was blue, but couldn't be sure about the numbers or letters, as it was nighttime." The deputy flipped through his notes. "Oh, if the plates were blue, it wasn't any next-door states, like Virginia or South Carolina. We're thinking it might have come from New Jersey—maybe a northern company trying to get away with dumping its waste down here, but we'll keep y'all posted." Linville thanked everyone for their attention and sat. His colleague had nothing further to add. At that point, Emily called on Sgt. Longacre of the Raleigh police. As the sergeant stood to his full six-foot-three frame, he had a twinkle in his eye that bespoke the cat that caught the canary.

"I think we have some tentative good news. Dr. Travis," Emily blushed slightly on hearing the as-yet-unawarded doctorate, "has been receiving some threatening calls—as it was her work that uncovered this whole dirty business. We got one positive trace on a call to her office and it came from a pay phone here in Raleigh. That in itself is not too significant—except for telling us that one of the culprits could be—and I stress *could be*—local. But what is significant is that the pay phone was located a few hundred yards from a transformer company—a company which uses PCBs...a *lot* of PCBs." Longacre looked around the room to gauge the reaction. "I can't give y'all the name of the company at this time as it's too early in the investigation; but it's not out of the question that the source of the PCBs is local. The carrier is secondary—important—

but secondary. Like you, we want to find who produced and then ordered the dumping of this waste." He paused and looked at the map, and then began tracing the circular routes with his hand. "You know," Longacre rubbed his chin in reflection, "the more I think about it, the fact that these dumpings have meandered all over the counties east of Raleigh, the more I am inclined to believe the source of the PCBs is local. No offense to Deputy Linville, but if the source of the waste came from up north, why wouldn't they start dumping on the back roads up there? It's a long way for a tanker to come, only to have to return and go back for another load. That's a lot of diesel fuel." People around the room spoke in approval of his theory. "In any case, I don't mind telling y'all that I have a personal interest in this case. My uncle's farm and family have been hit hard by this dumping. I'm just glad to be in a position to help bring the guilty to justice." Longacre nodded to everyone and took his seat.

The next to speak was Craig Marsden of the EPA—a friend and colleague of Emily. "I want first of all to acknowledge the hard and excellent work done by Emily and her lab assistants. Her assistants aren't paid, by the way, but they have their tuition costs reduced for the hours they have dedicated to this case." Craig pointed at Stewart, Alison, Mark and Terry, opening a round of applause. "I hope you'll be happy to know the cavalry is coming to your assistance—and no, sadly this does not include a tuition grant to cover the rest of your studies here at State...but I wish it did. What it does include is Federal aid, given that this is turning out to be one of the largest PCB spills in U.S. history. We'll be liaising directly with Governor Hunt, the Department of Agriculture," he nodded to that member of the team, "and of course, all of you. I want to stress that we're not taking over the work you're doing here at NC State, but we will help expand it and then work with the inevitable clean-up..." Craig shook his head in bewilderment, "and I don't even want to estimate what that might cost."

~ * ~

After all of the updates, lunch was brought in by the university's catering team. As people munched and chatted amiably, Sgt. Longacre leaned across the table to Emily and said, "Have you noticed police cruisers driving by your house more frequently?"

"I can't say that I have. Should I have seen them?"

"Well, yes and no," chuckled Longacre. "It's just that I have requested more presence along your road—as a deterrent—in the event that the threatening calls have any substance to them. But personally, I think the caller was just trying to scare you into backing off."

"Kinda late for that." laughed Emily.

"And by the way," continued Longacre, "The campus security is doing the same around your building." He patted Emily's arm. "We got you covered."

"Thanks for looking out for us," Emily acknowledged. "The extra security is reassuring." Then, looking around, Emily noticed that several team members were making ready to leave, so she stood and clunked her soda can on the table to gain everyone's attention. "In addition to wanting to thank all of you again for your time and energy spent on this case, I wanted to let you know that the next week or so I hope to drop off the radar, as I have my doctoral defense coming up. Although many of you generously refer to me as 'Dr. Travis,' that honor is yet to be bestowed. And, of course, all being well with my thesis and defense, then graduation is the week after next."

Before Emily could continue, Sgt. Longacre took to his feet and, in his best 'good ol' boy' fashion, said, "Ma'am, if that doctoral committee gives you *any* trouble..." he patted his holster, "just call me." He winked at the gathered group and sat down.

At another table, Deputy Linville called out, "That goes for us deputies too!" Along with the laughter which followed, everyone wished Emily the best.

Blushing brightly, Emily waved away the applause and said, "I just want y'all to know that my lab team have worked out a shift schedule so that there will be someone at the end of the phone here from nine to five every day. And they can reach me if the need arises."

~ * ~

Over at the Advancement Center, the afternoon heat was weighing heavily upon Stephen. Lincoln was out of the office and, as things were slow at the center, Stephen was flipping through a Sierra Club book of hiking trails in Great Smoky Mountains National Park. He had promised to organize an outing for Emily and himself, as her graduation present. Stephen still had a few days of annual leave to use before he finished his last weeks as a prison chaplain. As for Emily, she hadn't had a break since their honeymoon, the first week of January. In fact, Stephen reflected, between finishing her doctoral dissertation and discovering the PCB spills, his wife had scarcely had a full weekend off in five months. They both loved the mountains, but they also loved the idea of being where no one could reach them. In the year they had known one another, and in the nearly six months they had been married, life had been a cup that had "runneth over" most of the time—their intense romance, Stephen's being severely wounded, and now the concentrated effort made by Emily in both finishing her PhD while at the same time investigating the criminal dumping of toxic waste. They both felt the extraordinary and the extreme were becoming far too commonplace in their lives. What was needed was boredom...or at least low-key adventure. A week's camping sounded just about right.

"Mind if I bother you?" It was Delbert Moore. After Travis, Moore was the best-educated man in the center. He often liked to chat with Stephen just to shoot the breeze and discuss things that never passed on the radar of most men there. "Planning next Sunday's sermon?" teased Delbert.

Stephen lifted the book. "Not quite; but I am planning something slightly more interesting."

"Man, I'd love to get up into the Smokies...in fact, I'd love to go just about anywhere. This place is driving me crazy with boredom."

"I sympathize with you Delbert, but in your case, it could have been a lot worse. I could name fifty other prisons in which you'd really lose your mind. Sorry to say it, but it's true. Thank God you'll be released soon. What is it now—less than three months?"

"True enough, but I'll sure miss our talks..." And before Stephen knew it, Delbert was covering all of the same old ground again: the crooked county sheriff, the town council's plan to have the sheriff replaced, then Delbert's being framed by said sheriff with planted drugs...Travis had no idea how many times he'd heard the same complaints. And, yes, it was unfair, and yes, Delbert would have a criminal record for life—barring an investigation of the sheriff's illegal doings and/or arrest. Then the monologue moved to Delbert's master's degree in English—the only thing, apart from these chats—that was keeping him sane, and more latterly the fact that his girlfriend had dumped him because the enforced eighteen-month separation was too much for her...

And then it happened, something that had never happened to Travis during his years as a prison chaplain: he felt the urge to laugh. It was building up in him like sneeze one cannot fend off. *Laughing at an inmate? What's wrong with me? What kind of chaplain laughs at an inmate?* Stephen tried to think of things that made him sad, but no luck. For good or ill, Stephen had one of those transparent faces that told all. He could never have made a good poker player. Biting the inside of his jaw and lip worked for a bit, but he realized Delbert had taken notice of his facial gyrations—although this had not caused him to pause. Stephen wondered whether his impending departure from the prison system was working on him— perhaps making him feel the way inmates feel when their release is imminent. He had witnessed the unfettered joy on the faces of inmates and the transformation of worry lines into the creases of smiles, when it was definite that prison was a thing of the past. Stephen had seen the now-former inmates take a deep breath when stepping through the front gates of the prisons in which he had worked—as though the air were different. *Yes, a deep breath—that's it! Breathe in deeply and slowly....deeply and slowly.* Stephen burst out laughing. The shame, shock and disappointment written on his face were only matched by the look of surprise on Delbert's face. And Stephen continued laughing—as though he had just been told the funniest joke ever. He made helpless gestures at Delbert, whose countenance went from that of shocked bewilderment to unrestrained mirth. Shaking his head at himself and his predicament, Delbert joined in the laughter—at himself, at Travis, at the whole damn situation. The two men looked at each other, and every time their eyes met the laughter erupted again. Nearly choking, Stephen croaked, "Sorry Delbert...I...I don't even know why I'm laughing"—more spluttering—"I'm certainly not laughing at you!"

"It's okay, Stephen. You've just made me realize how many times I've told you the same old shit..."—gulps of laughter—"and moaning hasn't done me any good—but laughing sure helps!" It took several minutes for their laughter to subside, after which both men were wiping their eyes.

"I don't know what came over me, Delbert. I hope you'll forgive me," said Travis.

"Don't worry about it. Listening to me going on about my problems is enough to make any sane person laugh. But I think I can hazard a guess as to why you laughed."

"I'm listening," responded Stephen.

"My dad would have called it 'de-mob happy'—from after the war when men received notice they were about to be 'de-mobilized'. They went a little crazy because their lives were their own again."

"Makes sense," said Stephen.

"But here I am moaning to you about my situation, all the while forgetting that you—sitting right here in front of me—took a bullet to the head for the likes of me and all of the other men here. If that's not pathetic, then it certainly is funny."

"Life is more than a little crazy," offered Stephen.

"Let the congregation say 'no shit'!" came Delbert's response. "How about a rousing chorus of 'What a Friend We Have in Travis'?"

"Don't get me started laughing again!" Stephen held up his left hand, but began writing something on a notepad with his right. He tore it off and gave it to Delbert.

"What's this?"

"Well, first of all, it's a broken prison regulation. That's my home address and telephone number." Moore shook his head uncomprehendingly. "Well, you said you were going to miss our conversations. So now you'll know where to find me...and if you ever need me as a reference—as to what an ideal inmate you've been."

Although something of a cynic by nature, Delbert's eyes misted over. He held up the piece of paper. "Thanks, man. I really mean it."

"You're welcome. It's the least I can do. And listen, when you're a free man again, come over for dinner one night, okay? But don't forget to tell me where you're living."

"Thanks. You can count on it."

Thirteen

"How are things going?" asked Stephen's therapist, Anthony Morley.

"Well, I nearly screwed the pooch today," replied Stephen, although he was smiling. "I burst out laughing while I was listening to an inmate. Can you imagine that?"

"I suppose it's every therapist or minister's nightmare—that or falling asleep when someone is in the midst of telling something traumatic. But you don't seem that distressed—what happened?"

Stephen related the incident with Delbert Moore from a couple of hours earlier.

"Wow, that really was a close one, wasn't it? And he laughed too—that's really something! I'm glad it turned out the way it did. Why do you think you laughed?"

"As you might imagine, I've given that a lot of thought over the last couple of hours." Stephen poured himself a glass of water from the pitcher on the table between them. "I think it's a combination of things. First, there was certainly something in what Delbert suggested: that I am 'de-mob happy'—a bit high from the knowledge that I won't be working inside prisons any longer. You know, after all the years, I never got used to hearing the doors lock behind me. I always felt a tightening of my spine and, well, believe it or not, my sphincter muscle, when I heard the clunk of the steel key and lock."

"I take that as a good sign," offered Anthony.

"How so?"

"Think about it a moment. What would it say about you if that sound had no impact on you?" They both reflected in silence for a few moments.

"I suppose," began Stephen, "it would suggest I was either institutionalized or too numb to care. But maybe they are one and the same?"

"Exactly," responded Anthony. "And perhaps your laughter was in part a release of that tension you talked about—the tightening of your spine every time you entered a prison."

"That makes sense. I always said I didn't want to work too long in prison—to the point where I looked through people rather than at them. I've seen that too many times with chaplains, social workers and the like. They had stopped *caring*, but had continued to *function*. They left their humanity at the prison gates."

"You see? You could do my job for me," joked Anthony. "The thing is, all of that emotion—all of that tension—has to go somewhere. And while I wouldn't recommend as a rule to laugh at one's clients, the laughter in itself is a positive release. Many people in your shoes would turn to addictive behavior as a form of release: alcohol, tobacco, sex, drugs—you know the drill. Oh, and I wouldn't be doing my job if I didn't remind you to be deliberate in your endings at the various units where you've been working—it might help prevent laughing at someone who doesn't have a sense of humor."

"Understood," replied Stephen.

"If you go in each day with the idea of releasing more of your workload, counselling cases, etc., you'll be better able to manage your emotions. Maybe bring home some non-essential paperwork and burn it—as a symbolic way of putting the past behind you. Have you kept any newspaper clippings regarding the extorsion racket or concerning your being shot?"

"Yes, I suppose I have."

"Do you *need* them?"

"Can't say that I do."

"So why do you keep them? You see what I mean about being deliberate in your endings?

"I do now. Thanks, Anthony. In fact, this is the first job I've had as a minister, so it's my first departure. And truthfully, I hadn't given it much thought—other than to leave. I mean, I knew I would have to tell people in the chain of command, as well as colleagues and inmates. But ever since getting shot...and the nightmares...well, getting out has been my main concern."

"That is understandable. And speaking of the nightmares," Anthony raised his eyebrows inquisitively.

"Ah yes, the ol' favorite has been there every ten days or so. It's always in the women's prison, at the gate to the control center. I seem to be going into the maximum-security facility, and one of the guards tells me some people want to see me. And when I look again, there's a line of inmates—women and men—as far as I can see along the fence. And they all want to speak with me *now*. And when I tell them I can't see them all now, they start taunting me and mocking me. And then I wake up...or Emily wakes me—if I'm making noise."

"What do you think the dream means or is telling you?"

"At first," Travis rubbed his beard as he reflected. "At first I took the taunting to mean I couldn't really help the people..."

Anthony cocked his head. "Go on."

"But in fact, I know my work has not been a failure. Oh, I mean, I think most of us, after a number of years of seeing the endless supply of inmates, can think, 'What good am I doing?' But that's when it's time to focus on each individual and to do the best you can for her or him. With more than twenty-five thousand people in North Carolina's prisons, there's more than enough for any number of individuals. You realize you can't do it all."

Anthony nodded and motioned of Stephen to continue.

"And that leads to the second interpretation of the dream. If you want to do this kind of work and *still care*, then there comes a time for each of us when we realize we cannot do it indefinitely—and still care. Call it compassion fatigue or whatever." Stephen looked to Anthony for comment.

Anthony raised both hands. "There's not a lot more I can add. Except this—which is the reason you came to me in the first place: the trauma of being shot. I don't have to tell you it doesn't simply go away. Remember the training you received from the Marines that you told me about, to help you deal with veterans in prison? Well, just like those Marines who trained you to work with and understand the effects of trauma on veterans, you're now experiencing firsthand both sides of it: as healer and the one who needs healing. As you know, it's now being called post-traumatic stress disorder, and features in the new Diagnostic and Statistical Manual of Mental Disorders, III." Anthony hesitated. "I don't know that I like to use the term 'disorder' with someone like you...because a disorder can sound like something which can't be 'cured'—only treated. The men you've seen in prison—for the most part—did not seek therapy like you have. They let their stress build up to the point that it dealt with them rather than the reverse. I'm hoping the Veterans Administration will start to handle such cases better—but that's another issue. Stephen, you've got a good cognitive handle on the issue, not just of being shot, which is enough in itself—but also of having to deal with the intransigent prison system which let things get out of hand, despite your best efforts. And happily, you're aware of your intrusive thoughts and dreams, which are a product of the emotional baggage and stress. I believe they will settle down and in time, hopefully, disappear. And I haven't had to medicate you." Both men laughed. "The fact that you cycle to some of our sessions is also a good sign. Many trauma victims withdraw into themselves and cease physical activity—which begs another question: how's your sex life?"

"It's good actually...although we've both been quite busy of late, as you know. But a few weeks ago, when we were on the way to one of the farms involved in the PCB scandal, we actually pulled over along the highway and had sex in a pickup truck!" Both men laughed again.

'Well, I don't think I've had sex in a car since I was a teenager," mused Anthony, "but enough of that—and good for you and Emily!" Anthony swiveled back and forth in his chair for a moment, occupied with his thoughts. "Stephen, considering what's happened in your life in the past six months, you're doing remarkably well. Apart from the occasional bad dreams and intrusive thoughts, you're managing yourself well. I support your move away from prison chaplaincy—you don't need to be in the environment which nearly cost you your life. Any job possibilities on the horizon?"

"Not yet," said Stephen.

"Well, you already know what I think about parish ministry. I'm a non-institutional-church type of Christian...which is another way of saying I'm a bad Catholic. I read the *Catholic Worker* and sure as hell respect the work and ministry of people like Dorothy Day, the Berrigan brothers and such—for me, they have been the saving grace of Catholicism. But expectations placed on priests are ridiculous—as is celibacy—but this is your session, not mine. As someone who cares about you, I just want you to be careful where you go next. There's too much denial going on in the institutional church, and that's exactly what you do not need. Here endeth my sermon."

"Thanks, Anthony. This has been a big help. Is next week this time okay for you?"

Anthony spun around in his chair and picked up his desk diary. "That works just fine." He penciled in the date. "And as long as you're okay with it, Stephen, let's keep meeting through your work transition. We can spread out the sessions if you like. It's up to you."

"Oh—I nearly forgot," interjected Stephen. "Emily wanted me to ask you about the two of us coming to these sessions from time-to-time. She had a close brush with death that night as well. What do you think?"

"As I have been your therapist, that's a decision for you to make, but from my point of view, I'm happy to see you both and will only share what you want me to share. Work for you?"

"Couldn't ask for more," replied Stephen.

Fourteen

Stephen sat with Sarah Webster, Emily's mother, in the back of the lecture room. Emily stood at a podium, alongside which was a table containing a glass of water and an overhead projector. She was discussing something neither Sarah nor Stephen understood, while showing graphs and charts on the screen to her side. Her panel included four professors from NC State University, as well as two visiting interlocuters. All asked questions except one. Stephen nervously wondered whether he was saving up a 'knock-out' question for the end. He had heard such stories from friends who had received their PhDs, as well as from those who had failed. One of his minister friends had completed his dissertation in Hebrew Bible—which had been approved by his advisor and second reader—but on the day of his defense, the second reader told the panel, "I never thought this was a good idea for a research topic. I don't approve it." Stephen's friend was left in tatters as every member of the faculty panel got up and went about their business. Stephen silently prayed he would not witness such a debacle today. Every now and then, he and Sarah would exchange glances and smile grimly. Sarah was almost constantly wringing her hands.

After nearly an hour, the questions seemed to have dried up. Emily had long finished her presentation and had not been flustered by anyone's questions. But the one visitor still had not posed a question. As the heads of the other five panel members were nodding, the visitor leaned over and whispered something to Emily's doctoral advisor, who nodded; and then he stood up. The visiting panel member acknowledged first Emily and then his fellow panel members, smiling broadly as he looked around the room. Stephen began biting his lower lip, while Mrs. Webster's knuckles were blanched from all the squeezing. Neither of them was prepared for what he said.

"My name is Dr. Michael Kirkland, and I am both a researcher and serve on the board of directors at the FarmBio Laboratories in the Research Triangle Park. Many of you here will have heard of us. We have followed with interest the case of the illegal PCB disposal in several of the counties east of us here in Raleigh--not least because our company is concerned with both animal health and diseases which affect livestock not only in the U.S., but also in the rest of the world. Frankly, we have been very impressed with the work of Dr. Emily Travis—" he paused to let his words sink in. Involuntarily, Emily put her hand over her mouth, while her panel applauded her—soon followed by everyone else in the room. Stephen was surprised when his mother-in-law put two fingers in her mouth and let loose a loud whistle. Dr. Kirkland lifted his hand for silence. "As I was saying, we at FarmBio have been impressed by the assiduous work of Dr. Travis and her team...who I believe are in the audience today. If so, please stand." Alison, Stewart, Terry and Mark stood as one. Once more, Dr. Kirkland and everyone else, began clapping. "At

FarmBio we pride ourselves on *recognizing* quality work..." Once more he paused while taking in everyone in the room.

"This guy knows how to work a crowd," whispered Stephen to Sarah, whose hands were now *un*wrung.

Kirkland continued, "And we also pride ourselves for *rewarding* quality work." He turned toward Emily. "Dr. Travis, I have been in conversation with your departmental chairman, your doctoral advisor, as well as with the university bursar and chancellor, and FarmBio would like to offer you a two-year joint position between us and NC State University. We're used to providing research grants, so this is a new departure for us." Emily looked for a chair and promptly flopped into it. Stephen and her mother were waving wilding from the back of the room. Chatter erupted throughout the audience. Lifting his hand once more, Kirkland said, "Frankly, we'd prefer to steal you away, but the university folks seem to want to hang onto you, so we'll have to settle for half of your time. If you're willing, that is." He turned again to look at Emily. "And you do not have to answer right now—for one very good reason. In my twenty years with the company, we have never made a job offer in this manner, and while it has been rather fun for me, I realize it might have come as a shock to you. And the real reason you don't have to answer now is that if you said 'no,' my ego wouldn't be able to stand it, so why don't I just leave you my card?" Kirkland started to move toward his seat but stopped. This time he was genuinely nonplussed. "Oh, I nearly forgot. FarmBio has never seen such professional field and lab work from undergraduates. But as I've already taken enough of everyone's time, please, would the four of you," he gestured toward Emily's team, "come see me immediately after these proceedings?"

Following Kirkland's rather astonishing—and breathtaking for some—statement demanded brevity, so Emily's doctoral advisor simply reiterated the fact that she had been awarded the

PhD in animal science, congratulated her and said he was looking forward to working with her for at least the next two years. He then let everyone know that the department and FarmBio had arranged refreshments in an adjoining room. Emily still looked dazed as she shook his hand. Sarah and Stephen were hugging each other with delight as they made their way forward. While Emily received the congratulations of the rest of the panel, she was mobbed from all sides by her mother and husband, fellow grad students and, of course, by the Gang of Four. As they gave Emily a four-way hug, they asked if she had any idea what Kirkland had on offer.

"I haven't a clue, honestly. But maybe it would be a good idea if y'all followed him to the refreshments and found out." Nothing else needed to be said. Her four assistants made a bee line for Kirkland.

As Stephen hugged Emily, she pinched his arm.

"Ouch! What's that for?"

"I just wanted to make sure I wasn't in one of your dreams."

~ * ~

Dinner that evening was a raucous affair and was held at Emily's former residence, which she had shared with two fellow graduate students, Charles Hampton and Patricia Crawford. Charles was also receiving his PhD from State, but Patricia had another year to go. As Emily and Stephen's cottage was too small to handle a large group, Charles and Pat, as Patricia liked to be called, offered to have the joint celebration in their house, a two-story Victorian weatherboard with a huge porch. Charles was from an old South Carolina family, which meant they were white and had been former slave owners. His parents were happy Charles had decided to do his graduate work 'out of state,' as their son was self-described 'queer as a three-dollar bill.' It worked for Charles inasmuch as they were happy to pay his upkeep as long as he remained in *northern* Carolina. The now Dr. Hampton was a cytologist, or cell biologist, focusing on the human animal. Pat was working toward her doctorate in electrical engineering. Rounding off the dinner party were the Gang of Four and a few of Charles's colleagues.

As Charles and Pat had dinner under control, the rest of the group retired to the porch with drinks in hand. Stephen slipped in next to Emily and put his hand around her waist. "Finally, I get to congratulate you personally—and without a mob!"

Turning to her husband and mother, and with a cheeky grin, Emily asked, "So...how much of my presentation did you understand?"

Stephen and Sarah looked at one another. "I definitely understood 'lab work' and 'results.' Stephen nodded vigorously.

Following her son-in-law's lead, Sarah added, "And I understood 'cow' and 'disease.' How are we doing so far, Professor?"

Gently pinching the end of her mother's and Stephen's noses, Emily replied, "You two are...are definitely...going to fail." Stephen gave her backside a slap.

"Watch it, Rev! That's my mother standing next to you."

"That was quite some job offer," said Sarah. "Had you any idea that was coming?"

"None at all. I was flabbergasted!"

"It must feel nice," Sarah continued, "to have an embarrassment of riches—both your university and a pharmaceutical company wanting you."

"Yes, it really is something...I mean, I have to admit I had never thought about working for a drug company. To be honest, I hadn't thought very far beyond the fact that I have a paid, post-doc year ahead of me. The rest of my time has been taken up with finishing my PhD, investigating the PCB spill—and of course, my husband." She gave Stephen a squeeze and a kiss.

"At least you wouldn't be full-time in the pharmaceutical company," proposed Stephen. "And we live on the west side of Raleigh so access to the Research Triangle wouldn't take so long."

"And it means you don't have to take the first ministry post that comes along—unless you really want it." Emily gave Stephen a Groucho-style raised-eyebrows look as she fished an envelope from her back jeans pocket. "Kirkland gave me this at the reception—and I took a quick peek." She held it up for Stephen and her mother to read.

"Wow! I can be a house-husband!" exclaimed Stephen.

"And medical insurance" added Sarah. "I would say some prayers have been answered."

"Hey, is that for both of us?" queried Stephen, reading more closely. "I lose my insurance after I leave prison chaplaincy."

"Yep," replied Emily. "I did check that one closely—especially after the last six months."

"So have you decided?" asked Stephen, "Or do you want to think about some more?"

Emily gave a sly look as she sipped her drink. "Well, I already have the promise and funding for a post-doc year at State...so I thought I might let Kirkland sweat it a bit...and call him in a day or so."

"Oh Em! Why do that to the poor man?" Sarah gave her daughter a mock smack.

"Well, why not? Here I am, a woman in what is largely a man's profession. So why not make him wait?"

Stephen laughed. "Ha! I like it! My scientist wife—she's neither cheap nor easy!"

Sarah pretended to be shocked but was clearly enjoying the banter between her daughter and son-in-law. "You two are just right for each other."

"We're glad you approve," joked Stephen, "because we're already married." Turning quickly to Emily, Stephen said, "Wait—you said you'll contact Kirkland after a day or two...*and tell him what?*"

She looked at Stephen with question-mark eyes, "And tell him *yes?*"

"Em, if it's what you want, then go for it. You know you have my full support."

"Well, I'm happy for both of you," said Sarah as she put her arms around them. "Emily, you've worked so hard for this. I just want you to know how proud I am of you." Sarah leaned forward and kissed her daughter's cheek.

"From convict to assistant professor—not bad, eh, Mom?"

"Oh, hush you! You don't have to bring that up."

"It's all right, Mom; everybody here is cool."

"It's the reason I married her," blurted Stephen. "An ex-con? It makes her somehow even sexier—if that were possible—and more mysterious."

"Y'all keep this up and I'll get a taxi back to the motel," chided Sarah in mock derision, but she was smiling all the while. "How about a change of topic? What about your young lab assistants—what did Dr. Kirkland say to them during the reception?"

"Yes," added Stephen, "what about the Gang of Four?"

"I thought it best to hear it from them," replied Emily. "Mom, can you do your loud whistle, please?"

Stephen held his mother-in-law's drink while she gave her two-finger whistle, drawing everyone's attention. Then Sarah surprised everyone by calling out, "Gang of Four, front and center!" As Emily and Stephen gawped, she grinned and said, "Well, I was married to a soldier for a number of years."

The Gang of Four duly obeyed and presented themselves in front of Emily, Stephen and Sarah. "There is curiosity afoot as to what our Dr. Kirkland had to say to y'all," said Emily. "Would you like to share?"

The three young men deferred to Alison, who spoke first. "Well, first, if we want to do it, we all have paid employment for the summer to continue our investigation into the PCB spillage—courtesy of FarmBio. And second," at this point she pulled Mark to the fore.

He still seemed dazed by what he had to say. "Yeah, in addition to the offer of jobs this summer, we're all being given grants to cover next year's tuition costs." The Gang of Four all raised their drinks in a toast to their good fortune—the others joining in.

"That is fabulous!" said Stephen.

"It's all thanks to your wife," interjected Stewart.

"And your daughter," added Terry, raising his beer to Sarah.

"Let's not be too modest," Emily rejoindered, "you've all worked your socks off both out in the field and in the lab—just as Kirkland said. I'm just glad there's been some recognition—and recompense. Just let me know what you decide to do."

"Yeah, like that's going to be a tough decision," said Stewart. "Let me see, work on a construction site during the hot Carolina summer or work in an air-conditioned lab? Gonna be hard to decide."

"You haven't heard what FarmBio is paying us," added Mark. "We'd be crazy not to accept their offer. I had no idea what job I would have this summer anyway. Decision made."

It was clear to Emily that her lab team would be with her at least for the next three months, and perhaps during the next academic year. In a night of celebrations and toasts, she raised her glass. "To the Gang of Four!"

Fifteen

"We'll leave the car at Big Creek Ranger Station. As you can see, it's not far off I-40. I've arranged for us to stay there in the campsite overnight so there's no rush to get going." Stephen was pointing to a map of the Great Smoky Mountains National Park, which was spread across their dining table. "Then we'll have a nice butt-busting hike up Mt. Cammerer. It's just under six miles, but there is an elevation gain of three-thousand feet." He looked at Emily.

"I can almost feel my lungs burning now. What a wonderful graduation present," Emily joked. "Good thing we cycle so much."

"Then it's Mt. Cammerer to Cosby Knob shelter—not as strenuous as the first day. After that," Emily followed Stephen's finger on the map, "it's down to Walnut Bottom, camping by Big Creek. Then another big climb up Balsam High Top—which has fabulous views. We'll camp at Laurel Gap and then over to Mt. Sterling the next day via Pretty Hollow Gap, which can have an amazing array of wildflowers. And finally, *la pièce de resistance*"— Stephen's finger left the Great Smoky Mountains National Park and went eastward to Asheville—"we take our muddy, weary bodies to Asheville for two nights at the Grove Park Inn—so, Dr. Travis, we'll need to throw some Sunday-go-to-meeting type clothing in the car. Consider that as our honeymoon revisited." Stephen bowed deeply to Emily.

Emily threw her arms around her husband and kissed him fervently. "I love it! Thank you so much for arranging it." she exclaimed; and with that she steered him toward their bedroom. Emily mumbled, "PhD finished" kissed Stephen and removed his shirt. "You're leaving prison work," kissed Stephen again and removed her blouse. "A week where no one can find us." She tugged off Stephen's shorts and undies, kissed him again and pushed him onto the bed "Too much hard work over the last two months." Off came Emily's last garments "Must have my man!"

~ * ~

On their half-day car journey to the Smokies, Emily and Stephen began by talking about all of the things that had dominated their lives of late—particularly the PCB spillage and the ongoing investigation. After their brain download, they put a cassette of classic rock 'n' roll in the sound system and sang along with the music as they rolled along I-40. Three quarters of the way to their destination, a combination of hunger and Mother Nature led them to a family-style restaurant near Morganton. They parked the car on the main street of town just a short walk from the restaurant. As they walked hand-in-hand, Stephen and Emily passed a men's clothing store. When they were no more than five paces beyond the front display window, they heard the sound of someone running behind them. Before either could turn around, Stephen felt a hand grab his right shoulder, pulling him to a stop. Feeling alarmed at first—a daylight mugging?—Stephen broke free of the person's grip and spun around. He was looking into the face of a smartly-dressed young man. For a brief few seconds, neither of them said anything. Emily looked on, perplexed.

"You don't recognize me, do you?" The young man sensed Stephen's alarm and the puzzlement on his face.

"No, I can't say I do."

"Aren't you a prison chaplain?" the young man asked.

'Yes, I am," replied a somewhat less troubled Stephen. "Why?"

"Because I came to see you when I was an inmate at the youth center outside Raleigh."

"I'm really sorry I don't remember you—" Stephen began.

"No man, that's cool, but *I* remember *you*; and I remember what you said to me—and it really helped. So when I saw you, I wanted *you* to know I'm outta prison, doing fine, and I have a good job in this clothing store." He opened his arms, beckoning a look at his suit. "And I knew *you needed to know that.*" Stephen and the young man shook hands and he was gone—just like that. The young man never even mentioned his name.

Stephen and Emily looked at each other in wonder and then continued on their way. "What just happened there?" asked Stephen. "I mean, was that an angel or a man?"

"It was almost...as if...he *knew* you were coming," replied Emily with deliberate, measured speech.

Stephen appeared almost taken aback by the experience. "He could only have had a few seconds—at most—to have seen me. You and I walk at a fairly quick pace, and yet, in that brief moment, he recognized me. And I haven't worked at the youth center for nearly two years. What if we hadn't stopped here to have lunch? Or what if we had parked further along the street? What if he hadn't come to work today? And yet," Stephen looked back over his shoulder as if to see whether the young man—or apparition—were still there. "And yet here we are and here he is, today, at exactly the right moment in time and space for him to give me his message."

"What was the Greek word you used to describe 'God's timing'?"

"*Kairos*—and if ever in my life there was such a time, it certainly is now." Stephen and Emily stood at the entrance to the restaurant.

"Still want to eat?" asked Emily. Stephen answered by opening the door. The establishment was one of those wherein the owners wanted that old-fashioned, down-home look. Old signs and rusty farm implements decorated the walls. There were also plaques bearing well-used aphorisms. As their eyes were adjusting from the bright sunshine, they were accosted by an over-friendly greeter. "How y'all doin'? Hungry—I hope, 'cause we got some mighty fine specials today. My name's Charlene and I'll be he'ping y'all today."

"That's great," mumbled Stephen as they were led to a table.

"Y'all take your time and I'll be back in a jiffy." And Charlene disappeared.

"That was oxymoronic," muttered Stephen. "How can we take our time if she'll return in a 'jiffy'?"

"Don'chu jest *lu-uv* being South'en?" teased Emily.

"Way-ull sorta," responded Stephen in kind, as he glanced over the menu. Then, looking all around him, he asked, "Did you see a sign for the 'Twilight Zone' before we entered town? I mean, this has been a very *dis*-usual set of circumstances." Emily liked the way Stephen used neologisms or malapropisms to make a point.

Having not allowed her customers to 'take their time,' Charlene was indeed back in a jiffy. "Y'all ready to order?"

"Not yet," replied Emily, "but could you just bring us some iced tea while we decide?"

"Sure enough, hon," and 'poof'—Charlene was gone again.

"She should try out for the Olympics," said Stephen. No sooner had he spoken, and he and Emily had begun to laugh, than Charlene reappeared with the tea.

"Y'all seem to be havin' a good time. That's what I like to see!"

"We're on our second honeymoon," offered Stephen, as he winked at Emily.

"Oh, that's so ro-MAN-tic," exclaimed Charlene. "How long've'y'all been married?"

At this point Emily took over. Her elbows on the table and her chin resting on her folded hands, she sighed, "Six—whole—months," as she gazed dreamily at her husband. Stephen reached over, took one of her hands and kissed it.

"*Six months* and y'all are going *ag'in*?!" exclaimed Charlene. And then, in a just-between-us-womenfolk tone, she leaned toward Emily and said, "Hon, you got more stamina than me," and gave Emily a sisterly chuck on the shoulder. "Y'all are gonna need to eat."

~ * ~

Once their meals had arrived and they had been given a respite from Charlene, Stephen asked, "What do you think about our encounter on the street a little while ago?"

"Well, obviously you made an impression on him. Whatever you said has helped change his life for the better."

"And yet," mused Stephen, "I can't recollect him at all. Of the hundreds—maybe thousands—of inmates I've encountered, his face...his situation hasn't stuck." Stephen made patterns in his mashed potatoes with his fork. "You know, Em. This is the first time I have ever been recognized by a former inmate on the street—right now, just when I'm about to leave prison chaplaincy."

"Is it giving you second thoughts?"

'Heavens no!" responded Stephen. "But did you catch his words: 'I knew *you needed to know that*'?"

"I did. It was an odd choice of words."

"Exactly." Using his fork for emphasis, he added, "You know those dreams I've had?—about standing by the gate to maximum security with that long line of inmates all wanting me to do something for them?" Emily nodded. "Well, it seems unconsciously I *have needed* to hear that young man's words." Emily could almost see the wheels turning rapidly in Stephen's mind. "Have I ever mentioned that the Hebrew and Greek terms for 'angel' simply mean 'messenger'?"

Emily smiled as she shook her head in the negative. "We've only been married six months."

"In the scriptures, angels don't come with feathered wings and bright haloes—those liberties were taken by artists in the Middle Ages and the Renaissance. The only way one can tell if an angel—or messenger—is from God is in the nature of the message. In the Hebrew Bible, angels don't pitch up and say, 'Hi, I'm Michael...or Roger.' The person hearing the message is the one who discovers that these are 'heavenly messengers.' The New Testament...well, it's a bit showier—Hollywood-style—you know, heavenly choirs and all of that. But nevertheless, the meaning of the message always rests with the receiver. And you only know it's true if you test it. If it doesn't ring with truth, if it doesn't 'pierce the heart' as with Mary, Jesus' mother, then one would never say it was an 'angel,' in our modern understanding. Does this make sense?"

Emily gazed at Stephen for some time before answering. "Yes, absolutely. Testing the truth of a message sounds downright scientific." She wiped her mouth before continuing. For Stephen, she seemed to be rooting around for the right words—a good trait for a scientist. "You knew I was a scientist and a religious agnostic when you married me..." Stephen acknowledged. "Well, Reverend Husband, you have just helped make palatable certain aspects of faith to this weakening agnostic."

"That wasn't my intent."

"I know that. You have made good on your promise not to press your experience of faith on me. I don't know what happened out there on the street before we came in here. It all happened so fast. One second I thought you were being attacked and...and the next...well...I think God wanted you to hear something." She smiled and shrugged. "Before you explained the real meaning of 'angel,' I would have dismissed the idea. Now I am not so sure...having witnessed what happened...it all seems more plausible. Beyond that, I cannot say."

Sixteen

"Don't you just hate these switchbacks?" puffed Emily. Both she and Stephen were carrying at least forty-five pounds each. "Every time I see blue sky ahead, I think 'Aha—we're reaching the summit'...and then we turn the bend and there's another section of the trail...going up toward another patch of sky. Tell it to stop!"

"Well...we can always stop—whenever we want," replied Stephen. With that, he loosened the belt of his backpack and set it down beside the trail, taking a seat on a boulder. "I'm just glad the mist lifted." Stephen wiped his brow and took a sip of water. "We should have some lovely views once we reach the summit." He handed his canteen to Emily.

Emily nodded her thanks and took a long drink. "What altitude do you think we are?"

"I'm not sure, but I would guess around four thousand feet. If so, we have another nine hundred or so to go. Man, I can feel the burn in my lungs. You can tell we live much closer to sea level."

"Don't I know it! But didn't you say today's hike is the most difficult?"

"Indeed I did," Stephen replied. "We're doing the worst part first. And each day we'll adjust that bit more to the altitude, so climbing Mt. Sterling won't seem quite so bad." Stephen swung up his backpack and slipped his arms through the straps. He reached down to help Emily to her feet. "Ready, my love?"

"Lead on, Rev."

~ * ~

It was nearly three o'clock when they reached the fire tower situated atop Mt. Cammerer. Despite their weary legs, Emily and Stephen dropped their backpacks and scampered up the steps to soak in the views. They hadn't met any other hikers on the trail all day, and now it seemed they were alone on the summit of Mt. Cammerer—unusual, as the Appalachian Trail passed this point. Apart from a light breeze, they were enveloped in a sacred silence. The tower's balcony afforded them a three-hundred-and-sixty-degree panorama of the eastern end of the Great Smoky Mountains National Park. They moved slowly, taking in the rich shades of green, the rocky outcrops, the shadows cast by the afternoon sun.

"The climb was worth it," Emily said softly and reflectively. Stephen put his arms around her and then was surprised when she began to sob, pressing her face into his neck and shoulder.

"Em, what's the matter?"

Emily lifted her head and extended her right arm toward the surrounding mountains. "It's all of this...it's so beautiful—and peaceful. I...I don't think I realized how overwrought I was becoming over the last months. Your getting shot—and all that came with it, discovering the deliberate PCB spillage, the threatening calls, finishing my PhD—all of it. I feel as though I've been under water and have finally come up for air." Stephen fished a handkerchief from his pocket and gave it to Emily.

"So breathe then, my lovely scientist. Breathe in the peace and beauty and exhale all the emotional tension. I think we've both needed a release from all the negativity that has been dominating our lives for nearly a year."

"There's something about the immensity of these beautiful mountains and their seeming permanence," Emily spoke quietly, her voice breaking, "that makes all of the shit—which seemed so important just yesterday—shrink to insignificance...or at least gain its rightful perspective. Einstein was right, the passage of time is an illusion. We're simply in a beautiful state of existence." She kissed Stephen and said, "Thanks for arranging this trip. It's medicine for the soul."

"You're the one with the more-than-full-time job. Organizing this adventure has been a pleasure. Tell you what, why don't you just drink in all of this while I set up the tent? Then we can cook some supper."

"Are you sure?"

"Absolutely." Emily smiled at him through eyes brimming with tears.

~ * ~

As Stephen finished laying out their sleeping bags in the tent, another group of hikers arrived. They greeted Emily and Stephen, and then availed themselves of the views from the tower—the reward for aching muscles and tired legs. Emily perched herself on a log by a circle of rocks that had been someone's campfire. Stephen was mixing a packet of dried soup with lentils to make a thick soup.

Emily nibbled some trail mix while watching Stephen prepare their meal. "What would you think about squatting here?" she mused. "The fire tower's not a lot smaller than our cottage."

Stephen smiled at the idea. "We could charge people food in exchange for letting them enjoy the view from our balcony. That way we wouldn't have to leave very often."

They continued to build on their fantasy life as the soup cooked. As Stephen served up the thick mixture, along with whole grain bread and cheese, the other hikers invited them over for a communal meal. They consisted of two couples, all teachers. Like Stephen and Emily, they were hiking the Smokies to clear their heads. They were on their way to Davenport Gap to finish their five-day trek through the Great Smoky Mountain National Park, which had begun at Fontana Dam. The six hikers compared notes on their respective climbs up Mt. Guyot and Mt. Cammerer, and all were of one mind in their damnation of switchbacks and the false hope they engendered.

Nighttime seems to fall faster in the mountains; or at least bedtime comes sooner, as after dark there is nothing to do apart from gaze at the night sky, if there are no clouds. It is also the case that people are truly worn out and ready for the refreshment sleep offers. In any event, once the food was finished and the dishes washed, the yawning set in, so the three couples headed for their tents.

Emily and Stephen's sleeping bags were a pair, which zipped together, thus allowing for more body heat—as well as cuddles. As they snuggled in, Emily lay her head on Stephen's chest. "Tired?"

"Tired enough, I guess. Why?"

"Too tired?" Her hand traveled down his belly and south of his navel.

"We'll soon find out."

Seconds later she said, "Obviously not too tired," and she crawled on top of him. They made love slowly, with the last of their strength. They both fell asleep as soon as they had climaxed, bodies and limbs still entwined.

~ * ~

As soon as light shone through the sides of their tent, Stephen and Emily began to wake. Both were on bladder alert. "You go first." Emily kissed him on the nose and pushed him out of their nest. Stephen fished around for his underwear and the sandals he wore around campsites. As he exited the tent, his bare back brushed the rain fly, which was covered in dew. "Eek! Cold!" he uttered, as the water rolled down his back. He dashed to the nearest tree and carefully made sure no one had left any unburied bodily deposits. Then came the release and its concomitant relief. "Ah, that's better. But it is a bit chilly this morning. Your turn," he offered Emily as he re-entered the tent. He was surprised to see a look of concern on her face. "Em, what's the matter?"

"About last night..." she began.

"It was wonderful. Thank you. Nothing like making love before falling asleep."

"Yes, well...while I agree that it was wonderful, I uh...I just remembered I haven't brought my pills."

"It's only one time," Stephen tried to reassure her as he pulled on a shirt.

"Yeah, well...about that," Emily continued. Stephen could read the concern written across her face. "I have somehow forgotten to take them for the last week—what with work and finishing my PhD." She looked pleadingly at Stephen to gauge his reaction. "I don't know how I could be so careless."

"Ah..." voiced Stephen as the penny dropped. "I suppose if I were as liberated a man as I like to think, I would have asked you." The two lovers looked at one another for a few moments.

"But can you think of a more beautiful place to conceive a child?" asked Stephen, in genuine hopefulness that Emily would agree. She stared at him almost impassively for several seconds.

"No," replied Emily, "I can't."

"Want to try again?" asked Stephen mischievously, as he knelt by her side.

"Don't push your luck!" Emily chortled and pushed him over. "I gotta pee." When she returned to their tent, Stephen was lying on his side, propped on his elbow. Emily collapsed onto her bag, groaning, "Oh, I'm stiff!" Looking over at Stephen, she saw he was smiling in a way she had never quite seen. "Out with it, Rev. Travis!"

"I was just contemplating the idea of fatherhood."

"Does the idea appeal to you?"

"With you, it does. Seeing as how we've both made it to thirty without becoming parents; I realize I've been waiting for the right relationship—and that is you. But, of course, I'm not the one who gets to become a double-person."

"True," replied Emily. "You do get to miss that part. But I suppose I can make you suffer if hormonal changes cause me to have mood swings." Emily reached over and tugged Stephen's beard. Stephen took her hand and kissed it.

"I'm ready for whatever comes. I just want you to know it."

'Whatever comes..." mused Emily. "With all of the hiking we have ahead of us...even if I am pregnant, there's a chance of losing it."

"I'm aware of that," said Stephen. "But let me remind you that I married you for *you*. Not for the children you might or might not produce. But I'm ready for that adventure with you, if it should happen." He leaned over and kissed Emily. They wrapped their arms around each other and lay in that embrace for several minutes. It was when they could hear the other hikers talking and moving about that Stephen spoke. "Breakfast?"

~ * ~

The two lovers spent most of the morning trek talking over the possibilities of parenthood. They both admitted the whole idea was somewhat scary, as it was *terra incognita,* but it was a land they were enticed to discover. "I suppose it's something like walking these trails," said Emily. "There are the obvious ups and downs—but they are not as they first might appear."

"How so?"

"Well, I had thought the hardest bit would be climbing the steep trails—and it is tough, but the views are worth it. And going downhill seemed to be easier...until I tried it with this weight on my back. I'm actually feeling more muscle strain going down. Is any of this making sense?"

"As a trail description, yeah, it makes sense. But I'm not so sure how it relates to having children. I might add that it's not as clear as your scientific self would normally be." Emily used her walking stick to poke Stephen in the backside.

"Perhaps it's because this time *I'm* the subject of the experiment. How's that?"

"*That* I understand! And there is this: although *you alone* have to do it, you don't have to do it *alone*. How's that for paradoxical thinking?"

"Hmm, I think I got it."

"I'm saying that I'm with you all the way, Em. And although the first nine months are largely yours, I promise I will change diapers, feed, wash, dress and help care for the little critter."

"Gosh—you're making it sound like I'm actually pregnant. Maybe it's time to change the subject? Speaking of which, I need to pee." Stephen helped Emily off with her backpack, and she made her way into the laurel and other undergrowth off the trail. Then he heard a scream and something came charging past him through the brush—a wild boar.

"Em! Are you okay?" Stephen cried. The next thing he heard was a string of expletives from Emily. "What's the matter? Are you hurt?" he asked with some urgency, all the while making certain the boar had left the area.

"Yes...*I'm* okay...but I peed all over my jeans and panties, goddamnit! That boar literally scared the piss out of me."

Stephen began laughing, despite himself. "I'm sorry, Emily. I'm really not laughing at you—but the situation."

"Ha-ha," sarcastically came from the bushes. "Can you dig into my backpack and get me some clean clothes?"

"Will do. I am sorry, though. I'm just glad neither of us was gored by its tusks."

"Hmmm..." was all Emily had to offer as she exchanged her soggy clothes for clean.

"I'll tie these to the outside of our bags to dry."

"That's really going to look great when we get to Walnut Bottoms camp site," growled Emily.

"Well, at least we can wash them in Big Creek. This certainly won't be the first time something like this happened on the trail."

"I think my heart has left my throat now...and seems to be beating almost normally in my chest," Emily said.

"Same here," said Stephen. "I was startled as well. With your screaming and then the boar charging across the trail—all happening in a split second—I really was afraid you'd been injured."

"I'll look more carefully next time nature calls," Emily stated firmly.

"That makes two of us." They walked on in silence for some time, breathing in the rich smell of the forest's damp growth and decay—life and death intertwined in the same instant. They were both sweating from the exertion—adding their own bodily scent to the pungent arboreal fragrance. The trail took a sharp turn and began a steep descent.

"Is that the wind?" asked Emily, searching the trees for movement.

"It's Big Creek—welcoming us back to the valley. But we've still some way to go."

With each turn in the trail, the sound of rushing water grew louder. Before long they caught sight of the rocky torrent which they had heard a quarter of a mile away.

"It's like one continuous waterfall," commented Emily.

"I suppose that's exactly what it is," Stephen replied. "Water searching for the lowest level is a constant waterfall." They were nearly walking alongside Big Creek. Once the trail reached the bank of the creek, they stopped.

"Watching water flow is mesmerizing," Emily mused aloud. "It's like watching a log fire burn—the sound, movement, change..." She pointed at a pool beneath a small waterfall. "Look how one moment the water is rushing, only to be stationary in the next instant. It's almost as though the water needs a rest—just like my legs and back."

"Happily, we're only a short walk from the campsite," said Stephen.

"I've never wondered about water feeling tired before," murmured Emily, almost to herself. "After only two days here, it's amazing how vacant my mind feels...vacant enough to entertain idle thoughts. Raleigh, and all of the shit that was happening there, seems a million miles away—or another life."

"Yes, backpacking has a way of keeping one living in the moment—missing a tree root or a rock in the trail can mean a world of hurt. Being aware of one's environment can mean life or death," said Stephen.

"Yeah, you mean like dropping my jeans to pee without seeing the boar," added Emily.

"Exactly!" Then in Monty Pythonesque style, he said, "Say no more! Say no more!"

They carried on a for another forty-or-so paces, and Emily spotted a largish pool of water where the sun made its way through the canopy. "Fancy a dip?"

"It'll be cold!" said Stephen, but Emily was already setting her backpack down and peeling off her clothing. Stephen watched her undress and felt that familiar stirring in his groin.

"Come to think of it, cold water might be just what I need right now." He slipped off his pack and began digging in it for a towel. "Believe me, we're gonna need this when we get out."

Emily had already tip-toed over the algae-covered rocks and slipped into the water. "Oh my God!" she gasped.

"What did I tell you?"

Emily noticed his semi-erection and laughed. "This will be interesting. How many seconds to full-flop mode?"

Stephen pushed off into the pool and came up spluttering. "Jesus Christ!" Seeing a long, flat rock behind Emily, he propelled himself toward it and pulled himself out of the water. Looking down, he asked, "Does that answer your question?" Emily quickly joined him and they embraced—if only for the body heat.

"Our first skinny dip as a married couple," panted Emily. "How romantic!" She pulled her hair back in a ponytail and squeezed out the water.

"Just one problem," said a shivering Stephen, "We left our towels on the other bank."

Emily kissed Stephen's bluish lips and purred, "Carry me back over?"

"You've gotta be joking," came his quick retort. "It'll be all I can do get myself back through that water. "Man! How to go from hot and sweaty to hypothermic in ten seconds. Are you coming?" Stephen slid down the rock, covering his genitals with one hand—for what little good that would do. He held out his other hand to Emily. She gratefully took it and then they gingerly felt their way along the bottom of the midriff deep water. Once on the other side, Stephen helped Emily up the back. Noticing that she had not retrieved a towel from her bag, he gave her first use of his. At that point they heard female voices approaching along the trail from the same direction they had come—and they were close. In all of their frantic commotion to get out of the mountain stream, neither had heard the other hikers. Unconsciously, Emily had quickly wrapped the towel around herself, leaving Stephen bare-assed naked.

"Em?" Stephen looked pleadingly at his wife, who gave a Gallic shrug, made an 'oops' face, and folded her arms over the towel.

The hikers were in sight—three women—as Stephen made a grab for his underwear, mooning the women as they came along the trail. There was much laughter at the couple caught short. And then, as Stephen turned to get his jeans, one of the women blurted out: *"Chaplain Travis?"*

Part Two

Seventeen

"Frumpy?...I mean, *Annabelle Lee*?" Stephen hurriedly pulled on his jeans and shirt before handing Emily her clothes.

Then both Annabelle Lee and Stephen spoke at the same time, uttering the over-used question which ignored the obvious, "What are *you* doing here?" Then they both laughed at the inanity of the question.

"I knew Stephen Travis when I was in prison," Annabelle Lee said, teasingly, to her friends.

"I thought you were in a women's prison," commented one of her fellow hikers.

"I was...he was the chaplain."

"That coulda made prison a *lot* easier," said the other hiker, ostensibly to herself.

At this point Stephen, still flummoxed, turned to Emily to explain. "Annabelle Lee was my secretary for a while at the women's prison—four years or so ago. I'm sure I've mentioned her." He introduced the two women, following which Annabelle Lee's companions introduced themselves.

"Stephen has mentioned you." Emily smiled at Annabelle Lee and friends, as she tugged up her jeans underneath the towel, and added to Stephen under her breath, "but not how attractive she was."

"Where are you headed?" asked Annabelle Lee.

"Walnut Bottom. You?"

"The same. We'll leave y'all to get dressed and see you there." The three women departed, laughing and chatting in an animated fashion. One called back, "Nice ass, Stephen!" More laughter followed. Stephen and Emily could guess what they were discussing.

"Well," she said, drying her hair with the towel. "That was a surprise."

"It certainly was." Stephen pulled his T-shirt over his head. "And more than a little embarrassing."

"Well," mused Emily, "we've run into two former inmates on this trip—so far—whatever next?" After a moment's silence she added, "That Annabelle Lee is a looker."

"She is that," agreed Stephen, "but if it sets your mind at rest, she is not one of the inmates who hit on me, okay? That young woman went through hell with men—her father and her husband."

"She's not *that* young."

"Oh, come on, Em! Yes, Annabelle Lee is good-looking, but so are a lot of other women—but I haven't married them. I married you...and you're the only ex-con for me." Stephen put his arms around Emily's waist and looked at her. "I've never seen you jealous." He looked at her as if for the first time as he kissed her eyes, cheeks and nose.

"Isn't this scientist allowed to be human?"

"Yes, of course. I guess I've only seen your strong side over the time we've known each other, that's all."

"Yeah, but with a life involving death threats, toxic waste dumping investigations, car chases and getting shot at—you know, little everyday things—it's no wonder you haven't seen a more vulnerable side of me. But I do have normal feelings...and the occasional bit of insecurity. I'd rather this came out now than later when we're at the campsite—you know, with an old-fashioned cat-fight."

Stephen laughed at Emily's joke. "Yeah, how cool would that be?—two women fighting over me? Maybe you two could get covered in mud first?"

Emily deftly swung her foot against Stephen's backside. "Watch it, Rev." She emitted a little growl. "You might be first."

Once fully dressed, they donned their backpacks and set off for the campsite. As they walked, Stephen began to fill in some details of Annabelle Lee's background.

"So why did you call her 'Frumpy' when you first saw her?"

"Ah, yes. Well, that was a nickname she picked up in school, after being raped by her father. She stopped wearing any make-up and wore baggy clothes—to make herself less attractive to the male of the species. And one really can't blame her."

"Nice father. What happened to him?"

"He was shot dead by his father—Annabelle Lee's grandfather."

"God almighty!" blurted Emily.

"Sadly, it didn't stop with her beast of a father. She eloped immediately after high school graduation with a ne'er-do-well who committed common law robbery—with her along for the ride. They both got time for it."

"Did she have anything to do with it?" asked an increasingly irate Emily.

"She says not—and I believe her. As you have no doubt discovered living with a prison chaplain, our 'justice system' ain't all it's cracked up to be. Too many people are failed too much of the time. Our society sees prison as the answer to every crime—large or small. We seemingly live in a world wherein people feel good about sending people to prison—guilty or not."

"Poor Annabelle Lee. She's been treated like shit by men. What a start in life, huh?"

"No kidding—and she was just one among hundreds of women who came from such backgrounds. Almost makes me ashamed to be a man. In any case, her outward beauty hides a lot of ugly inner scars. I just hope she's been able to get help and support since leaving prison."

"Don't I feel like a jerk for having felt jealousy?"

"Hey, Em, we all make superficial judgment calls. I'm no exception. I'm sure many a person has looked at you for the spectacular babe that you are, never guessing that you served time in prison. When you get right down to it, looks tell us almost nothing about a person—it's just the canvas on which we can paint our prejudices and preconceived notions. Or—to put it another way—put anybody's face behind bars and that person looks like a so-called 'convict.' Funnily enough, I think you and Annabelle Lee might make good friends." Stephen stopped and had a drink of water. He pointed his canteen along the trail, "Campsite ahead. Time to change the subject."

Annabelle Lee and friends were nearly finished setting up their tents. Stephen and Emily waved and set down their backpacks several yards away from the women. There were two other tents set up further along Walnut Bottom.

~ * ~

Emily and Stephen had joined Annabelle Lee and company in collecting wood for a fire they would share. Stephen used some fire starters to get damp kindling burning. Emily was boiling water on their Optimus stove.

"I can't believe I ran into you this way," Annabelle Lee said to Stephen over the crackling fire. She brushed her long, honey-blond hair away from her face. "I had thought about trying to get in touch with you after hearing about you in the news last winter.

128

But I didn't know where to send a letter. I just knew you were recovering in the hospital from a gunshot wound, but had no idea if you'd go back to chaplaincy work or not."

Stephen and Emily then related, in abbreviated form, what had transpired at the Advancement Center for Men and the subsequent attempt on both of their lives by the brother of a prison officer.

"And that's how I came to have this." Stephen tapped on the steel plate in the back of his skull. "Guaranteed not to rust."

"Stephen actually proposed to me from his hospital bed," said Emily.

Annabelle Lee and her friends laughed. "How romantic!" said Barbara, one of Annabelle Lee's companions.

"All the more so because at that moment Emily couldn't be sure whether she'd be both bride and widow in a matter of weeks," joked Stephen.

"He can laugh about it now, but there's more than a little truth in what he said. Happily, Stephen has recovered well."

"I'm so glad you two have each other," said Annabelle Lee. "And I'm glad you had a wedding and not a joint funeral."

"Amen to that!" said Stephen.

"And weren't you two in the news again more recently?" queried Barbara. "Or at least you, Emily? All that business about PCBs being dumped in the eastern part of the state? Aren't you the scientist who discovered the spillage?"

"Guilty as charged. But truth to tell, that's kinda the reason we're here now—to put all of that out of mind, at least for a few days."

"Jesus!" interjected Frances, the third member of Annabelle Lee's party. "You two have had more drama in six months of marriage than most people have in a lifetime."

"Which is exactly why we're here—and to celebrate my brilliant wife's doctoral degree—conferred last week. How's that

129

for a change of topic?" Everyone joined Stephen in lifting canteens in a toast to Emily. "Annabelle Lee..." Stephen began.

"I go by Annie now," she interrupted.

"Okay, then, Annie, do you feel like catching me up on your life? If you don't mind an audience."

"Oh, these two? They've heard all of my stories. Hopefully Emily won't mind?" Emily shook her head and tossed some twigs into the fire.

"Funnily enough, we've all just graduated as well—from Appalachian. Barb, Frances and I were housemates in Boone."

"So we're not the only ones celebrating by punishing ourselves," joked Emily.

"Far from it! We've met other recent grads on the trail since we've been here," responded Annie. "But to answer your question, Stephen—I guess I can call you Stephen?"

"Certainly, I'm not your chaplain anymore." He listened attentively.

"After my release, I spent a couple of months at home—just trying to adjust, I suppose you could say. During that time, I reflected on all the women I met in prison...women who'd never get the chance to move beyond their status as 'convicts'—which was most of them. So, I decided to apply to Appalachian State, as it was practically in our back yard. Happily, there was some insurance money—from my dad...I suppose he did more for me in death than he ever did in life." Annie snorted an ironic laugh. "Anyway, I was accepted. I continued living at home until my mother remarried and then I moved in with these two reprobates, who needed another roomie to share the rent." Annie bumped her shoulders into those of Barbara and Frances.

"She's not bad for an ex-con," said Frances. "We didn't have to lock up our money or anything."

"Thank you, Frances...remind me not to ask you to be a reference in the future."

"We think Annie got royally screwed by the justice system—what about you?" Barbara asked Stephen pointedly.

"Whoa, Barb!" Annie grabbed Barbara by the arm. "Stephen's one of the good guys. And remember, he got shot going up against the system."

"I'm sorry," Barbara apologized genuinely. "It's just that Annie has been through so much shit due to her dumb-fuck former husband—not to mention what that dick of a father did to her, and now she's a felon for life. Who's gonna want to hire her? Sorry, Annie, but it has to be said. It's amazing Annie's as sane and together as she is."

"It's okay—and it's not as though I haven't thought about it—a lot," responded Annie. "It just doesn't do me any good to look backward."

"What did you study, Annie?" queried Stephen.

"Like any good former inmate, sociology—with an emphasis on criminal justice—and psychology."

"This former inmate studied animal science." Everyone looked at Emily.

"You too?" Annie searched Emily's face to see whether she recognized her from women's prison. Emily smiled and nodded. "Did you two meet at—"

"No," Emily cut in. "I know what you're thinking. I was in another prison, far from here. But that's for another time. And somehow, I think there will be another time. Please continue."

"Annie graduated *summa cum laude*!" interjected Frances.

"Barb and Frances have been my cheering section," continued Annie. "Sometimes I don't think I would have done half as well without these two."

"We could say the same," replied Frances. "Annie's got looks and brains. She helped us with academics and we got the boys she brushed off. What a deal!"

"What plans—jobwise—do you have?" asked Stephen.

"I'm looking." Annie shrugged. "The real search for a job begins when I get back to Boone. Frances received her degree in education and will start teaching in the Boone area in a couple of months. And Barb, here, is going on for her master's degree in health and physical education."

"That just means I'm not ready for the real world," added Barbara.

"So, for the time being, we still have a home together," Annie said.

Everyone sat in silence listening to their inner voices and the crackling fire. Around them, in the deep valley, night had fallen. Above the western ridge of the mountains, the early summer sky remained illumined. The steady crash of rushing water in Big Creek provided the soundtrack.

"Annie," asked Stephen, "what would you really like to do with your degree?"

"It's going to sound sentimental, but here goes: I'd like to work with girls and women who come from fucked-up families like mine. Maybe start a safe haven or halfway house, where women can find refuge and get the emotional and psychological help they need."

"Hardly sentimental," asserted Emily. The other two women said the same. Then, looking at her husband, Emily said, "Stephen, I can see those mental wheels turning even in the dark."

"Yeah...sorry, it's too early to say anything definitive. But I certainly have an idea...it's just that I don't want to create any false hopes for Annie."

"Oh, c'mon, Rev!" chided Barbara. "It's not as though Annie hasn't had to deal with disappointments in life." The rest of the women followed suit. Stephen didn't stand a chance.

"Okay, okay. It's like this. I'm still awaiting the outcome of a damages case against the state of North Carolina. It should be settled soon. If the results are anything like what my lawyer—who's my brother-in-law—says, I might, and I stress *might*, be able to help Annie realize her dream. But nothing is certain, okay?"

Stephen's protestations of uncertainty had no effect. At a time when aching bodies needed the salve of a night's sleep, the four women suddenly became his energized interrogators.

"He hasn't even told me about this idea," declaimed Emily. "Out with it, husband of mine."

"All right, I surrender. Here's what has come into my mind only this evening. In a couple of weeks, I'll be leaving the prison chaplaincy." Annie's head pricked up at those words. "As Emily knows, I am not a typical parish minister—I simply don't fit the mold. I've been looking for a ministry that actually means something to me and has a positive impact on society. If, and again I must stress *if*, the settlement with the state goes as my lawyer predicts..." Stephen took a deep breath, "I might have, say, several hundred thousand bucks to play with."

"Can we all marry you?" joked Frances. She immediately apologized to Emily, who waved it off.

Stephen laughed and continued, "So a halfway house *might* have financial backing, in which case, there would be need for a manager or director."

"You would do that for me?" asked Annie.

"Yes and no," replied Stephen. "Yes. I would do that for you because I know you; I know what you've been through, and you have the heart, intelligence—and training—to make it work. No. I wouldn't be doing it just for you—but for all the women you've described, women who have been let down by men—fathers, lovers, husbands, police, lawyers and judges—and, not least, by the justice system. But remember, this is all hypothetical at the moment. Let's stay in touch and I promise I will keep you updated." Barbara and Frances hugged Emily, excited at the very thought of what might be.

As though on cue, they all got up, stiffly, from the logs on which they had been sitting and bade each other good night. Annie came around the dying fire to Stephen and Emily. "Do you mind if I hug your husband?"

Emily smiled as she said, "I think it's in order."

Eighteen

The next morning saw the campsite come to life in two stages. Those who had only arrived in the Smokies the day before were up first, preparing their breakfast and packing their tents—keen to hit the trail. Those who had already hiked for several days arose only after the other campers had made sufficient noise to deny them any further sleep. Stephen and Emily gave drowsy waves to Annie, Barbara and Frances as they crawled out of their tent, bedecked in wrinkled T-shirts and hair that was electrostatically charged by the tent. Stephen laughed as his inner gallery pictured them as the witches from Macbeth—although those three were far from hags.

Before they set off in different directions, Stephen jotted down his and Emily's address and telephone number on a notepad. He took it over to Annie, who was in the process of preparing the same for him. "Please remember I cannot promise *anything* at the moment. But when things become clear, I *will* be in touch with you." He handed Annie his sheet of paper and put hers in his pocket.

"I understand...it's just nice to feel hopeful about something

...and it's been...well, amazing to see you like this. My mother would call it a 'God moment.' I'm so glad you survived the gunshot wound, and that you and Emily have each other. She seems a lovely person for you."

"She is. Why don't you tell her yourself?" Annie accompanied Stephen to say her farewell to Emily.

Annie hugged Emily and then Stephen. "I can't begin to tell you what this encounter has meant to me. I said to Stephen that it's...simply amazing."

"You don't know half of it, Annie. In fact, you are the second former inmate we've encountered on this trip." Annie cocked her head with curiosity, looking back and forth between Stephen and Emily. "We'll tell you about it the next time we see you."

"Be sure you do. And keep safe on the trail." Annie hugged both of them again and then joined her friends. Emily and Stephen helped each other on with their packs, gave a wave to the departing group and began trekking.

"Back up we go," said Stephen. "It's a similar climb to Mt. Sterling...but not quite as hard."

"I'm counting on you to carry me if my legs give out," teased Emily.

"Okay, but we go without the backpacks," responded Stephen. "I remember one summer, several years ago, when I went out for what was meant to be a four-day hike with an old college friend." Stephen shifted his backpack a bit and tightened his straps. "Actually, it was 1976—a summer of intense heat and drought. On our first day out—on Roan Mountain—I slipped on some loose rock and jammed my left knee. It wasn't so bad at first, but as the day progressed it began to swell. I found a solid branch along the trail and tried using it as a crutch, but it wasn't much help. I wanted to soak it in some cool water but every spring listed on our map was dry. This meant that if we camped on the mountain, we couldn't cook anything. So we shared out what little water we had, and Matt—bless him—took my backpack from me and headed down the mountain to a campsite area situated by a creek. I felt real trepidation as I watched him disappear down the mountainside."

"Sounds like it was rather risky for both of you," opined Emily.

"Too right. With both backpacks, he must have been carrying at least ninety pounds. But it was a chance we had to take. If he had stayed with me, we'd both have run out of water—and despite the altitude, it was hot. All I carried was one canteen, a flashlight and my crutch. I guess it was about three o'clock when we split up. Whew! I'm talking too much." Stephen stopped and breathed deeply.

"You could at least finish the story," chided Emily.

"Well...I made it back; otherwise, we wouldn't be here right now."

"Wise ass!"

"In short, I made it down to the campsite—well after sundown. If I hadn't kept the flashlight, I would never have seen the trail signs. Happily, I could see campfires through the trees down below me. Never have I had a more welcome beacon. And when I schlepped into camp, I saw that Matt had set up our tent and rolled out our bags. And dinner was waiting over the fire. I almost cried. The next day we bushwhacked through the undergrowth to get to the closest road. From there, we hitchhiked back to his place near Asheville."

"Glad you didn't tell me that story *before* we came out here," said Emily. "And people talk about how they want to 'experience nature on its own terms.' Sounds like her terms can be fairly harsh."

"That's for certain," Stephen said between breaths. They stopped and looked back down the trail. Big Creek was well out of sight, although the sound of its rushing water could be faintly heard. "I suppose this is the third time I've hiked this trail. For some reason it's always a bit melancholic when I lose the sound of that mighty creek—after listening to it all night and for the first section of the trail—it's like leaving a friend behind."

"Give me a kiss, poetic husband of mine!" said Emily, pulling Stephen close by his T-shirt. The two lovers kissed, hugged as much as their backpacks would allow, and laughed—simply for the joy of it.

"When do I get to meet Matt?" asked Emily.

"Well, funnily enough, when we're in Asheville. He works just behind our hotel."

"Oh, so he's the flute-maker you mentioned when we were on our honeymoon? You pointed out his workshop."

"Indeed I did. He was off skiing when you and I were there in January. And besides, I seem to recall we had other things on our mind during the week of our honeymoon."

"We certainly did!"

"Anyway, I called him before we left and said we'd try to catch up with him while we were there. He's offered to take us out for dinner—which I know you're going to appreciate after several days of my trail mush! Shall we continue?"

~ * ~

"Now you see why it's called Pretty Hollow Gap." Stephen indicated the forest floor ahead which was littered with wildflowers—red, white, yellow, and blue.

"It's amazing!" replied Emily. "I've never seen anything like it. It could be a cover of multi-colored snow!"

"It fascinates me that this saddleback between Balsam High Top and Mt. Sterling is so free from underbrush—such that these flowers can grow. Let's stop and enjoy it for a while." They released their straps and lowered their bags to the ground.

"It's hard to step anywhere off the trail without treading on the flowers," remarked Emily.

Stephen began singing "Tiptoe through the Tulips." Emily doused him with water from her canteen.

"So far, this has been our gentlest trail. Please tell me I won't be lulled into a rude awakening."

Stephen took off the bandana he wore around his head to catch the sweat. He shook it open and then draped it between his hands. "One end is Balsam High Top and the other is Sterling—which is slightly higher. Happily, we're approaching Sterling from the least difficult direction. We're more than halfway there. The climb from this trail isn't anything like our first day or climbing High Top yesterday." Stephen splashed water over his head and wiped his face with the bandana. Once more he indicated their beautiful surroundings. "You know, you can't reach places like this—such pristine beauty—without effort."

"It certainly makes the aching muscles worthwhile," commented Emily who added, "Shall we have a bite of lunch here?"

"Why not? Will trail mix, sweaty cheese and apples do?"

"Sounds exquisite." They munched and crunched their way to replenished energy levels and set off again.

~ * ~

"Is that the top?" Emily indicated the fire tower that could just be made out through the trees.

"Yep, and hallelujah. Our last climb on this expedition."

"It didn't take as long as I thought it might," said Emily.

"Well, two of our hikes have started at the bottom of the mountains," answered Stephen.

"Except for what my tired legs are telling me, it's hard to judge the height—we're surrounded by trees."

"We'll climb the fire tower when we get there. Then you'll have a magnificent three-hundred-and-sixty-degree-view," replied Stephen.

Soon they had reached the base of the tower. Both gladly dropped their backpacks and stretched.

"Looks like we're alone," mused Emily. She swung her arms wide open. "A mountain all to ourselves! Who could ask for more?"

"I thought you wanted to squat in the fire tower on Mt. Cammerer," said Stephen.

"That will be our summer home. We'll live here in the winter...and have our shopping brought in by helicopter."

"Nice to see my scientist wife has an imagination as well," Stephen said as he dug into the backpack for his camera. "Don'tcha think we ought to look over the property before we make a firm decision?"

"That's a fine idea, Rev. Travis." Emily took his hand and they strolled to the bottom of the tower. Looking up, Emily shook her head. "I think you're going to have a hard time carrying me up those stairs—or are they ladders?—and through the threshold—it's a hatch in the floor of the cabin."

"Maybe piggyback?" laughed Stephen.

"Oh well, so much for tradition," smiled Emily. "We seem to have our own way of doing things, in any case. Follow me, good sir." And up she went. "Heavens! This really is a succession of ladders." Emily stopped at one of the small landings. "Stephen, my God, the view is wonderful."

Stephen crowded in close to Emily on the small platform. "Want to go any higher?"

Emily looked up and then outward. "No. I don't think a few more feet are going to change the view."

Stephen put his arms around her and clutched one of the steps. "I'll be your safety belt." He nuzzled his way through her hair and kissed her perspiration-dampened neck.

As their gaze moved from the western horizon toward the north and east, they were mesmerized by the fleeting shadows of clouds, which seemed to undulate as they moved over the folds of the mountains.

"I could stand here for hours just looking at these mountains," mused Emily. "Their immensity seems to draw you in..."

"I find it interesting that, with the trees in leaf, you can only appreciate their ruggedness by the passing of clouds or, in winter, a blanket of snow—both of which define their ridges and folds."

"Mmmh," was Emily's response as she laid her head against Stephen's shoulder.

"Hate to break the mood," said Stephen, "but we'd better get our tent set up and start cooking supper. We can come back up afterward."

"S'pose you're right." Emily yawned, stretching out both arms.

As they began their descent, both realized at the same moment how stiff their legs had become, standing still on the tower. Thus the descent was at a much slower pace than the ascent. Each laughed at the other's ughs and grunts which signified muscle ache.

~ * ~

No one else camped on Mt. Sterling that night. Their only companions were the sounds of night creatures and the canopy of stars and constellations. After their evening meal, the two lovers made their way back up the tower and sat on one of its landings.

"Are you ever afraid in the mountains?" asked Emily.

"Of critters or people?"

"I suppose both."

"Apart from being occasionally startled by an animal—like on our first day, when the wild boar made its appearance—no, animals don't really worry me. Only people."

"What about bears?"

"Oddly enough, of all the miles I've hiked in the Smokies, I've never encountered a bear. I've seen them lower down the mountains, but that was usually when I was driving. People scare me more than anything else on earth."

"Even up here?"

"Occasionally...particularly the *praedator redneckiensis*."

"The *what*?"

"It's my fake Latin for predatory rednecks who, sadly, have been known to venture up the trails to carry out their felonious deeds. Hey, let's change the subject. I have too vivid an imagination from having worked behind bars for years. That's the problem for us town dwellers when we get into the depth of nature at night—we can project our fears onto the darkness."

At that moment, as though to wipe their frontal lobes clean of negative thoughts, a shooting star crossed the horizon. Reflexively, they both oohed and pointed at the same time. Then they laughed at each other and kissed.

"That was timely," said Emily, "Or should I perhaps say it was another *kairos* moment?"

Stephen gave a grunt of agreement. "The last four or five days have been quite incredible, haven't they? Running into the guy in Morganton—and then Annabelle Lee here in the Smokies. If I were a Calvinist, I'd tend to believe it has all been predestined...but I'll just stick with *kairos* and leave it for the mystery it is." They sat with their thoughts, gazing upward. With no other light to interfere, and their eyes well-adjusted to the inky darkness, the heavens displayed their full glory. All they could see below were the last embers from their dying fire.

"Life really is mysterious, isn't it?" reflected Emily. "As a scientist, there's always the urge to discover and learn more—to push back the boundaries of our ignorance...the desire to help humans and other animals. But when I look out there," her hand swept across the night sky, "and see specks of light, which have taken thousands of light years to arrive here...well, I realize how little we human beings actually know about existence...on one little speck of dust amongst billions of others. Yet, rather than think of it as ignorance, I prefer to think of it as mystery. I have you to thank for that. And this I know: I am glad to be alive and to be here with you." Emily turned and kissed him. "I'm ready for bed."

~ * ~

As Stephen and Emily snuggled together in their joined sleeping bags, she asked, "Have you thought any more about the possibility of my being pregnant?"

'Some," replied a dozy Stephen. "You?"

"Yeah, a bit."

"And?"

"It's been something I thought I'd always like—being a mother...but it was always in the future. I suppose being thirty years old kinda caught me by surprise. I'll be thirty-one when the baby's born."

"*When?*" queried Stephen—not with shock or surprise, but rather with keen interest. "So do you think?—"

"Not sure...I just have a feeling. So what have you thought about being a father?"

"Readier now than I've ever been, and there's no one else I've ever given a thought to having a child with. I think you'd make a wonderful mother."

"How will it work with two parents who have demanding careers?"

"Well...you know that settlement with the state? If it comes through, maybe I can continue to break ministerial molds and stay at home with Baby X? In any case, I know you and I will work it out."

"Baby X!" Emily chuckled. "I like that!" She took Stephen's hand and placed it on her belly. "Will you like me when I'm fat?"

"Em, I'll *love* you when you're fat—especially knowing the reason why." She placed her head on Stephen's chest and within a minute had fallen into a deep sleep.

~ * ~

"Don't tell me that's Big Creek I hear," Emily said.

"Absolutely right, my lovely scientist." Stephen took a bite out of their last apple and handed it to Emily.

143

"Have you noticed that everything we eat up here tastes wonderful? I mean, I eat apples three or four times a week at work, and barely think about them." She handed the apple back to Stephen.

"I guess that it's because we eat because we really are hungry and need the nutrition, as opposed to eating simply because it's 'time'." He made apostrophes with his fingers.

They each had a handful of the nearly depleted trail mix and resumed their descent. "Wouldn't it be nice to live next to the sound of a roaring stream?" mused Stephen. "It's a comforting sound—like waves crashing on a beach."

"Ah, it's the Carolinian's dilemma—the beach or the mountains?" responded Emily.

"It's a luxury to be able to think that way, isn't it?" reflected Stephen. "The people I've been working with are pretty much left with the questions, 'How old will I be when I get out of prison and where will I go?'"

"I suppose if your halfway house for women comes to fruition, some prisoners will have an answer to one of their questions. By the way, did you come up with that idea because we bumped into Annabelle Lee? Or were you cooking that up beforehand?"

"It had actually started forming after I handed in my letter of resignation—when I began wondering what I might do in the near future. Why?"

"Just curious really. I like the idea. If it helps abused women and keeps them from rejoining their abusers, it's gotta be a good thing. How long might it take to set it up?"

Stephen gave his answer some thought before replying. "Well, IF the money from the settlement comes through, then buying a property won't be an issue. Planning permission will probably be the sticking point—but it's not insurmountable. Then we'll need a board of directors to oversee the project and to help with attaining charitable status." Stephen paused to catch his breath.

"At least you won't need to search for a manager or director," added Emily.

"I must admit, running into Annabelle Lee had to be an act of God. It really helped the idea of a women's shelter take shape in my mind...and the fact that she—despite the obstacles in her path as a convicted felon—is seeking to help other women like herself...well, what can you say?"

"I can say it seems you've found your future vocation and created a job at the same time."

"I think so too," replied Stephen. "But to answer your question, if I really throw myself into it, I'd like to think we could have the halfway house up and running in six to eight months. Hey, wouldn't it be great if we could get Ben or Kate to work with the shelter?"

"Just watch out about the 'we' element—after all, this is your baby."

Stephen stopped walking and turned. "Sorry, Em, I just get carried away with the idea. You know, last night as I was falling asleep, it occurred to me that our two encounters with former inmates are almost the two sides of a door—on one side is my past ministry, on the other is the future...a future that is far from certain but very appealing. Imagine if we hadn't come on this trip—"

"I'd rather not," interrupted Emily. She kissed Stephen full on the lips. "I like the way things are. Don't mess with *kairos*, Rev!" And they continued their descent.

Nineteen

"I'd almost forgotten just how fancy this is," murmured Emily as they pulled their Volvo into a parking space behind the Grove Park Inn. "Can we go in dressed like this?"

"We'll go in, Dr. Travis, like we own the place," came Stephen's reply. "Backpacks into the trunk and suitcases out."

"I can't wait to have a shower!" exclaimed Emily. "I'm probably carrying a pound of trail grime. My body feels so light after having carried a pack for several days." Emily did a big stretch and then then attempted to touch her toes. "Eek! Hamstring muscles are rebelling."

"I know the feeling," answered Stephen as they shoved their backpacks into the trunk. "See any wastebins around here? I want to get rid of our trail garbage."

Emily glanced around and shook her head. Then with a mischievous look in her eye, she said, "What about that Mercedes convertible over there? It would help give it that hillbilly look. Bring 'em down to earth a bit."

Stephen just about burst a gut laughing. "I don't know whether I've spent too much time around you or you with me. Are you serious?"

"No...but then, why not? At least it's all wrapped in a bag. I'll keep a look out."

Stephen walked as nonchalantly as possible towards the Mercedes. He looked over at Emily who gave him the thumbs up. With one look in all directions, Stephen quickly pushed the bag of trail rubbish behind the driver's seat. Meanwhile Emily had one hand over her mouth and the other over her belly, which was shaking violently. Stephen quickly walked back to their car and said, "Let's blow, baby!" They grabbed their suitcases and headed for the front desk, laughing as they went.

"You two seem to be enjoying your holiday already," the desk clerk smiled at the couple. "Names please?"

"The Reverend and Doctor Travis," replied Stephen. "And fret not about our current appearance, my good man; we've just come off the Appalachian Trail."

The desk clerk gave Stephen an uncertain look as he found their reservation, but then positively beamed and said, "I see you have a premium club room, mountain view. Let me just get your keys. Oh, and there's a message left for you by the state attorney general's office." The desk clerk turned his back to find the keys.

Stephen and Emily looked at each other with confusion. "Premium club room?" whispered Stephen. "Is he pulling our leg? We can't afford that." He picked up the envelope addressed to him. The clerk was facing the couple again, keys in hand. "Do you mind if we just read the message first?" asked Stephen. "Could be important."

"Be my guest."

Stephen and Emily stepped away from the desk and Stephen began to read. "Stephen, thought this might get your attention. Good news, bro. The state attorney general has settled the tort case out of court, as I had hoped. We reached a settlement the same afternoon you left for the Smokies. Given the nature of the crimes committed, the injuries you sustained, and with the proviso that you might have future problems resulting from the gunshot wound, you have been awarded the maximum damages allowable of one million dollars. But given that Emily was also involved in the shooting incident, which could have resulted in the loss of her life, you and she have been awarded a second amount of two-hundred-and-fifty thousand dollars. Thus, I took the liberty of having your room bumped up to premium club. Enjoy, bro, because you two have earned it. Give my love to Emily, Dave."

The surprised couple looked at one another and mouthed the dollar amounts again, their eyes wide with disbelief.

"All Stephen could manage to utter was, "Holy shit!" The couple hugged each other excitedly before turning back to the clerk.

"I assume everything is all right?" he asked.

"Couldn't be better," replied Stephen, barely able to contain himself. Meanwhile their bags had quietly and efficiently been taken up to their room. When Stephen received the keys, he realized that he couldn't stop smiling.

~ * ~

There were a basket of fruit, chocolates and a bottle of champagne being chilled on ice awaiting them. They immediately popped the bubbly and drank a toast to the results of Dave's hard work. "Your brother-in-law must really love you," remarked Emily.

"He's the brother I never had. I'm glad my sister married him. I remember," said Stephen, sipping his champagne, "that when he started coming over for Sunday lunches, there was always a lot of laughter. He could always get my parents to laugh. That's the first thing I noticed about him. Despite our age difference, he always liked being around me—going to the movies, buying me the occasional illegal beer, etc." Whenever I hear people say, 'He's like a brother to me,' I think of Dave."

"Well, once again, here's to Dave," Emily raised her glass, upon which Stephen feigned an accidental slip and splashed his champagne over Emily. She returned the favor and began kissing her husband fervently through champagne-soaked lips.

"Shall we get out of these wet things?" mumbled Stephen through pressed lips.

"Thought you'd never ask. There's a king-size bed waiting to be tried."

~ * ~

Frantic lovemaking had been followed by leisurely lovemaking. This, in turn, was followed by a hot shower. As they were getting dressed for dinner with Stephen's friend, Matt, Emily asked for more background on their friendship.

"Although Matt never finished his degree program at college, I think he had learned how he needed to learn—which wasn't in an academic setting. Although it's better coming from him, Matt spent a few years moving about—doing all sorts of things— *Dharma Bum*-style. He took up playing the flute during that time, becoming quite proficient. Then came the day he got a job in a bicycle parts company—not all that far from here. With permission to use their metal-shaping and cutting tools after hours, Matt made a flute—and it worked well. That feat alone earned him several job offers by established flute makers in New England, so off he went. He lived in Massachusetts for a fair number of years, but then, after hours he started making Baroque-style wooden flutes with silver fittings—he can explain it much better than I can. Once he started showing them at flute conventions, the orders started pouring in and, as the saying goes, the rest is history. He can fill in the gaps when we meet him in his shop, which—as I have pointed out—is immediately behind our hotel. Shall we away?"

The desk clerk did a double take—particularly at Emily—when the two of them walked through the lobby. Emily caught the clerk giving her the eye, so she tossed her long hair, smiled at him, and then said in redneck, "We shure duz clean up real gud, don't we?" The clerk looked as though he had been doused with cold water. Emily laughed as they stepped through the door.

Stephen chuckled. "I saw him giving you the eye. Poor man; you spoiled his fantasy!" No sooner had they descended the steps than a parking attendant asked if they needed their car.

"Not to go from here to there," replied Stephen, as he pointed at Matt's flute shop. "But here's your tip anyway." Stephen pulled a ten-dollar bill from his wallet, handed it to the attendant and they left him in stunned, but pleasant, surprise.

Stephen and Emily walked the thirty yards to Matt's shop. When Stephen looked back, the amazed parking attendant was scratching his head, but when he caught Stephen's eye, he gave a cheery thumbs up. Inside, Matt was sitting at his desk with his back toward the door. His two apprentices were cleaning the machinery and the floors before leaving for the day. One of them greeted Stephen and Emily. "We're just about to close, but may I help you?"

"Yes, please, my wife is interested in purchasing a saxophone—"

"Now don't start!" interrupted Emily.

"I'd recognize that voice anywhere." Matt spun around in his chair and his wiry frame was quickly on its feet. Emily noted that he bore a resemblance to the Beat poet, Gary Snyder. "Hey, buddy!" Matt approached Stephen and gave him a big hug. "And I'm guessing this is Emily?"

"It would be embarrassing if she weren't," Stephen said with a laugh.

Emily hugged Matt, saying, "I've heard so much about you. I almost feel like I know you."

"Was anything you told her true?" Matt asked Stephen.

"A little...well, some...uh, nah. You can correct all of that tonight."

"I know y'all are probably tired, so we'll just go a short way for dinner." Then, as though reading Emily's thoughts, "I'll give you a tour of the shop tomorrow—if you're up for it."

"I'd love it," enthused Emily. "You're on."

They piled into Matt's VW and drove into town. The restaurant, Yo' Mama's Cucina, offered a hybrid Italian/Southern U.S. cuisine—serving grits in lieu of polenta, fried chicken with marinara sauce, deep-fried artichoke hearts, etc. The décor was also a collision of cultures—a mix of North Carolinian memorabilia with Italian bric-a-brac, but somehow it worked. The dining booths were of two types: Appalachian mountain-shack or taverna. Once they had ordered food, the catching up began in earnest for Matt and Stephen, all of which served to introduce Emily to their twelve-year friendship.

"Hey, remember that time we accidentally led the Fourth of July parade in Black Mountain?" reminisced Matt.

"Okay, I'll bite," said Emily between bites of food. "How did you two manage that?"

"Well," began Stephen, "We were stoned—"

"We were on mescaline," interrupted Matt.

"Ah...true." Stephen restarted his account. "We had decided to have a sort of 'farewell to hallucinogens'...so we dropped at some small pond off the Blue Ridge Parkway—where Matt liked to swim, and then we headed toward Montreat to hike Lookout Mountain. We somehow missed the fact that there was a midday parade to commemorate the Fourth."

"Hardly surprising, given the fact that you two were high as kites." Emily laughed.

"So anyway, we turned down the main street only to see the gathered throng waving at us and shouting, 'go back!'" continued Stephen. "We were kinda freaked, thinking they wanted us hippy types to get out of town."

"And then I looked out my window," Matt said, "And who should I see but the dean of our college standing about five feet away from our car—that was almost like running into our parents—and he was also waving us back. Next thing we knew, the crowd parted and there we were at the head of the parade. So your dear husband put the car into reverse and we led the parade for about a quarter mile until we could turn into a side road."

"After our initial surprise," added Stephen, "we simply got into the spirit of things and waved at everyone, as though we were part of the parade."

"Having performed our civic and American duty of leading the parade, we looked for a place to park, where we could pick up the trail for Lookout Mountain." Matt smiled and shook his head at the vision in his mind's eye. "We parked the car and began our trek. However, we hadn't walked very far when we passed a small field where people were gathered around a tall pole, cheering and clapping—we thought it was some weird cult and started to freak again—"

"Only to discover it was a greased pole climb!" interjected Stephen. "As we were really tripping by this time, we wanted to get away from crowds of people and just groove on the mountains, so we hotfooted it for the trail head. No sooner had we started our ascent than we ran into a group of well-dressed men coming down the trail! There were about twenty of them. Not exactly what you'd expect on a mountain trail."

"Are you sure they were actually there?" teased Emily.

"Well, I saw 'em, too," added Matt. "So either they were really there or we were in each other's head! I ventured to utter a shy 'hello' to all these guys and there erupted a torrent of 'hi, hello and hey there'—only to be followed by 'Praise the Lord!' But the clincher after 'Praise the Lord!' was 'He's up there, boys!' Stephen and I looked at each other and immediately turned off the trail into the deep woods. We were not ready to meet the Lord that day."

"Sounds to me like God really has a sense of humor, for all of that to happen on your last trip," observed Emily.

"It doesn't end there." Matt said. "Stephen and I stayed in the woods until evening. When we walked back into Montreat, a firework display was just starting by the lake. It had to be the most ham-fisted fireworks show I've ever seen." Stephen grunted his agreement. "One of the first rockets fired straight across the lake and lodged itself on someone's car—stuck between the windshield and the hood, spitting fire all the while. This dude comes running over, tries to vault the wooden fence between the lake and parking lot, only to catch his foot and fall headlong down the bank. And then: BOOM! The rocket exploded. In our altered state of mind, Stephen and I started laughing our heads off. Very few of the rockets actually made it into the air. Most went up a few feet and then turned parallel to the lake and went straight for the crowd of people, where they exploded. We were mesmerized by the reflection of the rockets as they crossed the water and headed for the onlookers. I've never seen crowds part so fast as when the rockets approached them. We were so transfixed by this cartoonish firework display in which the rockets went in every direction but up, that we hadn't realized when one was heading toward us. It took several seconds to register that we were watching it head-on. Stephen caught on before me and gave me a shove, shouting 'Run!' I moved my ass just in time. The thing blew up only a few yards away from us, showering us with sparks. Man, that was wild!"

"Sounds like you two are lucky to be alive," responded Emily.

"I suppose so," Matt said thoughtfully, "but especially your hard-headed husband. To survive a bullet to the head—wow! That's something!"

"Yeah, and it's something we won't talk about tonight, if you don't mind. We're here to leave the prison craziness and Emily's work behind," Stephen said gently but firmly.

"Copy that," Matt replied, miming zipping his lips closed. Turning to Emily, Matt asked if they had bored her to death with their reminiscences.

"No," she said, "It's fun listening to what you two have been through together."

"Well, then," responded an encouraged Matt, "has Stephen ever told you about the time he re-enacted Jesus's walking on the water?" Emily turned to Stephen, who simply shrugged and went slightly crimson. Matt ordered another round of drinks.

"Your marriage won't be complete without your knowing this. It must have been around 1970. Stephen had a roommate who was Roman Catholic, and his mother had made him a monk's habit— maybe as a hint? Who knows?" Matt laughed. "Our college campus was in the sandhills of North Carolina as Stephen has probably told you, and the land for building was largely dredged from cypress swamps. The water was contained in two large lakes, with most of the cypress trees having been cut off just below water level." Matt winked at Emily. "You see where this is going, don't you? Well, our mutual friend here borrowed his roommate's habit and got me to row him out into the lake—at least twenty yards from the bank. Locals were allowed to fish the lake, and on this particular afternoon, the banks were crowded. The good reverend stands up in the rowboat, shoulder-length hair and beard—you know, Jesus-style—makes a gesture of blessing the crowd, and then steps out of the boat and starts stepping from tree-stump to tree-stump!" Both Stephen and Matt were laughing hard at the memory. "Fishing poles were dropping into the water, shouts were going up from the witnesses, and then—to top it all off—Stephen starts motioning for the faithful to come join him on the water!"

"What happened?" exclaimed Emily.

Stephen took over while Matt guffawed. "A few tried to walk on the water...but as you might imagine, they didn't get very far." Stephen began to look sheepish. "I'm just glad no one drowned."

"So how did it end?" Emily asked.

"Will you tell her or shall I?" asked Matt.

"Be my guest," replied an abashed Stephen.

"Alas," spoke Matt gravely, "suffice it to say that no souls were saved that day. Your water-walker, upon seeing there were no takers, shrugged dramatically and shouted, 'I can see you are not ready!' and climbed back into the boat, whereupon I rowed him back to the other side of the lake—and we scrammed before anyone could drive around the lake to find us."

"You two pranksters!" Emily said, laughing. "It's amazing you had time to study with all of your antics."

"Ah, well there we differ, Stephen and I. As he's probably told you, I left college after my sophomore year, whereas Mr. Academic here went on to finish his degree and go on to seminary." Matt raised his glass. "Here's to you, my friend."

Stephen accepted the toast, but added, "You haven't done so badly yourself, Matt. I admire the way you've built your business. Academics are easy by comparison."

"But we're not comparing," interjected Emily. "We're celebrating: Matt's flute-making business, your leaving prison chaplaincy and my PhD! To mutual success, love and friendship!"

"So, Stephen—leaving prison ministry? Please tell me you're *not* going into a local, white-bread, American church!"

"Well..." began Stephen, "that story will see us through dessert."

Twenty

As with any much-anticipated holiday, the time for Emily and Stephen seemed to evaporate like a July shower on a scorching afternoon. On the drive back to Raleigh they each related the high points of their time away, which they would henceforth refer to as their 'second honeymoon.' By the time they had passed Winston-Salem, their conversation had begun the inevitable shift toward 'tomorrow': work, the PCB spillage and what next for Stephen. When they were less than an hour from home, Emily ventured to say, "I think I am pregnant." She glanced over at Stephen who was driving. He reached out and took her hand.

"And how do you feel about it?"

"Excited...scared...puzzled..." Emily's voice trailed off.

"Puzzled?" asked Stephen. "How so?"

"Oh, just wondering whether I subconsciously forgot my pills—maybe as a way of deciding about parenthood."

"Want to explain?"

"Yeah. I mean that if we kept discussing parenthood in a theoretical manner, I could come up with a hundred reasons to get pregnant and a hundred reasons to avoid it. As a scientist, theories are interesting...but sooner or later one has to pick a likely theory and try it out through experimentation. I don't like sitting on the fence."

"So...do you actually think you forced the decision? It doesn't seem like you," remarked Stephen.

"You're right...it doesn't seem like me. It's not my style—and I don't think I would do that to you. But it's also not like me to forget my pills. I'm just trying to process things, that's all."

"In any case, you might not be pregnant," offered Stephen. "Maybe it's time to visit your doctor—just to make sure?"

"I'm pretty sure," responded Emily. "And before you ask," Emily dramatically threw the back of her hand across her forehead and intoned wistfully, "A girl just knows these things," and then burst out laughing. Stephen joined her. "And yes, I will go see my gynecologist. The sooner we know, the better, eh, Rev?"

"Absolutely!"

"So then...how are you feeling?"

"It's hard not to let my mind get carried away with the possibility," said Stephen. "I wouldn't want to be disappointed."

"So you're really up for it?"

"As I said when we were in the mountains: with you, I am ready—and I'm already starting to get butterflies in my stomach just thinking about it."

"Hey, buster, I'm the one whose innards are supposed to be acting funny," teased Emily. "I wonder if we'll end up in the Guinness Book of World Records?"

"What do you mean?" asked Stephen.

"I should think we've had the most eventful first year of marriage ever—you know: car chase, gunshot wound, your blowing open the extortion racket, my breaking the case about the massive PCB dumping, your getting a million bucks in the tort case against the state—and now becoming parents. And the year is barely half over."

"Perhaps we should aspire to become boring?" suggested Stephen. "I, for one, would welcome it."

"Having a child just might help with that," said Emily. "As a colleague of mine said: 'Having children doesn't simply change your life—*they rule it!*' Diapers, feeding times, lost sleep!"

"Oh well, what else were we going to do with the next eighteen years or so?"

They were approaching the western part of Raleigh. Stephen guided the car off the interstate and soon they were in the leafy part of the city they called home. As they rounded the corner that led to their cottage, Stephen asked, "Shall we eat out tonight? There won't be much in the fridge, as we've been away for a week." As he turned his head toward Emily awaiting her response, Stephen saw the color drain from her face. Emily's left hand covered her mouth as her right pointed straight ahead. A fire truck was parked in front of their cottage and the firefighters were dampening down the remaining flames as dirty-looking steam poured from the front door and windows. Neighbors stood watching the Sunday afternoon drama, while a police officer was talking to one of the spectators. Stephen parked the car on the opposite side of the street and they got out of the car, their faces conveying their growing sense of disbelief. The neighbor speaking with the policeman pointed toward Emily and Stephen. The officer looked up from taking his notes, thanked the individual with whom he had been speaking and approached the stunned couple. After introducing himself as Officer Mason, he said, "I understand this is your house?"

"Yeah, we rent it...but it's our home." Stephen spoke slowly, looking over the officer's shoulder at their badly damaged nest.

"Well, we're all just glad you weren't in the house when it caught fire—"

"Do you know Sergeant Longacre?" interrupted Emily. "Has he been informed of the fire?"

Somewhat taken aback, Officer Mason said, "Uh yeah, ma'am, I know him, but I don't see what he—"

Emily cut him short again. "I'm sorry, I don't mean to sound rude, but can you call for him on your radio? It's important. I think this fire was deliberately started."

"Well, ma'am, the fire department will be conducting an investigation as to the cause of the fire," offered the policeman.

Sensing that Emily was about to explode with rage, Stephen placed his hand on the man's shoulder and said, "Excuse me, Officer Mason, but we've been receiving threatening calls recently—Sergeant Longacre is in charge of the investigation. Please, if you could just call him, that would be a big help."

"Okay, y'all just hang tight and I'll be back in a few minutes," and the officer returned to his car. In the meantime, Stephen's and Emily's neighbors, as well as their landlords, Carl and Denise Bennett, came to commiserate with them.

Denise spoke first. "We're just so glad y'all are all right—and that you weren't at home when the fire broke out. The whole place was engulfed in flames in a matter of minutes. We just can't understand it." She turned to Carl, who simply shook his head.

"We were sitting on the deck, reading the Sunday papers, when we smelled the smoke. At first, we didn't think too much of it—until we saw it belching out of the back porch of the cottage." Again, he shook his head in disbelief. "And then it seemed to be smoke and flames everywhere." He gave a Gallic shrug. "I can't think why it would burn so fast like that..."

"I think I can," said Emily. "I just can't be sure yet."

Denise and Carl pricked up their ears at Emily's remark—as did several nosy neighbors. Carl asked Emily to explain what she meant.

"Just this. You know the publicity I've received regarding the PCB spillage in the eastern part of the state?" The landlords nodded. "Well, I've been receiving some threatening phone calls. I don't think this fire was accidental—I'm really sorry about your property."

Denise reached out and touched Emily's arm. "Oh hon, don't worry about the cottage. Insurance will cover the damage. Carl and I are just so sorry that you and Stephen have lost all of your possessions. It's not as though you two haven't been through enough in the past year." Denise hugged both Emily and Stephen. "Listen, if y'all need a place to sleep—we've got room."

At the moment, Officer Mason returned. "I assume you've met our landlords," Stephen indicated Denise and Carl. "The cottage belongs...well, belonged to them."

"Yes, we've met," he said, as he nodded politely. "I've spoken with Sergeant Longacre—he's on another case right now—but told me to...uh..." Mason looked at the eager ears surrounding him. "Say, do y'all mind giving us some privacy here?" Shocked into awareness of their intrusion, the neighbors dispersed—except for the Bennetts as it was their property at issue. Looking at Stephen and Emily, Mason continued. "Are y'all okay if I share this information with all of you?"

"We don't know what it is you're going to say," replied Stephen, "but yes, I guess we're okay."

Mason nodded. "Okay, it's like this. Sergeant Longacre is going to carry out a full criminal investigation, but in the meantime, he uh...wants to know if you're okay going into the witness protection program?"

Emily and Stephen looked blankly at Mason and then each other.

Emily spoke first. "Is it really necessary? Does he think we're in that much danger? And besides, we aren't witnesses to this arson attack, if it is indeed arson."

"Let me clarify," responded Mason. "It's not the full deal—like with a change of names, location and all of that. It's more a case of finding you a safe place to stay—you sure can't stay here." He turned to look at the steaming cottage, its windows shedding sooty tears. "Look, at this stage we don't know whether someone was just trying to scare you or actually trying to hurt...well, kill you."

Mason waited for his words to sink in. When neither Emily nor Stephen said anything, Mason added, "There's only one way to find out if someone wants to kill you. Do you really want to find out?"

"No," responded Stephen. "We've already had that experience, thank you." His hand unconsciously touched the back of his head.

"Right, I'm sure y'all don't want that. Why don't y'all just follow me down to the station. The sergeant's already got someone finding you a place where we can both protect you and keep an eye on anyone snooping around."

For two young and fit individuals, Stephen and Emily stood like two hanged people. They took in the officer's words but were having difficulty making the full sense of them.

"Is Emily's car okay? I mean, have you checked it over yet?" Stephen's eyes drifted over Emily's VW. "We'll need both cars...to get to work...I guess."

Emily glanced at her husband, who hadn't sounded so 'absent' since his sedation after the gunshot wound. "Stephen? Are you okay?"

"Yeah, Em—that is, I guess. It's just this—" his arm limply indicated their smoldering home. Trying to engage his sense of humor, Stephen added, "Hey—at least we don't have to pack anything else to go into hiding." No one laughed. Looking at his distraught wife, Stephen said, "Everything we own is in this car."

Regarding Stephen with a wary eye, Officer Mason asked, "Is one of you all right to drive?" Both Emily and Stephen nodded. Turning to the Bennetts, Mason asked, "Could y'all keep an eye on your property and let me know if you see anything suspicious? *Anything.*" He handed them his card. "Sergeant Longacre, who has been working on the PCB spills and the threats to the Travises, will want to talk with y'all as well. He'll be in touch tomorrow. Meanwhile, if you think of anything you've forgotten, or if you have any questions, contact me or call the station, okay?"

"And what about my wife's car?" Stephen pursued the question. "What if this asshole has boobytrapped it?" Mason almost snapped to attention at the latter question.

"Let me call the department on the radio. And then let's go get you somewhere safe—and maybe a meal? How's that sound?"

~ * ~

Sitting in their hotel bedroom, backs against the headboard, Emily and Stephen stared at the wall where the television was mounted. It wasn't switched on, but both of them stared blankly in its direction, as though waiting for a sign to appear. They had both called their families—in the event they had heard about the presumed arson attack on the news—to let them know they were all right.

"Don't you just love doing good things for our fellow human beings?" Stephen asked rhetorically. "I mean, we wouldn't get the chance to stay in this nice hotel had you and I left those nice farmers to their own devices with the PCB spill."

"Sarcasm doesn't suit you." Emily spoke toward the blacked-out television. "You're a bigger and better person than that."

"I wish I felt it," moaned Stephen. "Maybe that bullet to the head last December did more damage than I thought. Or maybe there are simply more evil people in the world than I ever realized—despite having worked in prison."

"Or perhaps this is simply the real cost of discipleship?" replied Emily. "I've heard you say many times that following Mr. Jesus isn't for wimps—that evil rears its ugly head whenever people try to change the world for the better."

"Well, maybe there's more wimp in me since taking that bullet."

Emily turned to face Stephen. She took his face in both hands and said firmly, "Shut up!" Then she kissed him fiercely on the lips, holding it for a good while. "Sitting here is driving me crazy," declared Emily. "I'm going to the lab. Are you coming with me?"

"I'm not letting you go there alone," retorted Stephen. "But why now—apart from going stir-crazy?"

"I don't know...I just have this feeling," Emily replied distractedly.

"When a scientist trusts her intuition over empirical knowledge, then this minister listens. Let's go," said Stephen. They put on their shoes and stepped outside their room.

Officer Mason was sitting outside. He looked up from his newspaper and cup of coffee. "What's up?"

Emily led the way. "I need to go to my laboratory—at the university."

The officer looked at his watch. "At this time of the evening? It's nearly eight-thirty. And I'm really not supposed to let you out of my sight until my shift change."

"When is that?" Emily asked.

"Ten PM."

"That's okay," replied Emily. "Come with us to the university. You can keep an eye on us there. We should be back here within an hour."

Mason hesitated, shifting his gaze between his two charges and his watch. "Are you sure?"

"Certainly," chirped Emily, trying to make light of it all. "You can drive, if you want. Then you can radio your boss, if you need to tell him what's going on. I'll put in a good word for you." Emily gave him the best charming smile she could muster.

"Okay, I'll drive," Mason replied tersely.

After locking the door to their room, the three went downstairs to the parking lot. Emily sat in the front with the policeman and directed him onto the campus and to her staff parking area. There were two cars parked there. Emily recognized one of them—which belonged to her lab assistant, Terry. The other was an expensive-looking Mercedes.

"I've never seen that car," Emily noted for Stephen and Officer Mason. "The other belongs to Terry, one of my lab assistants. He must be working late."

163

They entered via a security door, for which Emily had the key, and climbed the stairs to the floor where Emily had her office and lab. As they entered the corridor, there were no lights on, except for the light which shone through the window of the door to her lab. The indirect light silhouetted a large bundle on the floor, as well as myriad reflections from shattered window glass. Emily stepped back to the light switch by the staircase.

"It's Terry!" gasped Stephen. The side of the young man's face was drenched in blood. As Stephen and Emily ran to where Terry lay, Officer Mason unholstered his revolver.

"Keep your voices down!" whispered Mason. "Chances are whoever decked your friend is still here!" Mason peered around the door's window into the lab. He saw a man, about twenty feet away, who apparently had not heard them, as his back was turned. In one swift motion, the officer had thrown open the door as he shouted for the man to keep still and place his hands on his head. There was a strong smell of gasoline. The intruder had been in the midst of filling various receptacles with his intended accelerant. Startled, he turned his sweaty, porcine face toward Officer Mason. The late middle-aged man was clearly nonplussed when he saw the gun pointed at him. He quickly placed both hands on top of his head. In a desperate panic he shouted, "If you f-fire your gun, y-you'll prob'ly ignite this gas—and you'll die with me. J-just let me walk outta here and we'll both be okay."

"Hell." Mason laughed. "I won't die! I'm not stupid enough to stand in this room and shoot you, unh-unh. All I gotta do is stand behind this wall and shoot into this room—in your general direction, of course—and you'll burn alive." Quickly casting a glance at Emily and Stephen, he made a furtive wink. "So either you start moving toward me real slow-like or you'll fry—you decide. Oh, in case you're wondering, I have backup—right, Travis?"

Following Mason's lead, Stephen replied, "If you don't nail him, Mason, I will."

The man's oinkish features twitched upon hearing Travis's voice. Seeing that his options were limited to death by incineration or jail, he began his slow walk toward the officer's weapon. While he moved, Mason judiciously read him his rights.

"That's right," coaxed Mason. "Nice and easy."

He was at the door.

"Very good so far," said Mason. "Now turn around slow and put your hands behind your back. My partner is armed as well, so if you want to be dead, just make a sudden move. Understand?" The man nodded his assent as Mason put the handcuffs on him and then began to pat him down. He removed the man's wallet from his sport jacket and looked at his driver's license. "Mr. Rex Porter," he read aloud. Mason then noticed the calling cards which proclaimed "Porter's Transformers, Raleigh, N.C." The officer laughed to himself at the way this case was falling right into his hands. "Oh, and while you're doing the right thing, Mr. Porter, why don't you tell me about what you did to this young man out here?"

"Oh, God! Is he dead?" the man was visibly trembling as he looked at the inert body.

"I don't know," replied Mason. "What did you do to him?"

"I-I didn't mean to hurt him—or anyone! He...he just surprised me, so I hit him with the hammer I used to break the window—to...uh, get in here. Honest—I didn't intend to hurt anybody. You have to believe me!"

"No, I don't *have* to believe you—that will be for the jury."

It was then Porter noticed the Travises. "They're not police!"

"Oh, really?" said Mason in mock surprise. "Well then, let me introduce you to my backup: Dr. Emily Travis and Rev. Stephen Travis—two of your *intended* victims. You've probably read about Dr. Travis in the newspaper—you know, your PCB dumping. We've just come from their house, by the way, which I'm guessing you torched. For a guy who doesn't mean to hurt anybody, you have an odd way of showing it—making threatening phone calls, setting fires and slugging this young man with a hammer."

"I...I want a lawyer," stammered the firebug, slowly regaining some measure of mental capacity.

"I'll just bet you do." Mason chuckled. "Y'all always want your lawyers—kinda like shouting for mama."

Stephen and Emily were still with Terry and they were having difficulty detecting a pulse. Mason looked at them and asked, "Is there a phone I can use anywhere in this building?"

Emily shook her head. "Not that I know of; I only have the keys for the main door and my lab."

"Okay, look," replied Mason, "I'll cuff this tub o' lard to the heating pipe over there, while I go to the car to radio for an ambulance and a crime scene team." Looking at Porter, he added, "The key is going with me, dipstick." As Mason started down the corridor, he stopped. "Oh—Dr. Travis, don't go into your lab, okay?"

"Could you also alert campus security?" asked Emily.

"You betcha," he replied—almost cheerily—now that he had netted a dangerous felon.

For Porter's benefit, Stephen asked Emily "I wonder whether Porter has ever visited Central Prison?"

Understanding Stephen's intention, Emily joined in. "I don't know. Why?"

"Well, it's where they have the gas chamber—which is where he'll be going if Terry dies, not to mention the possible victims whose land and water he's poisoned..." Porkish Porter tried to put on a defiant face, but his face had developed a twitch and he sweated profusely—both of which indicated that Stephen's words had hit home.

~ * ~

The ambulance arrived shortly after Mason returned to the crime scene, soon followed by the campus security. While Mason and Emily spoke with campus security, the paramedics determined that Terry was still alive, but severely concussed, and set about securing him on the stretcher for transportation. During this time, Porter was left cuffed to the heating pipe, being of no consequence at that moment. Stephen, whose blood was up with righteous anger, decided to regale Porter with stories of the gas chamber, which, he informed him, had replaced the electric chair in nineteen sixty-one. He discussed some of its most recent occupants—all short-term, of course—as well as the relative merits and demerits of each instrument of death. He asked Porter which he thought would be his preferred method of dying: electric shock or poison gas, all the while pretending Porter was interested in his discourse. Mason caught wind of what Stephen was saying to Porter and chuckled to himself.

When the crime scene unit arrived, it was time for Mason to take the much-chastened Porter to the police station. As he also needed to get witness statements from Emily and Stephen, they rode in the front of the cruiser.

Mason picked up Stephen's monologue regarding the gas chamber. "For my money, I would choose the electric chair; I mean, it's gotta be quicker. Of course, things have been known to go wrong...the prisoner just looks like he's been put in a toaster-oven but doesn't die. That's gotta be bad, right? What do you think, Mr. Porter?"

By the time they were inside the station and had completed the booking, fingerprinting and mugshots, Mason's graphic accounts of executions gone wrong—punctuated by occasional maniacal laughter—had loosened Porter's tongue to the point of asking for a plea bargain if he would finger the person or persons actually responsible for dumping the toxic waste. And his lawyer hadn't even arrived at the station. Porter's clothes were so sodden from nervous sweating, it looked as though he had just come in from the rain on this bone-dry summer's evening. Officer Mason could almost feel a promotion coming on.

Twenty-one

The evening television news was abuzz with the latest development in what had come to be called "the midnight dumpings." The Travises sat up in bed, sharing a bottle of Saint Emilion, while watching the report with interest. There was footage of their smoldering cottage, an interview with the presiding fire officer, a statement from the Raleigh police that Dr. and Rev. Travis were under their protection, and the clincher: the source of the PCB dumping was right there in the capital city— Porter's Transformer Company. There was also the news that there had been an attempted arson attack on Dr. Emily Travis's office and lab at NC State University by none other than Rex Porter, who had been caught in the act—although there was no comment from his lawyer. There followed a short clip of Officer Mason, who had earned his thirty seconds of airtime for not only preventing another arson attack, but probably saving the life of the young lab assistant, Terry Saunders. Much was made of the "savage hammer attack" on Terry, his condition being listed as "serious." Emily switched off the television.

"I'm exhausted." She turned to Stephen. "You?"

He nodded as he sipped his wine. "Yep. I feel like I did when the case of inmate extortion had reached its climax—and before getting shot in the head, of course." Indicating the television, Stephen commented, "At least anyone listening to the news will know why they can't reach us. Think they'll let us go to work tomorrow? I have some pastoral counselling cases I need to wind up."

"If the police will let me in, I will. I'd like to stop by the hospital first and see how Terry is doing."

"Oh gosh, yeah, I'd like to go with you. Poor guy...but I have an idea how his head must feel."

Emily smiled tiredly. "That you do, my lovely man." She stroked his head. "I hope they throw the book at Porter—the slimy bastard."

"Time will tell," Stephen responded. "He's white and he has money, so I wouldn't hold my breath. I should think there's some heavy-duty plea bargaining going on. I might call Sergeant Longacre and see if he has anything he can tell us...but I expect it'll be cloaked in secrecy at the moment."

"How can Porter plea-bargain if he was caught red-handed?" asked an exasperated Emily.

"There might be other people involved that he can implicate or hand over to the police. From what little I saw and heard of Porter earlier this evening, I feel he'd sell out his own mother to escape hard time. But we shall see. Ready to sleep?" Emily nodded dozily as she kissed him goodnight.

~ * ~

The following morning, Emily and Stephen were taken by police car to the county hospital, where Terry lay in intensive care. In the few minutes they were allowed to see him, they discovered he was in an induced coma while the neurologists discussed how to deal with the brain's swelling. It seemed that the visible lump, with an ugly gash, was mirrored by a hematoma pressing on the brain. Stephen and Emily each held one of Terry's hands as Stephen offered a prayer.

Their blue-uniformed chauffeur next drove them to Emily's office. Radio, press and television reporters were waiting for her when she arrived at work. It seemed the idea of their being driven in a police car was to deter anyone from following them after work, but both Emily and Stephen were doubtful as to the effectiveness of the plan. As the officer escorted Emily to her building, the news media crushed in upon her. As one canary had flown the safety of the police car, Stephen went unnoticed for several minutes. Having been prevented from entering Emily's building, several of them turned their attention to Stephen. With the cruiser's doors locked, Stephen decided to make light of his situation as best he could. The half-dozen or so hands knocking on the windows sounded like a flock of woodpeckers, so Stephen began laughing. As the reporters shouted their questions at him, Stephen cupped his hands at his ears and shook his head, indicating his inability to hear them. To those who pressed their faces against the glass, in order to blurt out their queries louder than the next reporter, Stephen gave shrugs and responded in various languages: "¿Que?" "Comment?" "Ich verstehe nicht," and the like. Happily, his escorting officer was soon back in the car and, as they pulled away, Stephen blew kisses at the puzzled and disappointed-looking crowd. *What else should I do when our home has been torched and we're under police security?* The officer took a circuitous route to the Advancement Center in order to make certain they were not followed.

As the policeman drove Travis into the Advancement Center parking lot, he looked over his shoulder and said, "As I told your wife, I'm on light duty today, so whenever you want to go home...um, well, to the hotel, just let me know, okay?" Stephen agreed, grabbed his briefcase and exited the car. No crowds of reporters waited for him—for that, he was grateful.

~ * ~

Sgt. James Fowler was on the front desk and had seen Stephen approaching through the glass door. He was on his feet and opening the door when Stephen was still several steps away. "Come on in, my man! Damn—you've been impossible to find. The police don't seem to trust their colleagues in corrections. Diane and I wanted to offer you a place to stay, if you needed it. But it sounds like you're buttoned down tighter than the guys in this unit."

The two friends hugged. "Thanks, James. It's been crazy days. We go away for a few days to celebrate Emily's doctorate and try to forget all the crap back here—and woosh! Our house goes up in flames. But at least Em and I are still alive and kicking."

"Lincoln's really been worried about you—but he doesn't like to admit it," said Fowler. "Let's go surprise him."

As they walked through the day room, the residents who weren't at work jumped up to greet Stephen, shaking his hand and clapping him on the back. One said, "Damn Rev, you sure those doctors didn't put a steel plate with a bull's eye in your head?"

"It's beginning to feel like it, but at least the police have the bastard that's been making our life hell."

"Let's hope he don't get easy time here," added another resident.

"You got that right," replied Stephen.

Lincoln Parker heard Stephen's voice before he saw him. Although he wasn't generally the hugging type, he actually threw his arms around Stephen. "Marcella and I thought you and Emily were put up in a bank vault or something. Both James and I tried to pull strings to find out where you were and if you needed anything. Man, trouble surely knows how to find you."

The three men went into the office that Lincoln and Stephen shared, and Stephen caught his colleagues up on the most recent events. Lincoln slapped the desk emphatically and exclaimed, "And the rev still refuses to carry!" He shook his head in disbelief, while looking to James for support.

"Don't look at me, Brother Man. I had enough of weapons in Vietnam."

"But our brother here gets shot, gets threatening phone calls, has his house burned down—and he still refuses to carry some protection."

"Frankly, Linc," replied Stephen, "I don't see what good a gun would have done me in any of those situations. I was shot from behind and it's impossible to shoot someone who threatens you on the phone..." James burst out laughing. "And it wouldn't have helped to put out the fire in our house. Let's face it, bro, I'm not going to carry a gun. But I appreciate your concern."

"Oh," interjected James, "Have you been up the hill yet to see Ben Katz? Both he and Kate McIntyre—and a bunch of others at the women's prison—have been worried about you and Emily."

"Maybe I'll go up there this afternoon," mused Stephen. "It depends on how much I get done here today."

"Well, at least call Katz and let him know you're all right. He probably wants to offer you and Emily a place to stay as well—at least, when the police let you go."

"Emily and I might take all of you up on your offer of hospitality. We don't want to wear out our welcome with any of you. But the truth is, we lost everything we owned except for what we took on our little vacation." Stephen rubbed his beard thoughtfully for a moment. "Who wants us first?" Then laughing to himself, he added, "Hell, you two and Katz were *all* my best men at our wedding. How about a week with each of you—until we find a place to rent?"

"J comes before L," said James, winking at Lincoln. "Why don't you start with Diane and me?"

"Sounds good," responded Stephen. "I'll let Emily know. And by the way, the police have us staying at the Hampton Inn. Here's our room number." Stephen jotted the information on a note pad for both men. "And now—I better get to work. I have a lot to finish in just over a week."

~ * ~

"Stop scaring me like this!" blurted out Ben Katz. "You're turning me into my mother! Every time you're out of my sight, something terrible happens to you. *Nu?* Who's going to help out at my wedding if not you?"

"Worrying about me and Emily seems to be going around. It's nice to have people who care so much about us, but maybe you could turn down the worry into moderate concern?"

Hearing her husband-to-be and Stephen talking in the corridor, Kate came out of her office and immediately gave Stephen a big hug. "He knows already," said Ben. "We were both worried about him and Emily."

"Of course, we were! Having your house torched—that...that's just horrendous. If Ben and I can do anything for you two, just let us know, okay? *And we mean it.* We both have space in our homes and will be glad to have you stay."

"I'm losing track of offers," said Stephen, "and I'm truly touched. You might be hearing from Em and me before you know it. James and Lincoln have offered us space as well. As soon as we're out of the protection program, we'll be staying with James and Diane for a week—then with Linc and Marcella. I guess one of you is next."

"Have you heard the news today?" interrupted Ben.

"No—I've been rather busy. Why?"

"Your nemesis, Mr. Rex 'PCBs-R-Us' Porter has turned state's witness. He's named the outfit who transported the PCBs and dumped them. The evening news will probably carry the story."

"So has he received a 'get out of jail card' already?" asked Stephen.

'Nothing's been said," replied Ben. "But don't be surprised if he appears down the hill at the Advancement Center.

"Another white-collar criminal dodges the slammer." Stephen frowned with disgust. "Just another reason to get out of this line of work."

"Yeah, Porter's 'white' in both senses of the word," chimed in Katz. "They certainly didn't have to sweat him for very long. But then, he most likely has a lawyer at his beck and call."

"That's usually the case," said Stephen.

Kate McIntyre, who had been listening quietly, entered back into the conversation. "How about some positive news? Ben and I have set the date for our wedding."

"That's great!" exclaimed Stephen, "When is it?"

"In the autumn—mid-October—when the worst of this heat and humidity is past," answered Kate.

"Just tell me where and I'll be there," said Stephen.

"You'd better be," piped up Ben, "Or we'll only be half-married! Oh, and would you mind being my best man as well?"

"I don't know..." Stephen responded with great seriousness. "Minister and best man? This is really gonna cost you."

"Shmuck!" Katz threw a fake punch at Stephen.

"Hey listen, both of you. May I bend your ears for a few more minutes?" Kate and Ben nodded. "Pick an office," asked Stephen. Kate pushed open the door to hers.

Once inside, Stephen began. "I have an idea for a halfway house for women who have been abused...for when they are released from prison. You both know how many go straight back into the same sort of relationships or even to their same partners." The two psychologists listened intently. "Well, I've just been awarded a substantial amount of money from my case against the state. I'd like to donate a large sum of it toward buying a property here in Raleigh that could be developed into a halfway house...and I'm wondering if either—or both—of you might be interested in helping it get off the ground."

Ben and Kate sat back in their chairs at the same moment and breathed out emphatically. "Wow!" uttered Kate. "It seems you really do have a plan for post-chaplaincy."

"It's only come to me of late," said Stephen, his voice full of energy. "Do you remember my secretary from several years ago? A young women named Annabelle Lee—but she went by 'Frumpy'?" Ben and Kate acknowledged they remembered. "Emily and I ran into her while hiking in the Smokies last week. She's just finished her degree at Appalachian—*summa cum laude*, no less—and get this: her degree is in psychology and sociology, with an emphasis on criminal justice and...well, she can't find a job as she's a convicted felon...so, I...um...thought, who better to run a halfway house than someone who's been abused and been through the system?"

"Chaplain Travis to the rescue," interjected Ben.

Somewhat stung by Ben's abruptness, Stephen asked, "Do you think I'm simply being a rescuer?"

"I don't think so," edged in Kate, sensing the immediate discomfort between the colleagues who were also good friends. Looking at her husband-to-be, Kate said, "I think what Ben is trying to say is, have you really checked out Annabelle Lee's credentials or spoken with her academic advisors? Or are you creating a job—out of the goodness of your heart—but also simply because you can?"

Stephen looked from Kate to Ben. "Kate's right, Stephen. This is a new venture—and an important one—I just don't want you to stick your neck out too far, only to have your head returned in a basket. Take my earlier outburst as my New Yorker way of saying I care about you very much. I actually think your idea is a good one—very good, in fact. But after everything you've been through in the last eight months—not to mention recently—don't rush things. Aside from all of that, *yes*, I'd like to help you pull the project together. Kate can speak for herself."

Stephen, slowly getting over Ben's outburst, looked at Kate, waiting for her to speak.

"A worthy idea needs a good business plan in order to get off the ground," began Kate. "When do you finish your chaplaincy work?"

"Next week," responded Stephen.

"Okay..." mused Kate. "Leave the idea with Ben and me for that time. Once you have fully left the prison system, let's start to put your ideas on paper. Do you envision the halfway house being a charity?" Stephen nodded. "Well, then you will need a friendly lawyer to help with that—and to help with planning permission. Have you anyone in mind?" Stephen mutely shook his head. "Don't worry about it at this stage, but just know that these are the very things that help make for a successful project. It's like building a house—if there's no solid foundation, it doesn't matter how attractive the house is, it will still fall down." Kate looked at Stephen and cocked her head. "Still feeling like we've rained on your parade?"

Looking a little less abashed, Stephen responded, "A friend of mine used to say, 'It's good to question authority; but when real authority speaks—listen. And I'm listening."

"And Stephen, I have nothing against Annabelle Lee in principle," added Ben. "But let me share something with you that might help clear up any reservations I might have. When I was an undergraduate, I took some classes in literature. One of the young assistant English professors was coming up for tenure. He was good at his job and popular with the students, but when the departmental chairman checked out his credentials, it turned out that his PhD was bogus. All I'm saying is that the head sometimes has to counterbalance the heart. It's always best to avoid any possible pitfalls that are, well...*avoidable*. Okay?"

"Message understood—from both of you. Maybe I'm just getting fired up because of leaving prison work and am simply keen to start anew. In any case, I promise both of you to slow myself down and consult with you—and others."

"Great!" intoned Ben, "Now let's talk about our wedding!"

~ * ~

"How long do we need to stay in the hotel?" enquired Emily of Sgt. Longacre. The sergeant had taken her and Stephen to dinner after work.

Between bites of food, Longacre replied, "This is probably your last night. We've already got word that the trucking firm which dumped all of the PCBs has been raided. It's a father and son outfit up in New Jersey."

"Damn Yankees!" Stephen slapped his hand melodramatically on the table. Longacre and Emily laughed.

"Extradition warrants are in process," added Longacre. "As far as we can tell, there is no one else out there that y'all need to worry about." The officer took a long drink of iced tea. "Have y'all got a place to go? If not, we'll cover a few more nights until you can arrange something."

Looking at Stephen, Emily spoke first. "I think we're both ready to leave this hotel. Happily, we have friends who are willing to put us up—"

"Or put up with us," interjected Stephen.

Longacre nodded thoughtfully. "Okay, but if you have any concerns whatsoever, just let me know. Deal?" Both Stephen and Emily acknowledged. The sergeant continued, "You know, Dr. Travis—and you too, Reverend—if y'all keep up all of your criminal investigations, you're gonna put people like me out of a job." He smiled broadly. "But thanks for the help."

"Just doing our jobs, Sergeant," replied Stephen.

"Hey look, we've spent so much time together, y'all can just call me Eric."

"Only if you agree to call me and Stephen by our first names," responded Emily.

Playing with the remains of the food on his plate, Eric said, "I've been doing a little background check on you two." Both Stephen and Emily raised their eyebrows, but Longacre only stared at his plate as he seemed to be searching for words. Tapping his plate for emphasis, Eric spoke slowly. "Y'all both came damned close to being killed last December. I wasn't involved in the case but I remember hearing a little about it."

177

Looking directly at Stephen, he continued, "You took a bullet to the head—isn't that right?"

"Happily, it was a ricochet," commented Stephen as he patted his steel plate.

"And you were left in a runaway car which crashed." Eric looked at Emily. He shook his head in admiration. "I tell you what, if y'all ever get tired of what you're doing, you can join my team anytime."

Both Emily and Stephen laughed. "I think we get enough crime-fighting excitement just doing what we do," exclaimed Emily.

"I'll second that," added Stephen.

"Well then, at least let me thank you on behalf of my uncle's family for all you've done for them and the other farmers affected by the dumpings. They surely owe you one helluva debt of gratitude."

"Eric, honestly, none of you needs to thank me. I don't want to sound overly modest, but this is why I chose the work I do—to help farmers and their herds. I'm just sorry that so much human and animal suffering can't be fixed as easily as identifying the problem. And as for the soil and water contamination...well, they will take more time to clean up than I like to think. I've never seen anything like this."

"But if you really want to thank Emily, you could make sure we're outta this hotel tomorrow," interjected Stephen.

"Okay, done!" said Longacre. "Just be sure to let me know where y'all're staying—just in case."

Then, seizing the moment, Stephen said to Eric, "As a law officer of some years' experience, may I put to you an idea I have for a halfway house for women coming out of prison?"

Twenty-two

James Fowler wasn't on duty the morning Stephen cleaned out his office at the Advancement Center, but in any event, Stephen would see him at supper as he and Emily were staying with the Fowlers for their first week out of police protection. Stephen had said his goodbyes to the residents two or three times during the past several days. It was starting to feel like the song, "How Can I Miss You if You Won't Go Away?" But it was also the case that Stephen was experiencing the way endings have of compressing time, such that his six years spent behind bars seemed more like a summer's vacation—until he started to reflect on all the people he had met, all that he had witnessed and done...including nearly losing his life. And Stephen still had his shared office at the women's prison to clear this afternoon. Up until then, Stephen had only ever left behind part-time and student jobs—work that had never been meant to last. Now he was actually moving on from his first full-time ministry post, and he was stuck with a great big lump in his throat.

As he stared at the blank cinder-block wall beside his desk, Lincoln came striding into the office. "You still here?" he asked in a joking manner.

Stephen was jolted out of his reverie. When he tried to speak, he uttered more of a croak. "Uh, yeah man...just kinda thinking about all that has gone down since I first came here." Stephen tried to take an unobserved swipe at his eyes.

"Hey, sorry if I scared you just now, Rev," offered Lincoln.

"Nah, it's okay. Just finding it a little more emotional than I expected. I'll be heading up the hill soon—one more stop before I finally bust outta the 'joint'."

"How's it going at Brother Fowler's place? The kids letting you and Emily get any rest?"

"Oh, they're great. Letitia enjoys braiding Emily's hair—she's even invited some friends to come have the experience of playing with 'white people's hair!' Emily finds it relaxing."

"Well, tell your good lady that at six months, Clarissa's a little young for braiding, but she can certainly put her sticky little fingers in Emily's hair!" Stephen laughed. He needed the relief.

Having already removed most personal items from the office, Stephen had only one small box to complete the job. He cocked it under his left arm as he thrust his right toward Lincoln. "See you next week."

"Marcella and I are counting on it," replied Lincoln. Stephen stepped out the door, and as he closed it behind him, he noticed Delbert Moore sitting in the dayroom. He was the one resident Stephen felt he needed to see before leaving his role as chaplain. Perhaps Delbert had entertained similar thoughts, because he was sitting where he could hardly be missed, poring over his books and making the occasional note on a pad.

"Portrait of the scholar as an inmate," joked Stephen.

Looking at the box under Stephen's arm, Delbert asked, with a twinkle in his eye, "Going somewhere?"

"Yeah—up the hill to women's prison so I can clean out that office as well. Want to come with me?"

"I didn't think chaplains were supposed to make cruel jokes at the expense of inmates." Delbert placed his hand over his heart. "I'm truly hurt by that remark."

"You'll get over it." Stephen laughed, with Delbert joining in.

Delbert said, "I'm gonna miss your sense of humor. It's been one of the few saving graces in this place." Then, tapping his pen on his notepad, Delbert asked, "Who's gonna read my dissertation chapters with you gone?"

"Well, remember how I broke prison regs and gave you my home address and telephone number?"

"Yeah."

"Well, the house is toast and the phone is so much melted plastic."

"Rev, you're incorrigible."

"I know. It's one of my lovable qualities. But look, seriously, Emily and I are staying at James Fowler's place. And after that, we'll be staying with Lincoln and family. So anything you want me to read can be given to either one of those gentlemen and I promise to give it the same attention as I did as your chaplain. And when you're finally free of this most accommodating correctional system, you're always welcome in our home."

"But your home is a pile of rubble," offered Delbert.

"True, but you're welcome in it."

"I think you've spent too much time behind bars...but suffice it to say, I am going to miss you." Delbert stood and offered his hand.

"I have every reason to believe our friendship is just beginning," responded Stephen. "Keep sending those chapters!" Stephen gave a nod and a wave and headed toward the front door.

~ * ~

Stephen chatted to the staff in the administration building at the women's prison before crossing the grounds to his office. On the door of his office someone had stuck a sign which read: "WANTED: Jumped Bail." Below was a recognizable pencil drawing of Stephen, but with a desperado's face. Someone else had scratched through 'Bail' and written 'Karma.' Stephen chuckled to himself. *Jumped karma! I'm actually going to miss the offbeat humor that's borne of the prison setting.* Once inside the office, Stephen found a *papier mâché* image of himself kneeling in the corner of the room—not at prayer, for there was an all-too-real gardening trowel in the right hand, as well as a ring of soil, representing an escape hole. Stephen burst out laughing. As the offices were only separated by partitions which ended well below the ceiling, Stephen's laughter drew the attention of his colleagues, Kate and Ben. Within minutes, both were standing in the doorway to his office.

"Is there a whoopee cushion on my chair?" asked Stephen. Indicating the *papier mâché* likeness, Stephen said, "Nice work. Did you two stay up all night?"

"Nah, we used free inmate labor. It seemed appropriate," quipped Katz.

"A few of the ladies in the art class were more than willing to get involved in the gag," added Kate.

"I just wish I had a camera," said Stephen as he looked at the inmates' handiwork.

"Ta-da!" interjected Kate as she produced a camera with a flourish. "I borrowed the Polaroid from the front office. Please stand alongside your escaping self and I'll take a shot of you by the poster on your door." Stephen dutifully complied as the camera clicked and whirred. Ben asked Kate to take a few photos to post in their offices, so Stephen once more took his position next to the gags meant to provide him with a cheery exit from the slammer.

"This…" began Stephen, indicating his two likenesses, "this is *good*. As you know, I decided not to have any sort of farewell service here—not after what the men did for me down the hill. Besides, I couldn't take *two* services as emotional as that! But *this* I can handle. Be sure to thank everyone for me, okay?"

"You got it, buddy," chirped Katz.

"Buddy? Since when do you call anyone 'buddy'?"

"Since I became engaged to a Southern lady. I decided I'd better try to fit in—you know, soften some of my New York ways. Start saying 'y'all' and all that."

"Well, take it easy," said Stephen, "you're scaring me. And don't stop telling Jewish jokes or I might not help out at your wedding."

"Oh, that stays!" exclaimed Kate. "It's in our prenuptial agreement. Half the reason I'm marrying Ben is for his sense of humor."

"Yeah, I'd probably explode if I couldn't tell jokes—they'd probably rescind my circumcision. Speaking of circumcision, have I told you the one about doing it Jewish-style?" Both Kate and Stephen shook their heads. "So, Hershel works for a New York bank that sends him to Paris to conduct some business. While in Paris he decides he might as well visit Pigalle and find a bordello a friend told him about. But first Hershel takes in a show at the Moulin Rouge and has a couple of drinks. Afterwards he asks a friendly taxi driver to take him to the bordello. Once inside, Hershel is asked what he prefers and he responds, 'I want a woman who can do it Jewish-style.' The madam shrugs and starts asking the ladies if anyone knows how to do it Jewish-style, but they all shrug and say, '*Non*.' So the madam sends upstairs to see if anyone can offer sex Jewish-style, but everyone gives the same answer: '*Non*.' Not to be deterred or to have a customer leave unsatisfied, the madam declares, 'I weel give two hundred francs to whichever of you weel give him sex Jewish-style." Silence.

Finally, one of the women says, '*Merde alors*, in order to find out what ees thees Jewish-style, I weel give him sex for free!" upon which, Hershel shouts, 'That's Jewish-style!'"

Stephen laughed and said, "You should have saved that one for your wedding speech."

"Um, probably better that he didn't," replied Kate, who laughed despite herself.

"Y'all want to share one last mug of tea with me before I bust outta here?" asked Stephen. "I only have a few personal things left to pack—you can even watch."

"Frankly, you're going to need a bigger box than that," said Kate. "Ben and I have some intra-prison mail for you."

"Just don't read them here! We've seen a few notes that were left with us and I don't want to see you cry. Meanwhile, I'll make the tea and Kate will bring over the letters." The two psychologists went their separate ways for a few minutes.

Kate returned first with a huge stack of notes written to Stephen by the inmates. "I'm going to put these straight into your box, okay? You know Ben and I didn't deliberately read them, don't you? When you weren't here, they put them in our trays."

"Sure." And then, in school-masterly fashion, Stephen intoned, "Nothing gets sealed that the inmates stick in the intra-prison mail—it's against regulations." He wagged a finger for good measure.

"Knowing that you were leaving after all these years, and especially after hearing about your house getting torched, a flood of women wanted to give you a farewell note. They make quite a leaving present. Oh—and be sure to check at the front office before leaving. I think you'll find some more there."

Stephen was momentarily taken aback at the number of sheets of paper—some bearing only a childlike scrawl from the women who were semi-literate.

"Right," said Stephen. "I'll check before leaving...wow. Look at these..."

~ * ~

As Stephen entered the administration building for what he hoped would be the last time, he set down the box for the officer at the metal detector to look through. *I won't miss all of this security.* He asked the officer to excuse him as he went to hand in his office and chapel keys and say goodbye to Warden Watkins. One of the admin staff saw him and beckoned him over. She, too, had a shopping bag filled with inmate well-wishes. While Stephen had a quick peek at the contents, the administrator buzzed the warden's phone to let her know the chaplain was leaving. Within a few seconds, Karen Watkins was walking briskly toward the front office and Stephen. Under her arm was a wrapped box. Before Stephen knew it, other staff started appearing: Lieutenant Jenkins, who had helped Stephen adjust to the world behind bars, Ben and Kate, teaching staff, and others. Even some of the kitchen staff made an appearance with a huge, rectangular cake, designed to look like an aerial view of the women's prison. The chaplain was caught totally off-guard. Ms. Watkins presented Stephen with his present and said, "I'm giving you one last order as chaplain—open this present *now!*"

Stephen made short work of the wrapping paper and produced a black and white striped prison shirt—much like one would see in movies. On the back it read, 'Stolen from N.C. Correctional Center for Women.' All around Stephen, there erupted cries of "Put it on!"

Warden Watkins said, "Stephen, as long as you wear this shirt, there stands a good chance you will be brought back here by some law-abiding citizen. Wear it as a token of our deep appreciation for your service." Stephen received his first and last hug from a prison warden. "And now to the cake."

Stephen was handed a kitchen knife to cut the substantial cake. He began his cut in the middle and soon ran into a problem as the knife would go no further. At that point Lieutenant Jenkins stepped in. "What seems to be that problem, Chaplain?" He took the knife from Stephen and cut an oblong section out of the middle. Reaching in gingerly with two fingers, Jenkins pulled out a shiny, new file. Along with the others, the warden was beside herself with laughter. Ben Katz shouted "Cuff him!"

"Solitary!" called out another.

"May I eat some cake first?" begged Stephen.

Jenkins offered the file to Stephen, "Aw, go ahead. You can lick this off! Just don't cut your tongue."

The leaving reception was short and sweet, as prisons wait for no woman or man. Although it had been made on one of the kitchen's largest baking trays, the cake was demolished by all of those who had stopped into the admin building to bid Stephen farewell. Stephen decided to leave before the last of his well-wishers had returned to work. He was not keen to prolong his departure, nor did he want to delay the turning of the page for what life held before him. Like the admonition to Lot and his family, Stephen felt this was no time for looking backward. So, with a smile and a wave, he walked to his car and was gone.

Twenty-three

Sergeant Longacre was sitting on the Fowlers' front porch chatting with James when Stephen arrived at his and Emily's temporary home. A few of the neighboring children looked on curiously from a safe distance. They weren't used to seeing white policemen sitting leisurely on an African-American's front porch. One or two of the braver children took a peek in the police cruiser. Both men gave Stephen a wave as he exited the car with his box of personal belongings and bag of letters. As he mounted the three steps to the porch, James stood to help him with his load and beckoned him to take a seat. "Can I get you a beer or anything?"

"A beer sounds good," replied Stephen as he greeted Eric Longacre. He noticed the officer had only a glass of water, so clearly this was no social visit.

"Have you had any news related to the case today?" Eric's face remained impassive.

"No. Should I have?"

"Not really. But as you're a man used to dealing with the hard realities of life, here it is, straight up: Terry Saunders has died of

187

his brain injury." Eric let Stephen sit with the news for a moment before adding, "If I could stay until your wife came home, I'd have been willing to break the news to her...but as it is, I'll have to leave that with you."

"I understand." Stephen bit his lower lip as he let the news sink in. "Poor Terry." Looking up at Longacre, Stephen asked, "Do his parents know?"

"Yeah. I called them shortly before coming here. It'll be all over the news tonight. That's no way for anybody to learn such news."

James returned with Stephen's beer and handed it to him. Stephen thanked him and asked, "You know about this?"

"Yeah." James nodded and placed his hand on Stephen's shoulder. "How do you think Emily will handle it?"

"I guess we'll both find out before long." Stephen took a swig of his beer. His face suddenly hardening, Stephen asked Eric, "Does Porter know?"

"Oh yeah, he knows. He's just been indicted for murder. It's one of the reasons I can't stay longer."

"No get out of jail free card," mumbled Stephen.

"Pardon me?" asked Longacre.

"Porter—he's white and middle-class. James and I—among others—were halfway sure he'd plea-bargain his ass out of hard time. That was his 'get out of jail free card'. At least now the bastard will have to pay for his crimes. It's not worth Terry's life...but it's something."

"I know the feeling," said Eric. "In the police, we sometimes call the justice system 'just the system'—it seems to have a mind of its own, regardless of the crime."

"Man, you can say that again," chimed in James.

Longacre stood to leave. "Sorry to have been the bearer of bad news...please tell your wife I'm sorry about her friend...really. And again, it there's anything I can do..." his voice trailed off.

"I know," said Stephen, "I know. And thanks."

~ * ~

Although certainly not without feelings, for Emily it was generally the scientist in her that took in information and processed it before handing it over to her emotions. The more she thought about her student assistant and his senseless death, the more her first emotion was that of righteous anger. "Goddamn that Rex Porter! It's not enough that he poisons half the counties in eastern North Carolina—no, he's got to kill Terry to protect his cocksucking ass!"

Stephen, James and Diane sat with Emily's seething anger. There was nothing else they could do for the time being. As people with a caring conscience always do, Emily worked through her 'what ifs' and 'if onlys.' If only Terry hadn't gone to the lab on that Sunday evening. If only she and Stephen had decided to go to the lab a few minutes earlier. Yet all of the 'if onlys' kept coming back to the one big 'what is.' Terry remained dead and nothing would change that. It was when Emily turned her thoughts to Terry's parents and the remainder of the Gang of Four that she gave free rein to her grief and tears. Stephen wrapped his arms around Emily as she wept into his shoulder. After a time, Diane asked if Emily would like a glass of wine. Wiping the tears from her eyes, she simply nodded yes.

When Diane returned from the kitchen, she handed the glass to Emily and said, "It's not going to fix anything, but it will help you to relax. I'm so sorry you've lost your friend."

Emily knocked back half of the contents in the glass and replied, "It was all so unnecessary. Terry had so much promise, and poof," she snapped her fingers. "It was all taken away." Emily finished her glass of wine and handed it to Diane. "If you don't mind?"

Taking the glass, Diane said, "Girl, after a day like this, the whole world needs a drink. I can keep them coming."

Emily smiled weakly at Stephen, Diane and James, saying, "Sorry for my outburst."

At once everyone responded the same way. "You don't have to apologize for anything! Your friend and colleague has been murdered."

Emily's mood mellowed somewhat into the second glass of wine. She asked Stephen about his final day as a prison chaplain. He smiled and said, "It went a lot better than yours." He told her and the Fowlers about the cake with the file in it, showed them the photos Kate had taken of him alongside his wanted poster and his *papier mâché* double. Then Stephen indicated the stack of inmates' notes. "Want to help me go through these?" He also invited Diane and James to join in, with each taking a turn to read out loud.

Most were positive, short and sweet, some were nearly illegible, and then James hit the jackpot. It was a message from Lola Rogers. James' eyes widened as he scanned the page and then he turned and asked Diane, "Are the kids in bed?" Diane nodded. "Doors closed?" Diane looked at him quizzically and James said, "I am not reading this one if the kids can hear it!" So he got up and quietly checked each child's door. Reassured, he returned to the living room.

"Honey, what's going on?" queried Diane.

"This," he said, proffering the letter, "is the damnedest farewell letter of the bunch." He shook his head in disbelief.

"I think I can guess," ventured Stephen. "It's from Lola Rogers, right?"

James sat back with amazement. "How'd you know that?"

"Well, I've had a lot of letters from Lola over the years. She's one of those women for whom prison is the best and safest life they've ever had," replied Stephen, who then turned to Emily and said, "She's the one I've told you so much about." Then, to everyone, Stephen continued, "Lola was physically and sexually abused by multiple men—including family—from childhood. She spends most of her time in Dorm C, which is maximum security. She's not a danger to anyone, she simply commits enough infractions to ensure she stays in solitary. Lola must have been released twice during my time at the women's prison, but as soon as she's out, she smashes a store window or the like and waits for the police to take her in for parole violation. So what has dear Lola got to say?"

James chuckled to himself again before he started reading. "Okay. Here goes. 'Dear Chaplain Travis, You sorry motherfucker, it's real good that your leaving the women's prison and I won't have to see your goddam face again. Love, Lola.'" James was still shaking his head in disbelief, while Diane had placed her hand over her mouth in shock that a chaplain would receive such a letter.

"That's Lola's way of saying she's going to miss me—seriously. Using vile language is her only way of expressing her needs or emotions. And in her letters to me, she has always ended them with 'Love, Lola.' It's both pathetic and funny."

"Poor thing must be all twisted up inside," offered Diane.

"She is," responded Stephen, "which is one of the reasons why I want to invest in a post-release refuge or halfway house for women like her—to help break the chain of returning to abusers. But now, thanks to the continuing hostage situation in Teheran and Carter's waning popularity, Reagan looks likely to be president in 1981. This, plus his valuing punishment over rehabilitation, might make it even more difficult to fund a women's refuge."

"At least you have a substantial amount of money to start with—you can buy a house," said James.

"Yeah, but you and I both know that getting the support of the community is essential—neighbors, local churches, businesses, etc." replied Stephen. "Look at the trouble Lincoln has finding homes for men leaving the Advancement Center. All he has to do is mention 'ex-con' and doors slam in his face. Forget that these men have paid their debt to society. I can't support the project for very long without the goodwill and financial support of the wider community."

"Well, that leaves you two obvious areas: black neighborhoods and working-class white," stated Diane.

"Kinda like where our prisons are located..." mused Stephen. "I wouldn't want the women to have to look at the fences they've just left behind."

"Well, Stephen, you know James and I will do whatever we can to help—starting with our church. Y'all come with us on Sunday and we'll make a start," offered Diane.

"Sounds good. Emily and I would be delighted," said Stephen. Then turning to Emily, he apologized for having been carried away with his idea—not only for his future endeavors—but for the abused women with whom he had worked for many years, and those who had yet to enter prison.

"It's okay, Stephen." Emily stroked the side of his face, giving his beard a little tug. "The fact that today was your last day as chaplain kinda got lost with the news about Terry's death. And frankly, it's been nice to have other things to think about." Indicating the pile of hand-written notes on the coffee table, Emily said, "It's not often we get to find out what difference we've made in other people's lives. Reading these has been good—and I get to discover another side to the man I married."

The four friends sat in comfortable silence for a while. Suddenly Emily spoke up. "I wonder whether I should call Alison, Mark and Stewart? Perhaps they haven't heard the news?"

"Are you up to it?" asked Stephen.

"I think so," responded Emily. "But we shall see. Still, I'd like to try." Stephen nodded in agreement.

Diane said, "You can use the phone in the kitchen, if you want."

"Would you like for me to sit with you?" asked Stephen. Emily answered by extending her hand to her husband.

~ * ~

The next few days were something of a dream-state for Emily and Stephen, with its touch of both surrealism and nightmare. At work, Emily had to deal with the emotions and logistics of her now-reduced team. For his part, Stephen was facing the first step of the journey toward realizing his vision of a safe haven for women, starting from scratch. He began by calling local pastors and rabbis he knew and arranged meetings with them to discuss the women's refuge idea. Having neither a home nor an office from which to work, Stephen decided to use his car as a mobile office and the trunk as a filing cabinet. Life was further complicated by the fact that he and Emily were due to decamp in the coming days to Lincoln and Marcella's home, after having stayed over a week with James and Diane.

Midway through the week came the news that Rex Porter, Terry's killer, had been arraigned on murder charges. This was quickly followed by Emily's receiving word that Terry's body had been released by the police and coroner. Terry's parents, Teresa and Peter, contacted Emily and asked if she would say a few words about their son at his funeral and she readily agreed. Stephen drove Emily and Terry's three student-assistant colleagues to New Bern, his hometown, the afternoon before the funeral. Terry's parents arranged places to stay for all of them, which, for Emily and Stephen, meant staying with Terry's family: his parents and a younger sister, Beth, a senior in high school.

Over dinner that evening, Emily was pumped for information about their son. Terry had kept his family abreast of his help in researching the PCB spillage in eastern North Carolina. He had become something of a local hero as the city's newspaper had carried numerous stories about the "midnight dumpings"—particularly as they were on the receiving end of the Neuse River before it reached the Atlantic, so their water supply was affected. Terry's work in identifying contaminated soil and water had been highlighted.

"Terry was so happy to be doing something...well, 'real' while finishing his degree at State. It certainly beat flipping burgers," said Teresa.

"It was very important work," replied Emily. "And it still is. We continue working our way through soil, water samples—as well as blood samples from animals. Terry's work has made a difference...and, for that alone, he will be remembered." Emily bit her lip as she thought carefully about what she wanted to share. Her hand squeezed Stephen's. "It was h-his dedication...to his work," Emily sobbed, "which led to his death. I mean...going in on a Sunday evening to check over lab results..." Emily erupted into tears. Hers weren't the only ones at the table.

After some time, Peter said, "That scholarship Terry was awarded by FarmBio?...we'd like to start a scholarship fund with that. Do you think you could help us? At least Terry's legacy will live on..."

"I assure you I will do everything I can—as soon as I am back at the university. I think I can also do some arm-twisting with FarmBio, as they want me to do some work with them." An idea flashing across her mind, Emily added, "Right now Stephen and I are enjoying a bit of unsought notoriety, so I think I can make that work in favor of a fund for Terry."

"Oh gosh, yes! We read about how you were burned out of house and home..." began Teresa. She reached across the dining table and took Emily's hand.

"It's all right." Emily raised her other hand. "Stephen and I are both okay. It's just 'stuff' that we lost."

"That's right," added Stephen. "More than once in our short married-life we have discovered that possessions simply don't matter in the greater scheme of things. It's our lives and relationships that matter."

Beth had been quiet for most the discussion, simply taking in what she heard about her brother. Finally, she opened up, addressing Emily, "Terry told me that he really liked working with you...and..." Then Beth suddenly went quiet and smiled to herself.

"What is it?" asked Teresa.

"Oh nothing," she blushed and dropped her head. "I probably shouldn't say it anyway."

"Well, now you have me curious," said Emily.

"Out with it, young lady," coaxed her mother.

Taking a deep breath and going for it, Beth blurted, "he said he really liked working with you and that you are a 'fox.' There." Beth then looked at Stephen and said, "Sorry."

Emily actually blushed, but Stephen laughed. "No offense taken," he said. "I am not the first man, nor will I be the last, to notice that Emily is beautiful—as well as extremely smart!" he pulled her close and kissed her forehead.

Emily waved her hand at her scarlet face and uttered, "Well, I am flattered."

Stephen raised his glass, "Here's to Terry."

~ * ~

The drive back to Raleigh was subdued. The Saunders family had entrusted Emily with all of the checks and cash which had been given as donations in memory of Terry. It was in excess of two-thousand dollars—and there was more to come from the funeral home.

As Stephen drove, Emily mused aloud. "I need to speak with the departmental chairman, the chancellor's office and legal department. They should be able to set something up fairly quickly. It is certainly not my area of expertise."

"You know..." responded Stephen, "You've come a long way for an ex-con."

"Stephen!" Emily shoved her elbow into his side. Three sets of ears in the back seat suddenly pricked up.

"Hey, watch it! I'm driving!" he laughed. "But really—you're pretty amazing. Don't you guys think so?" Stephen looked at Mark, Alison and Stewart.

"Is it true?" ventured Stewart, "Or are you just pulling our legs?"

"Thanks, husband of mine," groaned Emily as she gave Stephen another shove.

"I just thought the children might enjoy a story—to take their minds off recent events," joked Stephen.

The three undergraduates on the back seat looked like three young owlets waiting to be fed.

"All right," Emily began, "is everyone listening?—'cause I'm only going to tell this story once..."

Twenty-four

Stephen and Emily were sitting in the kitchen of their now nominal landlords, Carl and Denise Bennett, who were planning to have the cottage rebuilt as soon as possible and hoped the Travises would still want to live there. The Bennetts were old enough to be Stephen and Emily's parents.

"That's very thoughtful of you," responded Stephen. "I had supposed you might have been glad to see the back of us after all of the drama we've had in our lives."

"It might sound weird," offered Denise, "but Carl and I almost feel responsible for you two—especially after losing everything you own." Carl grunted his agreement over his cup of steaming coffee.

"But you know that's not the case, don't you?" asked Emily. "Stephen and I are grown-ups and the choices we made led to the torching of your property. We're only glad the fire didn't spread."

Carl spoke up. "Look, we've already had the insurance adjuster here, as well as a builder we know, so we can probably have the cottage rebuilt in a matter of weeks. Structurally, it's still sound." Everyone sipped their coffee or tea, absorbed in their own thoughts. For Stephen and Emily, it was a question of why the Bennetts so badly wanted them to stay.

Stephen broke the silence. "Carl and Denise, you know I've enjoyed living here—since I was finishing my divinity degree and all the years I've worked in prison. But you don't owe me—or us—anything. You've been great landlords, believe me, but you need to look after your own interests. Happily, we have several friends who are kindly letting us live with them as we start to buy new clothing and things we'll need for our household—wherever that may be. If it works out that we can stay in the cottage, then so be it. We have both liked it here."

"We'd so like it if you stayed," urged Denise. "And Carl and I have decided we won't raise the rent one penny."

"Well...um...about that," began Emily. "As Stephen has said, the cottage has been wonderful—and we love this part of Raleigh...*but*..." Stephen turned and looked at his wife with curiosity. "But the truth is, the cottage might not be big enough for us...*now*." Stephen's eyes widened with understanding and excitement. "*Really*?"

"Yes," said Emily, "I had hoped to tell you at home, but then Denise and Carl invited us over after I finished work." Emily raised both hands and her eyebrows in a 'whaddayouthinkaboutthat?' expression. Stephen leaned over on the sofa, kissing and hugging Emily, while the Bennetts, who were just beginning to grasp what was being communicated, gave each other a quizzical look. "It's still very early," cautioned Emily, "but it's positive."

"Em, that's wonderful!" beamed Stephen. Then turning to the Bennetts, he asked, "Think you could add a spare bedroom to the cottage?"

Denise, catching on to the news faster than Carl, said, "I think this calls for a drink!" Carl looked at his half-full coffee mug, trying to follow the logic. Noting his temporary paralysis, Denise said, "She's pregnant, Carl! Break out some champagne."

Hastening to his feet, Carl headed toward the cellar door, speaking over his shoulder. "How big does the spare bedroom need to be?"

~ * ~

Neither Emily nor Stephen slept much that night. Like most prospective parents, they discussed the possible gender, followed by preferred names for each gender, which, in turn, was followed by whom they would tell first...second...third, etc. Prudence dictated that they wait another week or two, rather than stir up the grandparent genes too soon. After all, their lives to this point had been quite unpredictable. Why should things change now? Stephen and Emily found it both amusing and appropriate that the child growing inside Emily had probably been conceived atop Mt. Cammerer.

"And we are not—repeat *not*—going to call this child Cammerer or Cammie or anything like it," stated Emily in mock anger.

"Not even Camille?"

"Well..." hummed Emily, her head on Stephen's chest.

"I know one name that's out for certain," offered Stephen.

"And that is?"

"Stephen Travis, Junior."

"No argument from me!" agreed Emily. "I have always wondered about men who name their firstborn sons after themselves. It's not fair on the child."

"Absolutely. The son will always live in his father's shadow," added Stephen.

"Okay then," yawned Emily, tracing circular patterns on Stephen's belly. "At least we've decided something. Want to decide something else?"

"Sure. Let's go for broke," replied Stephen.

"Want me to sign us up for pre-natal classes at the university? They're free for staff."

Stephen pulled Emily snugly against him and answered, "Absolutely! I already know how to make babies, so I guess it's a good idea I learn how to care for them."

"The big question for me is, when do I inform work about my being pregnant?"

"Is there anything archaic in your contract about not getting pregnant within so many months of employment—from either the university or FarmBio?"

"Happily, there isn't."

"Then, let's wait until we tell our parents," suggested Stephen. "Say, another two weeks?"

"Sounds good to me...um, darling?"

"Yes?"

"Are you hungry?"

"Not really. Are you?"

"Unh-huh. Would you go get me a bowl of cornflakes?"

"I guess I'd better get used to this. Let's just hope Lincoln doesn't think I'm a prowler. He keeps a gun at home."

"Oh. Well, just go downstairs with your hands on your head."

"Thanks, lovely wife. You think of everything."

Stephen needn't have worried because, as he tiptoed down the stairs, he noticed a light was on in the kitchen. A bleary-eyed Lincoln was in the kitchen with his nearly eight-month-old daughter, Clarissa—for whom Stephen and Emily were godparents. Lincoln was humming a tune as his daughter chugged down a bottle of milk. He turned when he heard Stephen's footsteps.

"Don't shoot," whispered Stephen.

"Preacher man, what're you doing out of bed at this ungodly hour? I don't see a baby on *your* shoulder."

"I have a hungry wife to feed," Stephen replied. "She wants a bowl of cornflakes."

"At this hour?" Lincoln began, but hesitated a moment as his eyes darted back and forth. "Hey, bro, 'scuse my asking, but have you two got a bun in the oven?"

"Well, since you ask—and because it's gonna be kinda hard to keep it quiet as we're living under your roof—yes. Looks like we'll be meeting this way more often, eh?"

Freeing one arm from holding his child, Lincoln threw an arm around Stephen's shoulders and gave him an energetic hug. "Man, that's great! When did y'all find out?"

"Emily had gone to the doctor a few days ago and received the results today. I found out this evening when we were at our landlords' house...seems like they're willing to add an extra bedroom to the cottage." Stephen smiled and shook his head at the thought of it all.

"So, no buying a house for you two?"

"Not at the moment," answered Stephen as he poured a bowl of cornflakes. "We're still trying to come to terms with Em's being pregnant. And we're also in the process of replacing our clothing and household goods...not to mention we'll need things for the baby...I don't think either of us has the mental energy to contemplate buying a house right now."

"Fair enough," replied Lincoln. "But you know property is going up in value in Raleigh all the time."

"Duly noted," said Stephen. "I'm heading back upstairs to sate my wife's hunger. You have fun with my goddaughter."

Once back upstairs, Emily tucked into her cereal, while Stephen let her know that Lincoln had come to the conclusion that Emily's wee-hours eating equaled pregnancy. "It would have been hard to keep the secret much longer while living with him and Marcella."

Emily smacked her lips and then drank the remains of the milk from the bowl. "Yep. You're probably right," she said. Then looking down at the empty bowl, she waggled it at Stephen and simply uttered, "Um?"

Twenty-five

Annabelle Lee, or Annie, was introduced to Ben Katz, Kate McIntyre and Malcolm Sparks by Stephen Travis. He noted—particularly for Kate and Ben—that Annie had gone back to her maiden name, McNair, following her divorce from Carl Locklear. They were meeting in Kate's house and were seated around her dining table. Each person of the interviewing team introduced him or herself to Annie. In fact, both Ben and Kate were familiar to Annie from her time in the women's prison, but they gave her more information about themselves and why they had chosen to work with the project to establish a halfway house for abused women leaving prison. Sparks introduced himself as a lawyer who was volunteering his services to the project and helping it work toward becoming a registered charity. Stephen was there as the principal funder for the project but would not be taking part in the actual interview.

Kate began the formal proceedings. "It might seem a bit odd to have a formal interview for a shortlist of one, but we want to make sure due diligence is carried out from the very beginning of this important venture. Stephen has made clear his support for you in the role of director of the halfway house. And we, as members of the board, are in the peculiar situation of having—at present—a one-man funding base, which is of course, Stephen. So, Ben, Malcolm and I will interview you in the same way as if there were additional candidates. And by the way, we have decided to use the name 'halfway house,' because it will only be for former inmates, as opposed to a refuge for women in the community—as important as that might be. Is everything clear so far?"

"Yes, very clear," responded Annie. "And I would also like to clarify that I haven't come here believing that I will be a shoo-in. Rev. Travis has made sure I understood that. And finally, may I add that I believe in this project enough that should you not find me suitable, I would understand."

"Good," stated Kate. "Then we'll get started. Each of us will pose three questions to you, but ancillary questions may be asked by any team member. Okay?"

~ * ~

The next thirty minutes were filled with questions, answers and animated discussion arising from Annie's responses. Annie found her nervousness had quickly dissipated as dialogue emerged both among the panel members and with Annie herself. The interview was conducted in a professional manner, yet remained good-natured and friendly. She was buoyed by the fact that each of her interlocutors was fully behind the project. At several points, Stephen found he had to bite his tongue when he had wanted to help Annie in some way, but he succeeded in keeping his support silent, while cheering her on inwardly. Annie handled herself well with the questions to do with the aims and objectives of the project, but Stephen was well aware that Ben and Kate each had their final questions, which would be of a personal and clinical nature. And that moment had arrived.

"Annie," Kate began, "as you will recall, you were interviewed by both Ben and me when you arrived at the women's prison, some half-dozen or more years ago. And you were also involved in some group work conducted by us. This is by way of saying that we are, of course, aware that you were abused by your father when you were a teenager. It is with that in mind that I ask my question: where would you place yourself on the spectrum running from victim to survivor? Please be as descriptive as you feel able."

Annie was not unprepared for this question and was actually glad it had finally been asked. She took her time before speaking. "The pathway from victim of abuse to survivor hasn't been a one-way street—at least not for me." Annie looked from one face to another around the table. "Apart from the sharing of stories with other women at the prison, and finding that I was not alone, the three people who helped me the most are here at this table today—particularly Chaplain Travis. Sorry Dr. Katz, but Chaplain Travis was the first man I ever opened up to...and who showed me—not so much by his words, but his actions—that not all men were like my beast of a father or my dork of a husband."

Ben raised his hand and waved off Annie's apology. "No offense taken, Annie; Stephen's a great guy. And please, call me Ben—you're no longer a client...or inmate. Please continue."

Annie smiled and nodded. "As I said, the pathway to surviving—or even thriving—has not been straight or easy. My mother and stepfather paid for counselling after I was released. And I continued to have psychotherapy on and off for several years..." Annie paused, drew a deep breath and resumed. "Particularly when I started dating again...actually, I never really dated before I got married at eighteen." Annie snorted a laugh at herself as she shook her head. "As you might recall, I eloped with Carl Locklear as soon as I finished high school and, thanks to his theft from the garage where he worked, I wound up in prison shortly thereafter. So, to answer your question, relationships with undergraduate men—well, boys really—were difficult. Due to my time in prison, I was older than most of my classmates by about four years, but in maturity, it felt more like a decade. I actually went to college to get an education—not to get drunk and get laid. And when it came to relationships, most of the guys were like horny puppies. I simply couldn't engage in casual sex—unlike most of the undergraduates. When I did go out with guys, they were usually upperclassmen. Even then, the ones I got close to were often blown away by the fact that I had already been married, divorced and spent time in prison." Annie laughed again at her memories. "I did have a couple of sexual relationships—when I felt safe with the guy. But for me, it was complicated—I needed to...shall we say, 'test the water.' To discover—perhaps for the first time—myself as a sexual being. In any case, I spent more time with my therapist than I did in bed." Annie stopped suddenly. "I can't believe I'm sitting here telling you all of this! Is it more than you want or need to hear?"

"It speaks volumes about your self-awareness," replied Kate. "And about how you have dealt with your past."

"Have you continued in therapy?" asked Ben.

"Yes, on an as-and-when-needed basis."

"Good." Ben nodded as he jotted some notes.

"So back to the spectrum..." prodded Kate.

"If I may alter your spectrum a bit, I would place myself somewhere between surviving and thriving...with, if I'm totally honest, the occasional relapse. As I said, it isn't a straight road to recovery."

"Thank you for your candid response," said Kate, as she smiled warmly at Annie. "It's been very helpful."

Ben voiced his agreement and then said, "So here's the final question...or questions." Ben smiled coyly. "Assuming you were appointed to the job, how do you think you would be affected being surrounded by women who have been abused? Might it reignite your trauma or cloud your judgment?"

Annie felt the import and impact of Katz's words in her gut. She inhaled and exhaled slowly while pondering his question. Then, letting a puff of air out her nostrils, she began. "I cannot predict how the work might affect me. I think I will feel differently at different stages in the development of this project."

"How so?" queried Katz.

"I could see that the first six months to a year would be a time of enthusiasm as the halfway house gets on its feet. As I wouldn't be working in a therapeutic capacity, my main focus would be on the firm establishment and smooth operation of the project. Then, after the excitement of getting the halfway house up and running, I could see where the search for funding, maintaining relationships with funders within the community, managing the day-to-day details, etc. could take some of the shine off the venture, but again, I would not be serving as the therapist for the women, but as the director of the project."

"But surely the women will share some of their histories with you," pushed Ben. "Would you not reciprocate?"

"Yes, I suppose I would—but only to a point. I do recognize my limits as regards my training and abilities. If I understand the setup correctly, you and Kate are making yourselves available for ongoing therapeutic needs. In short, I think it might help the residents to know I have been where they have been and that I can relate to their situations."

"And what about enforcing the rules of the halfway house?" interjected Malcolm. "Might your identification with the women tempt you to bend the rules, say, as regards drug or alcohol use on the premises? And given your age, how assertive do you think you would be with older residents?"

"Look, y'all, I know I'm young—and I can't help that—and I didn't come looking for this job. It was mentioned to me by Chap—um—Stephen Travis. And he made no promises to me. And yes, I'd like to be given the chance...first of all because I believe I can do this job. I firmly believe that. I'd even accept a six-month probationary period instead of three. And secondly—and I shouldn't need to tell you—it's damned hard to find *professional* work when you have a criminal record." Annie's eyes sparkled with passion and a hint of mischief. She went for broke. "So, in both regards, I'm a perfect fit." With that Annie sat back in her chair, feeling surprisingly relaxed and at peace with herself.

Twenty-six

"*Mazel tov!*" cried the few Jews in attendance at Ben and Kate's wedding. The gentile majority simply shouted, "Congratulations!" Stephen and the Reform rabbi, Michael Weisman, shook hands at the conclusion of their mixed-marriage ceremony which had gone without a hitch—no small thing considering they were in the chapel on the grounds of the women's prison. A number of the trustees were in attendance, accompanied by a female guard.

A few weeks prior, in the pre-nuptial consultation, Kate, Ben, Stephen, and Michael had agreed they would keep each faith tradition's rituals to a minimum, so they could focus on what both traditions held in common. Thus, from the Hebrew scriptures, Michael read from Song of Songs 8:6-7 and Stephen read from Ecclesiastes 4:9-11; and from the New Testament Stephen read from 1 Corinthians 13. All three readings focused on love and relationships. The one exception with regard to ritual was that Ben had bought Stephen a prayer shawl and yarmulke—which he insisted Stephen wear, as Stephen was both an officiant and Ben's best man.

"Who knows?" Ben had said, "with your dark hair, eyes and beard, when my family sees the photos, they'll probably think you're a rabbi and not worry so much about my having married a *schiksa*."

Kate simply rolled her eyes and asked the two clergymen if she could kick her husband-to-be. Michael and Stephen conferred briefly and agreed it would be appropriate. She said she'd save it for an unexpected time.

Before the free guests could prepare to depart for the feast at a restaurant in Raleigh, Rabbi Weisman called out for everyone's attention. He stated, in a very serious tone of voice, that he had forgotten something important in the wedding ceremony: the smashing of the glass. Most of the non-Jews, being unaware of the tradition, looked puzzled. Ben's sister, Esther, her husband, and three cousins from New York all began to whisper among themselves. Michael went to a chair and picked up a paper bag, which he brought to the wedding couple. "Look, I know we said we'd keep ritual to a minimum. Call me a sentimentalist, but I'm from Texas..." upon which he pulled out an empty Lone Star beer can and held it high so that everyone could see. Laughter erupted from all corners of the room. Then turning to Ben and Kate, he said, "Humor me," as he placed the can in the bag and set them at their feet. "On three." All of the guests counted, whereupon Kate and Ben smashed the beer can. Ben then snatched the flattened bag from the floor.

"*Nu*? This is going to hang on my office wall...or maybe our bedroom? I'm not sure."

Kate decided this was the time to release the kick she had been reserving for Ben. She hiked up her long dress and planted her foot gently on his backside.

"Husband abuse!" cried Ben. "You're all witnesses!"

Michael asked Stephen, "Did you see anything?"

"Me? No." Stephen shook his head. "And besides, he's already in prison." Stephen pointed at the bars on the chapel's windows.

A few photographs were taken of the happy couple, the small wedding party, and other guests. Afterward, a few of the inmates approached the newlyweds carrying a large rectangular box. The guard kept a watchful eye at a discreet distance.

"Hope y'all don't mind opening this present now," said Hattie Sampson. The other women nodded their assent.

"Not at all," replied Kate and Ben.

"We just finished it yesterday!" blurted one of the other inmates, who then put her hand over her mouth.

"Shut up, girl! Don't spoil it," declaimed another.

"Ha! I know what it is," shouted Katz as he and Kate received the sizeable box.

Kate looked at her new husband with curiosity, upon which Ben said, "Heavy! That's what it is!" He feigned that his knees were crumbling under the weight of it.

"Gosh! It really is heavy," added Kate. "You hold the bottom and I'll open it."

"Rabbi!" called Ben. "She's bossing me around already."

Michael simply patted Ben's shoulder and laughed as he said, "Get used to it."

"Oh my goodness!" uttered Kate. "It's a quilt!" She and Ben then each took a corner and held it up for all to see. Esther and one of Ben's cousins took photos of it.

"It's queen size!" boasted one of the women who had helped make it. "About twenty of us worked on it. We been using the remnants from the clothing factory," explained Alfreda. "The women stitched their names on the areas where they worked...and a few other things!" Alfreda giggled.

"Ben, this is really fine work," mused Kate as she marveled at the quality of the stitching. All of a sudden, Kate burst out laughing. "Look at this square!" she urged Ben. "Read it out loud!"

Pushing up his spectacles, Ben read, "A match made in prison." He joined Kate in laughing and then pointed out another which read, "Married for life without parole." Ben looked at the wedding guests and said, "With this, who needs a marriage license?"

"It oughta keep y'all warm in this chilly fall weather," spoke up one of the inmates.

Alfreda replied, "Honey, they got each other to make heat, if you know what I mean." Kate and Ben joined in the laughter which followed. They both thanked the women for the practical and amusing wedding present.

"But now, our wedding feast awaits us," said Kate. She and Ben received hugs from the trustees, who were then escorted back to the main grounds by the guard. They next made certain that everyone either had the directions to the restaurant or had a lift with someone who knew the way there—particularly the New Yorkers. After assuring that no one was left behind—or locked in!—the wedding party set off.

~ * ~

"Those who know me," began Ben, when asked to give a speech, "will know that I make my living by getting other people to talk about themselves and to share their deepest feelings—something I'm not very good at myself. I hide behind being a brusque New Yorker and express myself in the way that makes me most comfortable: humor. With that said, you will have noticed that there is a dance floor in this restaurant, I mean what's a Jewish wedding without dancing, right?...except that ours was a Jewish-Christian wedding, so instead of the bride and groom being lifted in chairs, as in a khasidic wedding, you can feel free to just lift a chair, which is kinda like dancing with me. I mean, I was born with three left feet, but circumcision took care of that."

211

Kate put her head in her hands and asked aloud, "What have I got myself into?" She leaned across the table toward Stephen and Michael, who were sitting with their wives. "Is it too late for an annulment?"

"So here I am," continued Ben, "finally getting married at thirty-eight...and to a non-Jewish woman. *Nu?* Most of my family died of shock—which is why there are only five of them here today." Ben lifted his glass and called out "*lekhai'im*" to his relatives. "So, speaking of death brings to mind a joke..."

"Death, *really*, Ben?" asked Kate. "It's our wedding day!"

"Don't worry." Ben remained undeterred, "This is a joke about marriage...well...*and* death! So, Myron hadn't been feeling well of late. He goes to see his doctor, who tells him he'll take some blood and get back to him in a few days with the results. Three days later, Myron goes to see his doc, who tells him to sit down as the news isn't good. Myron sits down and says, 'Doc, tell me what's wrong.' 'Myron,' says the doctor, 'you've got only a few months to live—five tops.' Well, needless to say, Myron is distraught and says, 'Doc, isn't there something you can do?' The doctor shakes his head and apologizes, the test results are clear. Then, all of a sudden, the doctor says, 'There is something. Are you married?' Whereupon Myron says, 'No, Doc, why?' 'Myron, my best advice is, go find yourself a nice Jewish girl and marry her.' Myron seizes upon the doctor's advice and asks, 'Will this help extend my life?' The doctor says, 'No, but trust me, five months will feel like five years.'"

After pausing for the laughter which followed, Ben turned to Kate and said, "The moral of the story...*I think*...is, that I didn't marry a Jewish girl...I married an Episcopalian—which I can barely spell! But the thing about being with Kate is that time goes too fast...and if I lived another fifty years, it wouldn't be enough." Ben lifted his glass to Kate. "To my beautiful wife."

All those present raised their glasses, calling out, "Hear! Hear!" and "To Kate!"

As Ben sat down, he leaned over and kissed Kate.

For her part, Kate lifted her knife from the table and, in a stage whisper, said, "I'm just glad you ended the joke the way you did—otherwise, who knows?"

Appealing to Rabbi Michael, Ben pleaded, "Twice in a day! First a kick and then she threatens me with a knife. Surely, Rabbi, the Talmud must have something to say about this!"

"Ah well," started Michael, "The Talmud is a very long collection of writings...not to mention that that there are two Talmuds—the Babylonian and the Jerusalem—so this could take me some time. Let me get back to you in, say...a couple of years."

"*Oy veh!*" uttered Ben, who then did a sudden about-face, saying to Kate, "I love it when you treat me rough!"

Stephen turned around in his chair and spoke to Annie McNair, who was at the next table. "How are you handling Ben's manic style on your management team?"

"If Ben's sense of humor is all I have to worry about, then I'm leading a charmed life! Actually, I find it refreshing. If I did his job, I'd need to laugh, too. I'm just glad y'all trusted me for the post. Oh—I hope that Ben and Kate understand why I didn't want to attend their service. I simply didn't feel up to being back on the prison grounds—at least not today. This day should be a happy one—I didn't want to be focused on my past. In any case, I was surprised to receive the invitation in the first place."

"Hey, you're a colleague now. And believe me, Kate and Ben respect your decision completely." At that moment—and as if to underscore what Stephen had just said to Annie—both Kate and Ben saw her and gave her a wave. Annie smiled and waved back. Then she touched Emily's shoulder and added, "I can see Kate and Ben aren't the only ones deserving congratulations." Annie indicated Emily's bump.

"Ah, yes," replied Emily. "Our little surprise. But thanks, Annie, we are pleased...if not a little overwhelmed by impending parenthood...and my love/hate affair with food at the moment. But at least we are back in our little cottage again—to which our landlords kindly added a second bedroom! No more moving from one friend's house to another. *That* was tiring."

"How far along are you?" asked Annie.

"I'm early in the second trimester," replied Emily, unconsciously rubbing her bump as expectant mothers often do. "Bumpkin is due in March."

"Bumpkin! I like that! Stephen?"

"Who else?" smiled Emily as she placed her head on her husband's shoulder for a moment.

"I'm really happy for you two. If ever I can be of help, let me know, okay?"

"Be careful what you offer—our parents don't live nearby, so we might take you up on it. Happily, I've parlayed my 'celebrity' status of late into four months off work—one month before my due date and three afterwards—as needed rest time." Emily dramatically placed the back of her hand over her forehead, feigning a delicate Southern flower of womanhood.

"Yes, I've followed the 'midnight dumpings' case in the newspaper, particularly now that the court case is under way." Annie paused. "It's awful about your colleague who was killed...frankly, for that alone, you've earned several months off."

"Thanks," said Emily. "Stephen and I have given our depositions and have had to appear in court once...but this case is far from over...and then there's the state's felony case against Porter for the PCB dumping. My fear is that our baby will be born all stressed-out...and I'm off all alcohol for the duration of the pregnancy." Emily made a miserable face. "At least my dear man has joined me in the alcohol fast."

214

"It only seemed fair." Stephen raised his glass of sparkling water to Emily.

"Hang on to him," said Annie. "He's more unusual than you know."

"Oh, I plan to keep him." Emily gave a wicked grin. "Because when I go back to work, Stephen gets to be the prime carer for Bumpkin!"

"Yes, despite Reagan's promises to turn the clock back socially if elected, some of us still have hope for a more progressive society, wherein dads can play a bigger part in the nurture of their children," said Stephen. "Thanks to the court settlement, I'll be my own boss for a few years—maybe more—who knows?" Stephen suddenly snapped his fingers, "Talking about Bumpkin reminds me: I need to find a good bike seat. Gotta get him or her started young."

"I somehow think they won't be flying off the shelves," replied Emily. "Maybe we should concentrate on decorating and furnishing the nursery first?"

"Ah, my ever-practical, scientist wife—where would I be without her?" said Stephen.

"Single and not expecting a baby! How's that for a start?" joked Emily.

"It doesn't bear thinking about! Fancy a third honeymoon?" Stephen asked playfully as he kissed his wife on the cheek.

"Not if it means winding up like this again." Emily rubbed her tummy.

"Hmm, there is that," mused Stephen. "Remind me how it happened."

"Not in polite company." Emily patted his hand. "I'll tell you tonight...I might need charts to explain it to you."

Annie laughed, along with others, at the couple's good-natured teasing and banter—but with a sense of, not so much envy or jealousy, but rather a deep *longing* for the warmth and security of such a relationship, and wondering whether she could ever trust herself so fully with a man. She had met Stephen when she was eighteen and worked as his secretary for nearly a year. He had been the only man to that point in her life—apart from her grandfather—who had not used or abused her. It was only natural, as she had admitted to her therapist, that she had developed a crush on him and had wondered what it would be like to have been in a relationship with him. And now, here he was again in her life, not only married, but also the funder for her new job. Annie hoped that whatever vestiges of romantic notions she had carried about Stephen would not be obvious to anyone— particularly Emily. Her fervent prayer was, "Please, God, let me discover Stephen's disgusting habits—nose-picking, gambling, secret drinking, or anything—in order to take the shine off the man." But her method of choice was derived from what she had learned reading Thomas Merton, whose writings had introduced her to the works of early and medieval Christian mystics. This was, in short: develop an attitude of gratitude. In addition to her therapy, Annie had spent time on guided retreats, discovering how to let go of her emotional engagement with the past, and simply accept what her mistakes and life's hard knocks had taught her. They couldn't be undone, but they could be left *unrepeated*. And if truth be told, she had learned a lot from what those negative experiences had taught her.

As a result, Annie was 'ahead of the curve' for most people her age—something that, to a marked degree, left her estranged from the typical culture of her age group. Dating required too much energy, because if the guy truly meant it when he said, "Tell me about yourself," they were usually spooked by the time she finished a short version of how she managed to be both divorced and an ex-con at the tender age of twenty-four. Being with Stephen, Ben and Kate was easy as they all knew her story and accepted her for who she was. The same went for Emily, as she had done prison time herself. It was so much easier to be with people to whom there was no need to explain oneself.

"Hello? Anybody home?" asked Stephen as he tapped Annie on the shoulder.

"Oh, Stephen...gosh...sorry! I was a million miles away," replied a flummoxed Annie. "What did you say?"

"I said that Emily, being a double-person, doesn't feel like dancing, so she has suggested that I ask you. Fancy hitting the dancefloor? It's a half-Jewish wedding, so I think it's required."

Annie turned to look at Emily who simply gave her a thumb's up and patted her tummy as an explanation.

"Kate has finally dragged Ben out for a dance—I just gotta be on the floor to watch it," said Stephen. He and Annie grinned from ear-to-ear as they moved up next to Kate, who was patiently trying to get Ben to loosen up and go with the music. However, Ben looked more like he was stamping on cockroaches than doing dance steps.

"It's called fun, Ben!" cracked Stephen. "You should be smiling at your bride and not breaking into a sweat!"

"Not helping," groaned Ben.

"He promised me one fast and one slow dance," said Kate. "I hope we can make it to the slow dance!" She waved to the band to cut the tempo, who duly complied.

Stephen and Annie slowed their pace as he took her left hand and placed his right on her upper arm. "Who'd a thunk it five years ago—that you and I would be working together again or be here celebrating Ben and Kate's marriage?"

"You left out the bit about running into each other on the Appalachian Trail—with you and Emily skinny-dipping."

"Oh yeah..." Stephen blushed a little. "That was a little embarrassing."

"But at least it led to my finding a job," said Annie. "Still, you couldn't have planned any of this... You know, I did think about writing to you once or twice over the intervening years—particularly after reading about how you had been shot last December."

"What stopped you?"

"I don't know...it just didn't seem like the right thing to do—if that makes sense. Do you ever hear from former inmates?"

"Actually, no—apart from running into a guy in Morganton whom I knew at the youth center just before we started our backpack trip; and then you, at Big Creek." Stephen shook his head at his silent musings. "Both of those encounters seemed almost destined to happen—and both within a week of each other. I'll tell you about the guy in Morganton another time. But meanwhile, here you are in Raleigh again—a free woman this time—and helping to realize my dream of starting a halfway house for women who have been through the same shit as you—sorry for bringing that up, but it is simply amazing."

"I am surprised," said Annie.

"Surprised? At what?"

"That you never hear from inmates after they're released," Annie clarified. "You really helped me—a lot. And if I never said it before, then let me say it now: thank you."

"Annie, seeing you doing so well since your time in prison is enough for me," replied Stephen.

Annie kicked him on the shin. "I'm still saying 'thank you'."

"Ouch and message received—and you're welcome! Now about your not writing to me—it actually makes sense."

"How so?"

"I think that for most people, a prison chaplain is just that: a minister who works in prisons," replied Stephen. "Once people have moved on, it's natural that they would identify me with their time behind bars. Writing to me might be seen as looking backward instead of forward. And looking back didn't exactly work out well for Lot's wife!" Both Stephen and Annie laughed. As the slow dance was just coming to an end, Stephen blurted, "I'll give you ten bucks if you can keep the groom on the dance floor for one more song."

Accepting the challenge, Annie replied, "You can keep your money. I'll do it just for pure mischief!"

As the two couples moved back toward their seats, Annie put on her best Southern charm and said to Ben, "I have never in my life danced with a groom. I would be just so grateful if I could have this next dance with you." There followed Annie's world-winning smile, along with the added touch of batting eyelashes. Stephen covertly winked at Kate, who nodded in comprehension.

"Oh, Ben," fawned Kate, "That's lovely! How could you say no?"

The psychologist in Ben was no match for the wiles of his colleagues and wife. "It's your feet," grumbled Ben. "Don't say I didn't warn you."

Stephen went back to his seat and got his camera. "Okay, you two, smile!" Travis clicked one picture, wound the roll and took another.

"You're gonna need a very good proctologist to remove that camera if anyone sees those photos," growled Katz.

"Just relax and enjoy yourself," chided Stephen. "I know I am!" There was friendly laughter and applause from Kate, Stephen, Emily, Rabbi Weisman and his wife. When the song ended, Ben couldn't get back to his seat fast enough.

"Some best man you are," puffed Ben to Stephen. "Leaving me to the designs of women on the dance floor."

"Ben—one of them was your wife of two hours, and the other a colleague," responded Stephen. "Relax! It's your wedding day." Stephen reached in his suit pocket and produced an envelope. "Here, perhaps this will help."

"What is it?" asked Ben.

"Well, gosh, Ben, as it's your wedding day, I thought an eviction notice might be a good idea. What do you think?—It's your present from Emily and me."

Katz tore open the envelope, already forgetting the torment of dancing. Kate looked on with curiosity. As they both read the contents of the envelope, their mouths dropped open.

"Stephen! Emily! You can't do this!" gasped Kate.

"Actually, we can—and we did!" laughed Stephen.

"And there's nothing you can do about it—except enjoy," said Emily.

"Consider it a *mitzvah*," added Stephen. "And yes, it's exactly what my family did for me and Emily for our wedding present. Y'all have two households to combine, so you're not exactly short on china, linens and the like. Em and I thought you might enjoy something totally gratuitous."

Kate began showing the letter to others at their table. "Five nights at the Grove Park Inn in Asheville—all expenses paid!" Ben was flabbergasted. Both he and Kate got up and walked around the table to hug Stephen and Emily.

Stephen discerned a tear in the corner of Ben's eye as he squeezed his shoulder and, in a breaking voice, said, "*Todah, khaver.*"

Emily gave Stephen a questioning look and he mouthed, "Thanks, friend."

Twenty-seven

Emily and Stephen were in court for the closing arguments in the case against Rex Porter for the killing of Terry Saunders, as well as the attendant arson charges. Also in court were Emily's remaining three lab assistants, Terry's parents, Carl and Denise Bennett, and Sgt. Longacre. Porter's defense attorney had been pushing for a verdict of involuntary manslaughter, which ignored the fact that Porter was engaged in a felonious break-in and attempted arson when he attacked Terry. He had tried using the folksy, good ol' boy approach with the jury—citing the many good things Porter had done for the people of Raleigh: creating employment through his company, giving money for remodeling the Baptist church he attended—and which, his attorney added, was home to one of the largest Scout groups in the city—and his status at his Masonic lodge. A third of the jury members were African-Americans, so the white, good ol' boy angle cut no ice with them. The judge had to remind Porter's legal counsel that Porter's previous reputation was not on trial, but rather that it was Rex Porter's felonies which were under scrutiny.

For his part, the district attorney had stuck to the facts: a young man with a promising future was dead—killed by Rex Porter, who struck Terry Saunders on the head with a hammer, while trying to set fire to a building on the NC State campus. The building contained the laboratory of Dr. Emily Travis—and here the district attorney indicated Emily to the court. This same Emily Travis and her husband, Stephen, a local minister, had been burned out of house and home by Rex Porter prior to his breaking into the science building at State with the intent of committing yet another arson. Given his violent and desperate actions prior to striking down Terry Saunders, the DA explained that the jury had no real choice but to return a verdict of second-degree murder. Porter had confessed to striking the victim on the head with a hammer, while committing the felony of breaking and entering— and he had confessed his intent to commit another, namely, the torching of Emily's laboratory: substantiated by the possession of gasoline—found at the scene. Finally, and here the district attorney stuck his neck out, *all* of the preceding crimes had been committed as a means of hiding the evidence of the illegal dumping of toxic PCBs—poisoning land, water, people and animals in numerous counties just east of Raleigh. But before Porter's legal counsel could object to this reference or the judge could bang his gavel, the district attorney rested his case. The jury members were then instructed by the judge and retired to determine the verdicts.

~ * ~

Stephen found he was grinding his teeth as they waited for the jury to return. Emily gripped Stephen's hand so tightly the knuckles on both their hands were turning white. The only thing which had finally broken their 'vice grip' was the movement of their baby, now twenty-two weeks in the making. The expectant parents whispered with delight with each push or kick, and loved gently pushing back, to let Bumpkin know that they were there and waiting. It was a major relief to have something positive on which to focus, when both simply wanted the business with Porter to be finished and gone. Each had managed to slip out at some point to have something to eat or drink—sustenance for the nerve-wracking wait for the verdict. It was during one of Bumpkin's more acrobatic wiggles that the jury announced they had reached a verdict—and it was unanimous. It had taken less than ninety minutes, which caught many people by surprise—none more so than the press and reporters who had slipped out to local watering holes, only to be caught out with regard to getting their stories released first. Concerning the unlawful killing of Terry Saunders, the jury found Porter guilty of second-degree murder. A murmur of reactions ran throughout the courtroom, but the judge let it pass. There followed a succession of guilty verdicts on arson, breaking and entering, as well as attempted arson.

When Porter heard each of the verdicts being read out, he looked as though he were being slapped—his face twitched and his eyes blinked with each count. He looked pleadingly at his lawyer, who refused to meet his gaze, but simply busied himself with the paperwork on his table. Porter turned toward the judge, who viewed Porter dispassionately, as perhaps simply another citizen-cum-criminal for whom the Fates had allotted a reckoning. Emily and Stephen were so enthusiastically hugging each other and expressing their joy at the convictions, that they nearly missed the sentencing.

For the crime of second-degree murder, Porter would serve twenty years. For the crimes of arson, attempted arson, breaking and entering, the judge handed down a sentence of ten years to run consecutively with the sentence for second-degree murder. Stephen sat back dumbfounded—he had been nearly certain that Porter's sentences would run concurrently. As a now former prison chaplain, he wasn't used to wishing anyone time behind bars, but Porter had burned his home and killed his wife's colleague, and Stephen was only human. Porter had thus more than earned himself prison time and was now facing thirty years—

and all this *before* his pending trial for the illegal dumpings of PCBs. Life as he knew it was finished.

~ * ~

In the courtroom foyer following the sentencing, all those acquainted with Terry, Emily and Stephen gathered together. The first to embrace Terry's parents were Emily and Stephen. Terry's mother spoke first. "Twenty years is longer than Terry's life...He would have turned twenty the month after he died." She put her hand over her mouth and wept into her husband's shoulder.

"I didn't know that," replied a tearful Emily. "But please know this, Terry's field notes and lab tests will be used to convict Porter again when the PCBs case is heard." She placed her hands on the grieving parents' arms. "And more than that, Terry's findings will help all of those affected by the 'midnight dumpings'—and there are many. Please know that his work will live on." At that point, Terry's colleagues, Alison, Stewart and Mark, came to express their satisfaction that Porter had been convicted. Excusing himself, Terry's father took Stephen aside for a moment, gripping him firmly by the shoulder—as though helping himself to remain standing—and said, "I never really gave much thought to what it takes to be a prison chaplain with men like Porter...and now...well I don't know how you did it all of those years. I-I hope God can forgive him...because I don't know that I can."

Stephen reflected a moment before speaking in measured tones. "I have come to learn that God's timing is always the best...and frankly, I'm glad I won't have to worry about being Porter's chaplain. It would strain my compassion to the limit—at least at this point in time. I could only speak to the man through clenched teeth and sadly, a closed heart...that's hardly what I'd call Christian charity."

Saunders dabbed his eyes, cleared his throat and, indicating Emily, said, "Take care of that child of yours...they don't stay little

for long...a-and you think you'll be able to protect them forever..."
He broke down at this point and turned to embrace his wife; each
burying their grief in the loving hold of the other.

Denise and Carl Bennett stood at a discreet distance, chatting
in low tones with Sgt. Longacre. Reporters, who had finished
feasting on the district attorney and Rex Porter's lawyer, now
came in search of fresh blood, namely the victims of Porter's
crimes: the Saunderses, Travises and Bennetts. Seeing the distress
written on the faces of these six individuals, Longacre decided to
place his considerable frame between them and the approaching
pack of story-hounds. This presented the Bennetts with just
enough time to whisper to the others an invitation to come to their
house for food and privacy. They also offered the Saunderses a
bed for the night, if they felt too emotionally exhausted to make
the journey back to New Bern. All accepted the welcome offer.
Emily asked if it might include her lab assistants, all of whom had
been Terry's friends. Receiving the affirmative, she squeezed
herself through the encircling reporters, making sure that she trod
on as many toes as possible. Seeing Alison, she pulled her in tight
and whispered the invitation. For her part, Alison nodded and
made her way to Mark and Stewart. That accomplished, Longacre
made himself into a human crowd breaker, behind which the
others formed a sort of 'flying wedge,' which worked a treat. They
were soon outside and heading toward the parking area, with the
dispersed trail of newshounds following and shouting questions.
The Bennetts kindly took Terry's parents with them, offering to
bring them back for their car when things had calmed down.

Twenty-eight

"Don't y'all move a muscle," Marcie commanded her guests, but in a dulcet tone. "Clarence and I can clear the table—and besides, dessert's comin'." It was early December and the fire in the wood stove crackled as Marcie opened the warming oven to remove two homemade pumpkin pies. The whipped cream came courtesy of the local supermarket, as the health of their dairy herd remained uncertain. The Moores had invited Emily and her lab assistants, and of course, Stephen, for lunch at their home. It had been three weeks since Rex Porter had received his prison sentence. The Moores had rightly perceived that the Travises would have suffered enough from the persistent pestering of reporters. The press, TV and radio stations were still hungry for stories of the fallen local captain of industry and were anticipating the upcoming case of the state versus Porter's Transformers, along with the trucking firm hired to dump the PCBs. Emily and her team would be prime witnesses. In fact, the Moores had offered all of their guests a bed for the night in their gracious, rambling farmhouse. It was Sunday, a day of rest, and on Monday, Emily's team had agreed to retest the water, as well as take samples of the cattle's feces and blood. But that could wait. Now was a time for fellowship and reflection.

The table conversation had ranged widely and had ventured into deep waters. Both Clarence and Marcie averred that the problem inherent in waiting for something to be over—such as the PCB hearings—was that it allowed one to make the mistake of assuming that what came afterward would necessarily be better. "We did that when Alan, our son, was serving in Vietnam," said Marcie. "We just kept saying, 'When the war is over' or 'When Alan gets home.' Trouble is, when he came home...it wasn't what we'd hoped for or expected." Marcie reached over and patted Emily's growing bump. "Don't rush any of it, honey."

As Marcie cleared the table, Clarence walked to a bookshelf and returned with a photo of Alan and a folded flag. "This is Alan in 1969...somewhere in Vietnam. And this is the flag we received when they buried him in the county cemetery. We fly it on public holidays...doesn't seem right to leave it sitting on a shelf." The guests passed Alan's picture around the table.

"I can't imagine how much you must miss him," commented Emily, as she and Stephen looked at the faded photograph.

"You don't ever get over it...you just get on with it. He's still here..." Clarence placed his hand on his chest, "in our hearts." He smiled sadly and collected the other dishes from the table.

"You know, I felt our work here was important before," offered Mark in a quiet voice. "But now...now seeing how the Moores have lost their son and we've lost Terry...I guess I'm just beginning to see how fragile everything is. I never thought one of us would lose his life over this. I mean it coulda been any one of us who walked into the lab that night."

"We were on our way there," said Stephen as he took Emily's hand.

Mark continued, "And now that Terry has..." he searched for words, "has paid with his *life*. I just want to do my utmost to keep the likes of Rex Porter behind bars *for the rest of his goddamn life.*"

"I heard that," laughed Marcie.

"Sorry, ma'am," apologized Mark.

"Oh no, honey. I couldn't agree more...in fact, I say 'Amen!' to that! Can I hear another?"

"Amen!" resounded around the kitchen.

"That one man, Rex Porter, has nearly cost us our dairy farm—and the same goes for other farmers in the area—not to mention that he killed your friend," said Marcie with conviction. "So I hope he spends his goddamn life behind bars."

Clarence chortled as he listened to his wife's impassioned statement. "They shoulda sentenced him to clean up the contaminated soil and water," added Clarence. "We could have made life interesting for him." He laughed at an image only he could see. "Sometimes prison isn't enough. People need to see the results of their crimes—and be made to feel the impact on their victims...if that's even possible."

"Oh, it is *possible*," chimed in Stephen. "Many countries have such restitution programs, but sadly it's not what our politicians want. Prison is our answer to everything—and it's a big business; another fact that our increasingly conservative government doesn't like to admit. But then, there are some crimes—like murder—wherein restitution is never fully possible. Yet, I remain convinced that if we embark simply on the path of revenge, that usually leads to more violence." Stephen paused for a few moments. Then looking from Emily to Mark, Alison and Stewart, he added, "In the case of the PCBs, Terry's 'revenge' will be his copious field notes that he left—and his lab work—as well as what all of you do to bring this investigation to a close and to ensure that Porter's company pays. That's the best thing you can do for Terry."

"And what about you?" asked Marcie. "Now that you've left prison chaplaincy?"

"Oh, somehow I think my hands will be full. There's Bumpkin on the way," Stephen lovingly stroked Emily's belly, "and then there's my new project, a halfway house for abused women who are released from prison. I have decided there's too much to be done outside of prison walls to prevent people from returning to the lifestyles that put them there. And the residence manager is a young woman who used to be a secretary at women's prison some years ago.

"Think you'll miss the 'buzz' of prison work?" asked Stewart.

"Ha!" laughed Stephen. "I never quite thought of it as a *buzz*. It's more like an adrenaline high to deal with all of the unexpected events, the violence and the pain borne by those behind bars. No, being an adrenaline junky for my work is not my idea of 'the good life.' But in any case, if my life with Dr. Travis to this point in time is anything to go by, it will certainly be as exciting as my years behind bars—but frankly, for the foreseeable future, I'd prefer dull and boring."

Meet Jack N. Lawson

Jack Lawson grew up in North Carolina. As an ordained minister, he worked as a prison chaplain in North Carolina and Ohio, and later served as a parish minister in the US and the United Kingdom. After earning a PhD in Hebrew Bible, he taught both ministerial candidates and lay people in the English counties of Kent and Norfolk. After leaving parish ministry in 1997, Jack worked for the Countryside Agency, focusing on rural economic regeneration and managing a European Social Fund grant between Kent and Nord-Pas-de-Calais. In the process he developed an intense love of France and the French people. Later, Jack spent more than 12 years as training and development officer for the Methodist Church in East Anglia. Jack is married to Chris, a former mental health specialist who worked with children and families in the UK. They reside in Lower Normandy, France.

Works from the Pen of Jack N. Lawson

No Good Deed - A Vietnam veteran seeks to find peace within himself, first as a circus clown and later as an ordained minister. Events in his church conspire to reignite his PTSD.

Criminal Justice - A prison chaplain uncovers criminal victimization of inmates by the staff and must decide to risk his job/life for the sake of justice.

The Woods - Life in an enchanted retirement community opens the residents to their deeper selves—for mirth or madness, good or ill.

Dirty Business - An animal scientist uncovers the deliberate dumping of toxic waste, but the notoriety opens the door to further intrigue, danger and murder.